Secrets
OF THE
Forgotten heir
Heather G. Harris & Ella Stone

PUBLISHED BY HELLHOUND PRESS LIMITED

HELLHOUND
PRESS

Heather's Dedication

For my awesome supporters on Patreon, with special mention to Amanda Peterman, Kate Potter and Melissa Snyder. Thank you so much for going that exta mile!

Ella's Dedication

I dedicate this book to Roberta Mary, who is unfailingly kind and supportive at every turn.

Heather's Addendum

I wholeheartedly endorse Ella's dedication because Roberta is awesome!

Contents

Foreword

If you'd like to hear the latest gossip, bargains and new releases from us, then please join our newsletters!

If you'd like FREE BOOKS then join Heather's newsletter on her website and you can get a couple of free stories, as well as pictures of her dog and other helpful things.

Ella will also give you FREE BOOKS, but she will send you cat images instead! Sign up to Ella's list here at her website.

Content Warnings

Please see the full content warnings on Heather's website if you are concerned about triggers.

All of Heather's books have occasional poor language and scenes of violence.

Please note that all of Heather's and Ella's works are written in British English with British phrases, spellings and grammar being utilised throughout. Here you'll find extra U's and S's, and less Z's.

If you think you have found a typo, please do let Heather know here.

Chapter One

'Demon or squirrel?' I whispered to my retriever, Eva.

She let out another low rumbling growl that made my scalp prickle; I'd only ever heard her sound so fierce once before and that had been because of a demon. My heart rate picked up, beating a fast staccato as we stalked forward.

Sometimes I wished my parents hadn't imbued me with such a fierce need to protect; anyone with any sense would be walking away right now, but they had taught me to run *into* danger, not from it. If there was a demon here, I couldn't leave the humans to deal with it.

At least I had magic, though admittedly only a teeny drop of it, a raindrop compared to my parents' ocean, but it was still better than nothing. That was a refrain I'd repeated to myself many, many times.

Tension roared through me as the bushes in front of us rustled again – then a small red squirrel scuttled out of the foliage. Eva barked fiercely as it dashed up a tree.

A squirrel. I glared at my three year old dog; I'd been shitting myself. I'd faced a demon once before and once was more than enough.

'I honestly thought there was a demon,' I groused. Eva grinned at me, tail wagging, tongue lolling. 'Laugh it up, fuzzball. You're not getting any treats when we get home.' Of course my threat was totally empty.

Eva's eyes turned sorrowful and her misery hit me like a wave, making me hold up my hands. 'Dude, that's emotional manipulation.'

She whined.

'Fine. You win. You always win. You are an unstoppable force of neediness.'

The tail was wagging again. She had me wrapped around her little paws and she knew it. Three years earlier I'd saved her from that demon, but she'd been saving me ever since.

'Come on, let's go home,' I told her. 'That's enough excitement for one night.' Eva happily turned tail to trot back to my flat.

Walking in darkness had made us both edgy and it was all my fault we were out so late. My self-defence class should have finished by midday and since I had no open PI cases, I'd expected Eva and I to take our final walk while it was still light – but then I'd taken a call.

One of my students had rung to tell me she was going travelling in two weeks and wanted to make sure her skills were up to scratch. Could I fit her in for an extra lesson? Now? I sensed that she was a little nervous and needed some reassurance. I didn't mind, giving an extra lesson meant money. Despite the inheritance tucked away for me in Witchlight Cove, I've spent the last ten years struggling to get by. There was no way I would say no to earning some cash.

I'm a witch with minimal powers living in the non-magical world. My day job is being a PI, but I also teach young women how to protect themselves. It certainly isn't the life my parents had imagined for me – I doubted any of us could have foreseen this future. No one would have expected me to abandon my place as guardian of the Eternal Flame, least of all me. Weak witch or not, I'd been dedicated to that mission.

I rubbed my eyes as I remembered my passion and zeal. Now I recognised it for what it was: youthful naivety. How could I ever have protected the Flame adequately when all I had was a shitty bit of empathy magic?

Yes, I can fight: my parents had taught me a mix of Krav Maga and Brazilian Ju-Jitsu. Krav Maga teaches you practical self-defence, like strikes and quick takedowns, but BJJ focuses on submissions, escapes and control on the ground. My skills may be good but they don't compensate for my magic being about emotions. If someone with strong magic had come to take the Eternal Flame, what could I have done? *Loved* them until they went away? *Hugged* them into submission?

When my grandmother had come for it, I'd done next to nothing – except get my parents killed.

The old heartache threatened to overwhelm me. Next to me, Eva let out a sorrowful whine. I swallowed. 'I'm okay,' I murmured as I patted her head. 'Let's get home.'

Home is a crappy apartment in an even worse area, but the rent is cheap; when you live paycheck to paycheck, that's important. And it has books, which are always a plus in my column. There was a psychological thriller by H M Lynn waiting for me at home and I was more than ready to curl up with it.

Crummy as my home was, I was looking forward to getting back to its relative warmth. It was late and I wanted nothing more than to sit on the sofa with Eva and a good book, and let her adoration, unwavering loyalty and unadulterated love soothe the raw edges of my soul.

The pavements were full of rat-race workaholics on their way home. At least seventy percent of them seemed to be on their phones, either holding them directly in front of their faces so they couldn't see where they were going or chatting on Bluetooth speakers at a volume that suggested they wanted to share their conversation with the whole world.

One of the first things I teach my women is to pay attention to your surroundings. Seeing people walking with their headphones on, attention scattered, is my pet peeve because they make such easy marks. You should always leave out one earbud so you can hear the world around you; that way you hear the car or the jogger behind you.

The lady across from me was a prime example: she was so focused on her screen that she didn't notice the roadworks on the path in front of her. The workers were long gone but they'd left barriers around an open drain; unfortunately, the hustle and bustle of the street had dislodged them and the barrier that *should* have protected her from walking into it was now missing.

She was oblivious.

'Hey!' I shouted, trying to get her attention before she catapulted into the hole. She didn't react. Instead, her head kept moving to the beat that was clearly ringing in her ears.

I dived across the path to save her, letting go of Eva's lead so I could seize the hapless woman with both hands. I grabbed her shoulders and stopped her inches from the open drain. She whirled around. 'Hey!' she said, outraged, and popped out one earbud. 'What the fuck?'

I gestured to the drain she'd been about to tumble into and her mouth dropped open as she realised how close she'd come to a broken limb. A wad of chewing gum fell out of her slack jaws. Nice.

Behind me, a man was swearing loudly. The words 'Bloody dog!' caught my interest and I turned to see Eva cringing with her tail between her legs. There was a man on the ground in front of her and her lead was tangled around his legs. He picked up his phone and resumed his video call as he shot me a death glare and pointedly dusted himself down.

'Control your damned dog!' he snarled. His fury was so powerful I actually felt a flutter of it; for me to feel emotions coming off a non-magical person means their feelings have to be *seriously* strong.

I have far better control over my dog than most pet owners, but sometimes you have to accept that they are animals and occasionally they do whatever they like. This situation hadn't been *my* fault, though, nor Eva's or even the woman's; if the suit had been watching where he was going, he wouldn't have got tangled up.

Eva pressed into my side and I patted her reassuringly, ignoring the rude man in favour of checking over my dog and the shaken young woman whose head was no longer bobbing cheerfully. I gave her my standard spiel about being aware of her surroundings and passed her my self-defence business card, because ... well, why not?

By the time I reached home, I had replayed the conversation with the rude phone man at least half a dozen ways and come up with a number of witty replies he would never hear: *Ah yes, because my dog was the one staring at their phone and not watching where she was going. Classic canine behaviour!* My other favourite was: *Oh no, I didn't realise my dog was controlling **your** feet too! I'll have a word with her about that.*

It's such a pain when the witty repartee comes to you too late, but it's the story of my life. I was still thinking up cutting comebacks as I slotted my key into the lock.

That was the moment the whole debacle evaporated from my thoughts.

Because my front door was unlocked.

And I sure as hell knew I hadn't left it that way.

Chapter Two

I nudged the door open a couple of inches with my foot and peered inside. Whoever had decided to break in had badly misjudged what they would find: my camera and computer were so old that they were close to worthless, and there was zero in the way of designer clothes or jewellery. Courtesy of an elf, I still had a greenhouse full of thriving plants, but I doubted there was much of a black market for stolen ferns. And even if the burglars had raided the fridge, all they'd have found was a bag of grated cheese and half a bottle of Oyster Bay. I hoped they liked questionable dairy and disappointment.

Whoever had broken into my house had made a dire mistake. I'd spent the first sixteen years of my life training to be the guardian of the most magical, powerful relic in Witchlight Cove, and I'd started learning to fight as soon as I could stand. Neither was I on my own: I had Eva and, as she'd proved time and time again, she was an asset in numerous ways. We were *not* an easy mark; in fact, we were the worst possible mark. We were the kind of mark that stole the wallet back before you'd even finished lifting it.

'Ready, girl?' I asked, glancing down at Eva. Her hackles were up, but instead of the vicious snarling I'd expected – or even the low rumbling growl she'd given the damned squirrel – her head was tilted to the side and she was sniffing the air curiously.

I tried to tap into her emotions to see if I could glean anything from her, but all I got was a mild sense of curiosity. As I was trying to dig out what she might be thinking, however, I was hit by a dozen other emotions – and none of them were coming from Eva.

Houston, we had an intruder.

'Get behind me, girl,' I ordered. Half of me wanted to grab her by the collar and move her away, but I couldn't lose focus because I was feeling the emotions of whoever was in my flat and they were *strong*. Strong was bad. The only time I'd felt emotions this intense was when I was emotionally close to the person, and that wasn't possible here because everyone I cared about was either dead or in Witchlight Cove. Or they were seriously magically powerful.

There was one possibility that made the old fear rise up and threaten to consume me: my grandmother. Her body had never been found, and though she'd been banished,

I'd never been sure that she'd been truly vanquished. The possibility of her return filled every single one of my nightmares. You don't get over the potential resurrection of a homicidal magical matriarch.

'I know you're in there,' I called, trying to keep my voice steady.

Much as I didn't want to admit it, I was bricking it. Facing a non-magical assailant didn't bother me as long as they weren't armed with a gun – and given the UK's gun laws that was unlikely. I was fairly sure I could disarm and immobilise almost anyone, regardless of their size or training; I'd successfully taken on ex-military types countless times, plus an assassin a few years back.

But when you're up against someone magical, it's a whole different ball game. For all I knew, the intruder could already be reading my mind, stealing my best moves and judging my life choices. Even if they weren't witches, shifters had crazy strength even in human form. As for vampires, who combined speed with that whole pointy-teeth thing, they weren't something I wanted to deal with either. Not without some weapons in my hands to level the playing field.

'I don't want anyone to get hurt,' I called, hoping they'd think I was referring to them. 'Whatever you're after, I promise you've got the wrong person.' Unless it was dear old Grandmama, in which case, ding, ding, ding! She was on the right track all right.

That was when the emotions hit me again and this time it was a full-on tsunami, even with my mental shields up. Anger was being aimed straight at me, as well as hurt and fear and so much confusion. But it was the last emotion that had me gripping the doorframe to keep myself upright.

Love. Love for me so deep and fierce that it melted away the anger, disappointment, and hurt.

The fact that I could discern those feelings told me that I was emotionally close to my intruder, and the blend of emotions melded so perfectly with sympathy and grief that it could only belong to one person.

Straightening up, I stepped into my apartment and switched on the light. 'Maddie?' I whispered as I stared into my best friend's eyes.

'Hi, Bea,' she said brightly, giving me a finger wave and a smile as if all that hurt and upset weren't coursing through her veins. 'How's things?'

When you say you've got history with someone it can mean anything. It can mean you had a drunken hookup one night, or maybe you were work besties who fell out over a promotion, or maybe the history goes back as far as high school. But when I say it about Maddie, it would be more accurate to say that she *was* my history.

She was my ride or die, my best friend since I was old enough to land my first uppercut. Maddie was the only person who knew everything about me, from which guy I was crushing on – I tended to have a thing for shifters – to how much it hurt me to have such pathetic magical powers when I was the offspring of one of the most potent witches around.

Maddie had been the only one I could let it all out to. When the shit really hit the fan and my parents were killed, she and her grandmother, Yanni, had moved into my family home. She'd even taken over my position of guarding the Eternal Flame when everything had become too much for me.

I had run away from the task I had been born to do and left Witchlight Cove the moment I was eighteen. For the last ten years Maddie had taken over the responsibility for the Flame, lived the life I thought would be mine. I'd been pushing her to the back of my mind ever since, trying to pretend that I didn't miss her and the cove every second of every day.

That was a damn sight harder to do now that she was standing in front of me.

'You got a dog.' She crouched down, made kissing noises at Eva and stroked her, then frowned at the ever-present, purple-black smudge on Eva's bum. 'Hey, beautiful girl,' she said soothingly. 'What's your name?'

Finally I found my voice. 'Her name is "*What the hell are you doing here, Maddie*"?'

Maddie looked up with the cheeky grin I knew so well. 'Maddie for short? Aw, you named your dog after me. I knew you'd missed me.' She winked.

'Her name is Eva,' I ground out. 'What the hell are you doing so far from Witchlight Cove? The Flame—' Yeah, that, the giant magical relic that neither of us was supposed to leave unguarded.

Guilt spiked from her, hot and heavy, and I felt ashamed. Here I was berating *her* about leaving the Flame unguarded when I'd done exactly the same.

'Pot, kettle, black,' she shot back, her open grin disappearing as if I'd wiped it off a whiteboard.

Regardless of the reason for her presence, you don't break into someone's house – especially not someone who lived with the sort of fear that I did. She knew that. She knew what I lived with every single day.

Maddie stood up and Eva looked at me pointedly, wanting praise for resisting the fuss and attention. She trotted to my side and pushed herself into my leg, Team Beatrix all the way.

The silence was tense and uncomfortable, making it harder to breathe with each passing moment. And all the while, the hurt in Maddie's eyes cut me to the depths of my cowardly soul. I'd run away and left her with so much to deal with and it showed. I looked at my best friend, truly *looked* at her. Concern lanced through me. She was visibly tired; she had bags under her eyes big enough to pack for a trip around the world, and her shoulders were slumped and dejected. Alarm bells were ringing: something was up. She looked so different to the upbeat teenage girl I had left.

Now she was an adult and so was I. For all our shared history, we were virtually strangers – and it was my doing.

'You got a haircut,' I blurted. It was a ridiculous thing to say given how long we'd been apart because she'd probably had dozens, if not hundreds. But this one was extreme and a sharp contrast to the hair that used to flow down almost to her bum. Now her dark hair was cut into a bob that was short at the back and came down past her shoulders at the front. The ends were dipped pink.

That wasn't the only change: she had at least five more tattoos that I could see, though I couldn't tell if they were magical ones she'd given herself or traditional ink. And she had totally mastered the winged eyeliner look.

She obviously considered my comment as stupid as I did because she didn't respond. The silence returned almost instantly, hanging thick and oppressive as we studied each other.

Finally she shook her head and the pink tips brushed her shoulders. 'Something's happened. I need you to come back.'

Had she really said that? She knew it was impossible. I licked my lips. 'Come back? To Witchlight Cove, you mean?' I stared at her like she'd suggested I fly to the moon. 'Mads, you know I can't do that.'

Her eyes hardened. 'You're confusing the words *can't* and *won't*, Bea,' she said firmly. 'Look, I get that this is out of the blue, but the reason I need you to come back isn't something I could discuss over the phone. I wouldn't ask unless I needed you.'

That was a direct hit – and that was when I felt it: a flash of fear that radiated straight from her into me. My best friend was terrified. But why?

My heart stuttered. 'It's not Yanni, is it? She's okay, isn't she?' Yanni meant almost as much to me as Maddie did. She'd practically raised us both because, as best friends, we'd pretty much split our time between each other's houses. Maddie's mum had died in childbirth and her deadbeat dad had left when she was three months old.

Yanni had brought her up single-handedly, and taken me on too. If something had happened to her, if she was dying... I couldn't even imagine it.

Yanni had been a force of nature; it was easier to imagine the sun dying than to imagine her succumbing to old age or illness. A fierce bear shifter and the chief of police in Witchlight Cove's tiny, underfunded police station, she'd taken an active role in every community activity from the am-dram group to the constant fayres. I'd always thought of her as Superwoman, but she had to be in her mid-sixties by now.

Maddie's fear was still gripping me and I was moments away from a full-blown panic.

A smile crept onto her face at my visible distress. 'Nana's fine,' she reassured me. 'Working too hard as always, but she's not the reason I need you to come back.' The smile dropped away. 'Look, you must know that I wouldn't be here if it wasn't serious.'

I nodded. 'Okay, I'm listening. Why do you need me to go to Witchlight? What's happened?'

'A couple of reasons. It's easier to show you. Come with me.'

'I'm not coming anywhere without a proper answer, Maddie. *Why?*

Her lips pressed together so tightly that they almost disappeared. The fear was still rolling off her, but if it wasn't to do with Yanni then I had no idea what was causing it. As I stood there trying to think of a reason for her appearance, her fear intensified – and in the midst of it was guilt. Crippling, immobilising guilt.

'Maddie,' I started softly. 'What did you do?'

A sob escaped her but then she braced herself; whatever came next from her lips would be the truth. I tensed, ready for I didn't know what. Then her eyes shifted and rolled back into her head. A burst of white light glowed at the end of her fingertips and a second later, she dropped to the floor.

'Maddie!' I screamed.

Chapter Three

'Shit, shit, shit!' I fell to my knees and pulled her into my arms. The glow in her fingers had gone, which I supposed was positive – except they shouldn't have been glowing at all. It might have made sense if she'd been casting a spell or creating one of her tattoo inks with the Eternal Flame, but she'd just been *standing* there.

Panic rose through me. The nearest person who could help her would be in Witchlight Cove and that was a four-hour drive away. 'Come on Maddie, wake up. Wake up! Please wake up.'

Tears welled in my eyes. I was freaking out and also filled with frustration. If I'd inherited even a fraction of my mother's magic the way witches normally do, I could have done something but, as usual, I had nothing.

'Maddie! Maddie!' I carried her to my stained sofa and Eva immediately jumped up and licked her face. I was about to tell her to stop – it didn't feel like the most hygienic thing to do to an unconscious woman – when my friend stirred. Great, just what we needed: dog slobber as a medical cure.

'What...?' she mumbled, her voice groggy and confused.

'Maddie, can you hear me, love?' The old endearment slipped out before I could stop it.

She sat up, touched a hand to her head but left her eyes scrunched closed. 'Did I faint?'

'Yeah, you fainted all right! Let me get you some water. Stay still.' I ran into the kitchen, filled a glass of water then stood over her protectively and watched eagle-eyed as she took a few sips. She swallowed hard a few times then carefully set the glass down.

I folded my arms. 'That wasn't a normal faint, Maddie.'

'Sure it was,' she lied airily. 'I didn't eat on the way down here. It was probably low blood sugar, that's all.' She tried to look at me innocently as if I was actually going to believe her, which obviously I wasn't.

My weak empathy skills don't let me know if someone is dishonest but I didn't need magic to tell me she was lying because I had a whole childhood of fibs to compare it to.

'Your fingers were *glowing*, Maddie. Fingers don't glow from low blood sugar!'

She sat up a little straighter and rubbed the back of her head. She hadn't hit it when she fell but I guessed she was battling a serious headache. 'I had to put a couple of new wards on the house before I came out,' she said finally. She picked up the glass again. 'Big wards.'

'Why?' I asked. The house was always heavily warded. My combat training was meant to be used as a last resort if someone breached the defences and came for the Flame, but we'd never truly expected anyone to get that far.

I narrowed my eyes at my best friend; I didn't believe putting up those wards had made Maddie collapse. As an alchemist, she had some crazy skills and she'd been warding for years. Some of the witches before her – my great-great-grandmothers – had been guardians for decades and in all my training they'd never mentioned magically glowing fingers and fainting as something I should expect to face.

If Maddie had needed to increase the wards past their usual level, that sounded like a pressing issue. 'What did you need new wards for?'

Her lips pursed and that flutter hit me again: nervousness, fear. Yes, fear was definitely the strongest. My stomach clenched.

'There's a guy – an entrepreneur who's into real estate. He's been poking around.'

'Poking around? What does that mean?'

Maddie's gaze shifted uneasily. 'He's put in an application to take over as patron of the Eternal Flame.'

My jaw dropped. '*What*? He can't do that! The protection of the Flame has been in my mother's family for centuries.'

'I know.' Maddie's voice had quietened. 'But he found out that you're not there. That's one of the reasons I came – you have to show your face in Witchlight Cove, be around the house for a bit, so he knows that getting his hands on it won't be as straightforward as he thinks.'

'It's *my* house!' I protested. 'My family has a tenancy that's passed down the generations.'

She looked resigned. 'Sure, but you haven't been a tenant for ten years, Bea. It's only because Nana's the police chief that people haven't been skulking around and trying to get the guardianship before now.'

I clenched my teeth with frustration – and shame.

Maddie continued, 'This is really serious, Bea. You know I wouldn't be here otherwise. If he gets the guardianship, he can do what he wants with the house. I figured that with your PI skills, maybe you could dig up some dirt on him, make sure that he can never take our home.'

I should have anticipated this day would come at some point but I'd avoided thinking about Witchlight, the Flame, everything. 'Digging up dirt on someone magical might not be that easy. In the non-magical world I have sources, access to databases and information. I won't have any of those in Witchlight. It's going to take time, time I can't afford.'

She leaned forward. 'I didn't come here cap in hand like an idiot. I knew you'd need an income if you came home, so I sorted you a job at the station with Nana. You'll have access to the magical police files.'

I stared at her. 'You got me a job?' I wasn't sure whether to be grateful or horrified. Next thing I knew, she'd be finding me a husband. Still, it was telling: if Maddie had set up some massive wards and arranged my future employment, she really was worried.

She tried to look casual. 'I knew you were working as a PI and I thought you'd want something similar. Besides, Nana's been struggling without someone to man the phones at the station since Victor retired. You working there would kill two birds, so to speak. And you never know, maybe you'll like it and stick around for a bit.'

That was the job? Answering the phones at a police station? I had a ridiculous vision of myself plugging phone lines into a board like they'd used to do in the olden days. 'What's the other reason?' I said, aware that I was ignoring her previous comment.

'Other reason?'

'You said there were a couple of reasons you'd come. He's one. What's the other?'

'Oh, yeah.' Her emotions flickered again, changing as if she were deliberately trying to quash them so I couldn't get a proper hold of them. 'Tomorrow's the village's autumn fayre, and you know what that means.'

Her eyes twinkled and I couldn't help grinning. 'You're serious? They still do it?' I asked.

'Of course. The fastest person to eat twenty-five Cornish pasties wins five hundred quid and a year's supply from Chunkies!' It had been one of our favourite things as kids, laughing as adults gorged themselves on a tonne of pasties.

Maddie went on, 'We'll need to leave first thing in the morning so we can get back in time. After the competition, I'm running a stall. A load of mermaids said they'd be coming by to get their tattoos renewed.'

'You're tattooing mermaids now?' I asked with genuine interest. When I'd been living in Witchlight Cove, Maddie had been learning how her tattoos worked. There had been a couple of werewolves like Ezra that she'd practised on, giving them special tattoos to stop the transformation being forced on them at full moon, but mermaids? That sounded like serious business expansion. I wondered what the mermaids wanted? Stopping their fins from forming?

'Yeah,' she said proudly and beamed at me. 'I tattoo anyone who needs it these days.'

'Vampires?' I asked. Tattoos to protect them against the sun was big business, but she'd always been too nervous to approach them.

'Yep. I've got more than a dozen on the books – high-profile ones, too.'

'Wow.' I sat down next to her and realised how desperate I was to learn everything I had missed in our decade apart. Absurd as it sounds, I honestly couldn't remember the last time I'd had a conversation that lit me up inside. Sure, I had conversations with my students or the people I was doing PI jobs for, but they weren't like this. They weren't with Maddie.

Having her with me again made me wonder how I'd ever found the strength to leave her, but I hadn't seen it that way back then. I'd been hurting so badly; all I'd known was that I had to get away, away from everything including Mads.

'Hot chocolate?' I asked tentatively.

'Sure.'

I busied myself in the kitchen before bustling out with two hot chocolates. I didn't have squirty cream or marshmallows so it felt like a paltry offering but it would have to do. I handed her a mug and she wrapped both hands around it like she needed the warmth. Concern niggled at my insides. Something was wrong with Maddie; I was sure of it.

We sipped our drinks and made stilted small talk until Maddie decided to address the elephant in the room. 'You never rang,' she said finally. 'You never came home. I knew you needed space, Bea, but I didn't expect a whole decade of it.' The hurt radiating out from her cut me to my core.

'I'm sorry,' I said weakly.

'That all you got?' she spat, her tone harsh.

I swallowed, hard. I'd been working through some of my issues with a psychologist – removing anything magical from the narrative, of course – and I had a better grip on some of my behaviour now than I'd had at the time.

I swilled the cold remains of my drink and stared into their murky depths – anything not to meet her accusing eyes. 'I moved to London, I did my PI training, and if I didn't talk to you, Yanni or Ezra, I could imagine that Mum and Dad were still living in Witchlight Cove. Dad puttering around in his library, Mum fussing over the garden.'

My voice broke. 'If I spoke to any of you, I'd have had to face up to them being gone. It was denial at its best – or worst. For the longest time, I couldn't deal with the fact that they were dead, that they were truly gone. And after I finally did, avoiding Witchlight and all of you, was ingrained in me too deeply. I thought you were better off without me.'

'Better off without you?' she shot back, straightening her spine in outrage. 'I'm an outcast to the covens, Bea. I'm alone. I have Ezra and Nana and that's it. *You* were my person, and then ... you weren't.'

'I'm still your person,' I whispered, my eyes filling with tears.

'Are you? Because I need you to come to Witchlight. But if you're going to cut me off again afterwards, I need to know now for my own self-preservation.'

'I won't,' I promised fiercely, 'I swear I won't. When I return to London, I'll keep in touch.'

She slumped. 'But you will return to London?'

'My life is here.'

She gestured at my shitty apartment. 'There's nothing of you here, Bea!' she said fiercely. 'Some books and some ferns. Where are the photos? Where are the friends? Where is the evidence you've *lived* this last decade?'

I wish she'd pull her punches, because I was battered and sore. 'You're right, but I...' I shook my head. The thought of going back to Witchlight scared me, and that sense of fear pissed me right off.

I'd spent the last decade teaching women to face their fears, and now it was time for me to face mine. 'I'll come with you to Witchlight, okay? Baby steps. That has to be enough for now.'

'All right,' she said finally. 'I'll take that, for now. But I need to be clear, if you disappear after this and you don't stay in touch, I'm done. History only gets you so far. I deserve more.'

I had a lump in my throat the size of Gibraltar as I nodded. A big part of me was so proud of her for setting out her needs like that. Toxic friendship was no friendship at all, and I was determined that things would change from here on out.

Maddie gave the biggest yawn ever. Dark circles shadowed her eyes, and her skin was paler than usual. 'Sorry,' she said quickly. 'I think it's the driving and the magic. It's been a big day. Is it okay if I pass out?'

For a second I worried that she meant it literally. 'Sure,' I said quickly, 'and like you said, we need to get up early. Do you want the sofa or my bed? I really don't mind – but bear in mind that if you take my bed you'll have to share it with Eva.'

Her smile didn't quite reach her eyes. 'The sofa's fine for me,' she said before taking my hand and squeezing it tightly. 'It's truly good to see you, Bumble Bea.' There was the slightest hint of a waver in her voice and she looked at me like I was something precious that had an expiration date. It wasn't a good feeling.

My throat was suddenly tight. 'It's good to see you, too. Really good.'

Maddie turned to Eva. 'And it's good to meet you.' She ruffled my dog's fur. 'I'm guessing you need an early night as well – I assume you're coming with us to Witchlight Cove tomorrow? Unless you want to stay here, that is?'

Eva gave a low rumbling growl. 'I guess you're coming then,' Maddie laughed.

'We couldn't be apart,' I confessed.

'Like you and I once.' Maddie's voice was small. And yes, that stung too.

I pulled out a blanket and threw it onto the sofa. 'We'd better get to bed. Goodnight, Maddie.'

'Night, Beatrix. And Bea?'

'Yeah?'

'Thanks for agreeing to come.' She laid down and pulled the blanket over herself then, from one breath to the next, she was asleep. I started to worry again because that wasn't normal for Maddie; she was a sprawled octopus sleeper who tossed and turned for ages before sleep claimed her.

She was tired, that was all. That was what I tried to tell myself.

As I studied my friend, the weight of what she was asking pressed down on me. This wasn't a friendly visit; this was a call to arms. Someone wanted to take the Flame; someone wanted to claim my family's legacy.

I turned off the lights and stared out of the window. The wards had needed strengthening and Maddie had collapsed from the effort. And now some stranger was making a move for the house.

Something was coming. And I had a feeling it was already too late to stop it.

I grabbed a blanket and curled up in the chair opposite Maddie. She wasn't well, and I didn't want to leave her alone in case something happened again. 'If her fingers glow,' I murmured to Eva, 'wake me.'

My dog laid down facing Maddie.

For a long time, the two of us watched her chest rise and fall.

Chapter Four

'So, what can you tell me about this guy? This property developer?' I asked Maddie as I drove.

Eva was sprawled across the back seat of the car. If ever there was a sofa, a seat or a bed of any kind, she claimed it instantly – usually after a lengthy roll that left a substantial sprinkling of her golden fur behind. I admired her for it: she saw what she wanted and took it. It was the kind of confidence I aspired to but could never quite achieve, mostly because human society frowned upon rolling around on furniture in public spaces.

I didn't blame her for getting comfy; we had a long journey south ahead of us. Witchlight Cove is in Cornwall, the southernmost county in the UK. The rugged landscape, with its miles of coastline, undulating hills and epic scenery, is a favourite with both magical and non-magical tourists, and Witchlight Cove itself is one of the premier holiday destinations for magical folk. The small village has it all: quaint houses, stunning views and some gorgeous coffee shops.

Nostalgia and longing hit me like a sledgehammer: Witchlight Cove had never been a place to me but a living, breathing entity that I had loved as much as my own family. I'd been born there, taken my first steps there, had my first kiss there. Everything important in my life – the good, the bad and the downright ugly – had happened there.

I remembered that when I was young lots of holiday visitors talked about moving there but very few ever did. It had that small-town vibe that always felt good in the short term, but after a while it could grate on you if you weren't used to it. And even if you *were* used to it, it could get frustrating: you couldn't sneeze without half the village hearing about it. And dating? That was even worse. Not that that had been something for me to worry about because in order to date someone, they had to be willing to speak to you. Even people I'd gone to school with had given me a wide berth after my grandmother's visit. Fear is a cancer in society, eroding friendships and raising walls instead.

Yanni, Maddie and Ezra, the scrawny werewolf kid we'd grown up with, were the only friends who'd stuck by me.

They'd tried to make me feel it wasn't my fault and I'd always appreciated that – no matter how wrong they were.

Gods – Ezra. The thought of seeing him made a flutter of excitement and nerves rear up and take residence in my stomach. Would *he* be happy to see me? Or would he want to chew me out too? Maddie was dragging me back not quite kicking and screaming, but close; how would *he* feel about seeing me, the third of the Three Amigos?

I wondered what he'd look like, what he'd be doing. Maybe he was married by now with a pup or two on the way. He'd been fairly scrawny but he was good looking in that guy-next-door kind of way, and he had a warm sense of humour. He could always make me laugh back when I still had something to laugh about.

'He keeps to himself.' Maddie's voice interrupted my thoughts and I realised abruptly that she was talking about the property developer prick, not Ezra. That made more sense because Ezra was part of the werewolf pack, and that meant he was as likely to keep himself to himself as a goblin was to wait politely in line.

'His name is Fraser Banks,' she continued. 'He's already bought up a couple of businesses in the village. He lives by the coast, so I reckon he's some sort of water shifter – or maybe he likes the view. Plus that's where all the rich people live and he wants everyone to know he's loaded.'

She sighed loudly, obviously annoyed that she knew so little about him. 'He's arrogant and broody – honestly, just seeing him is enough to make me rage. He's one of those men who always dresses perfectly – he looks like he walked straight out of a luxury cologne advert, except instead of running through waves in slow motion he's ruining my village! I'm sure you can dig up something on him. There's no way a man with that many designer suits doesn't have skeletons in the closet next to them. You can't get rich without getting your hands dirty.'

Maddie wasn't in a place where logic could prevail, so I didn't point out that plenty of people had family money or successful businesses without being unscrupulous. Still, this guy was looking to steal my inheritance; that alone was enough to seal my dislike of him.

I'm never perfectly dressed; I sniff the clothes on the floor to decide if they're lying there because they're dirty or because I'd emptied the dryer and couldn't be bothered to put them away. It is a sophisticated system; some might call it lazy but I think it's efficient. Laundry is my most hated chore and frankly I'd rather poke hot needles in my eye than do the ironing.

'Okay, I'll start digging as soon as I can,' I promised, hands on the wheel. I slid Maddie a sidelong glance. 'I might dig into what made you faint, too, because that wasn't normal.'

She huffed. That same nervousness that I'd sensed the previous night was still rolling from her body; every now and then it got more intense as if she were thinking about something unnerving. 'So, how are the other aspects of your life going?' she asked, pointedly changing the subject.

'Other aspects?'

'Are you dating? Is there someone special?'

I snorted. 'Seriously? Who'd date me? I'm such a rubbish witch that no one with magic would want me, and normal men seem to be intimidated because I can quite easily break several bones in their body without so much as breaking a sweat.' I looked at her hurriedly. 'I hardly ever do that,' I reassured her.

I felt the need to add that last part in case Maddie thought I'd turned into some violence-loving vigilante. I hadn't, but some guys didn't accept that no means no and a few lousy dates had ended with me proving it to them.

Still, I don't enjoy violence for violence's sake, and because I can deliver it doesn't mean that I have to be cruel. One of the biggest complaints my students have is that they know I could go harder on them but I won't. It was bad enough risking broken bones and fractures in Witchlight Cove, where one of the covens could sell you a brew that had you healed in half an hour; there was zero chance I'd get over the guilt of harming one of my students.

'I don't think Ezra would be intimidated by that.' Maddie smirked. 'And just so you know, he's still single.'

My neck warmed. I'd been thinking of him but not like *that*. 'Ezra? You've got to be joking,' I said evenly. 'Ezra's very sweet, but he's not the type of guy I want to get down and dirty with.'

'I think you'll find that he's changed,' she said, the smirk still firmly in place. 'And he still asks after you. Not that I ever have much to tell him. He texts now and again to see if I've heard anything.'

I ignored the dig; I deserved it, after all. 'That's sweet, I guess. Since I'm going to be in Witchlight Cove, I expect I'll pop in and say hi to him.'

Like Maddie's, Ezra's family had been a solid feature in my childhood. His parents – and his huge posse of siblings and cousins – had welcomed me into their homes despite me being a witch and them being shifters. His dad was the pack's alpha so he was a little bit scary, but it had always been his authority that intimidated me; the man himself couldn't have been more welcoming.

'Ezra will probably be at the fayre,' Maddie went on. 'Maybe even taking part in the pasty-eating contest.'

I grinned. 'No way! He takes part now?'

'You bet.'

'You?'

She looked horrified. 'Gods, no!'

I laughed even though a slight tension rose in me. I'd felt so excited when Maddie had said I'd be back in time for the fayre, but in hindsight I couldn't think of a worse time to arrive.

Talk about a hard launch. In such a tight-knit community gossip travelled fast. In an ideal world, I'd have given myself a couple of quiet days to let the news of my return spread slowly, like a tortoise planning a flashmob. If I went to the fayre, my presence would be a flame to a powder keg. Maybe I shouldn't go. Maybe it would be better to lie low for a couple of days.

I slid a glance at my best friend and grimaced.

For her, I'd go to the damned fayre.

Chapter Five

We pulled over at the next service station and Maddie insisted on taking over the driving. I let her because her colour was up and we were driving *her* car; she'd taken one look at Rustbucket Rosie and insisted that we use hers. It had been impossible to argue, and anyway it was unlikely Rosie would have made it all the way to Cornwall. I was ninety percent sure her engine was held together by sheer willpower – her existence definitely defied science – but I wasn't ready to put her out to pasture just yet. She could rest at home and guard the flat for me instead.

After some brunch and a wee stop, I fell asleep. When I woke up again, the scenery made my heart clench: the rugged cliffs, the hidden sandy inlets, the bright blue water crashing into white waves.

My body tingled as I tried to steady my breath. Everything in me screamed that I was finally *home*. How the hell could I have spent so long away from all this? I knew the answer: I'd *had* to get away, had to leave, but now I was back it felt as if this landscape was a part of my very being, like my bones weren't made of calcium but of Cornish rock.

We drove into Witchlight Cove through the barrier that only we magical beings could sense. My nose was practically glued to the window. So much of it was achingly familiar. There were the same shops, brightly painted with large bay windows. There was the square where the large remembrance memorial rested. I didn't need a statue to remember the names of the dead and fallen, and I shuddered at the thought of my parents' names etched in the cold metal.

I looked around and my heart started to race. 'Maddie,' I started as panic wormed its way in. 'Where's my fucking house?'

'Don't worry about it,' Maddie replied airily, keeping her eyes on the road.

'Don't worry about it?' My voice rose an octave. 'Maddie – I can't remember where my house is. Where my *generational home* is! What the hell is wrong with me?!'

She smiled. 'Chill, Bea. Nothing's wrong with you. Trust me, it'll be fine in a minute.'

Her words didn't soothe me; there was nothing like being told to chill when you were mid-breakdown to really make you feel worse.

There was something fuzzy about my recollection of the house; it wasn't quite clicking into place. There was a big front garden – no, surely the garden was at the back? And what colour were the roof tiles? Hold up – did it even have roof tiles? I swear, I could have been ten feet from my home but if Maddie had left me there I couldn't have found my way to it. Why couldn't I remember the place where I'd spent the first eighteen years of my life?

Did I even have a house? Had I dreamt it? Maybe I'd actually been raised in a hedge – my hair often looked as if I had been.

My heart was pounding. 'Maddie, this isn't right!'

'Actually,' she turned to me and grinned, that old mischief I knew so well finally twinkling in her eyes. I'd missed it. 'It's absolutely right. To be honest, I'm a little relieved. It means the ward is still in place.'

I stared at her aghast. 'That's how you warded the house? You made it so nobody could remember where it was?'

Her smile transformed into one of her trademark smirks. 'Clever, right?'

Clever? Yes. Absolutely batshit? Also yes. She was unbelievable. No wonder she had collapsed – the amount of energy required to hide something of that size was huge.

'Clever, yes, but dangerous,' I chastened her. 'So that was why you fainted!'

Something in me eased now that I had a reason for her collapse; she didn't have a rare magical disease, she'd just overstretched herself like a favourite jumper pulled out of shape.

She waved off my worry. 'Don't worry. It's done now and I'm fine. The house is around the corner. You'll see it any minute now.'

As we turned another corner, I felt the ward give way – and there it was: a chocolate-box cottage with a thatched roof, vines climbing the stone, wisteria blooming purple in spring, and a large sky-blue wooden door. This was it. This was my home.

An idiotic part of me still half-expected the door to open and my dad to be standing there, pushing his glasses higher up his nose whilst my mum's arms slipped around his waist. They'd stood there together so many times to wave me off as I'd walked into the village. Tears blurred my vision.

'Are you okay?' Maddie asked softly.

I couldn't speak.

There was the garden where Mum had made flowers bloom with a touch of her fingertips, where Dad barbecued, where Maddie, Ezra and I mixed pretend potions out of herbs and mud. For a second I could hardly breathe for the crushing sense of loss. This was why I hadn't returned. God, it hurt to *feel*.

'The garden looks good,' I said finally, my voice wobbling. 'Mum would approve. Thank you for that.' It did look good, but I couldn't shake the feeling that something was wrong. The house always had a certain feeling to it – a vibe or whatever it was – and it was gone. A cold shiver of dread rolled down my spine.

'Sure,' she said quietly. 'I loved Iris too.' Of course she had, the way I loved Yanni.

I cleared my throat, desperate to stave off tears. Something was *off* – and it wasn't the lack of my parents. I frowned as I tried to put my finger on it. 'It feels different,' I said finally.

'You've been gone for ten years.' Maddie gave my shoulder a sympathetic squeeze before opening the back door of the car so Eva could jump out. It was so fancy that all of the doors worked; only the passenger side of Rosie worked so this was a luxury I wasn't used to.

I was prevaricating. I took a deep breath and followed, slinging my bag over my shoulder and trying to look casual, even though everything inside me was screaming *wrong, wrong, wrong!*

Maddie walked purposefully towards the cottage but my steps faltered. This time, it wasn't grief holding me back; something was buzzing in the back of my mind, something I couldn't quite put my finger on. 'There's something missing,' I mumbled.

She sighed. 'Yeah, there is.' She opened the front door then stepped aside, tucking her brunette strands around her ear, flashing the pink tips. 'Look, like I said there's no easy way to tell you. It's easier to show you.'

Finally relinquishing my place by the car, I walked down the crazy-paving path. I paused at the threshold, lingering by the blue door. The feeling of wrongness was even stronger now.

I dropped my bag to the floor and stepped inside.

As my eyes adjusted to the dim light, I looked around and soaked in the feeling of home. So much was familiar: the paintings on the walls, the curtains on the windows, even the mugs on the coffee table. But that feeling of absence was pressing down even harder on me – and it wasn't my parents' absence.

And then I saw it – or rather, I *didn't*.

My stomach dropped.

Maddie's face was ashen, her eyes wide with the worry she'd been trying to hide from me. I finally understood the fear that had emanated from her since the moment she'd broken into my apartment the previous night.

'Yeah,' she whispered brokenly. 'That's the main reason I needed you to come back.'

Chapter Six

It should have hit me the moment I'd walked into the cottage. The Eternal Flame was gone.

When I went in, the cool air should have set off every alarm bell in my being. The cottage was always warm – not warm, it was *hot*. You never needed more than a T-shirt; the raging Eternal Flame kept us hot in winter and scorching in summer. Now the cottage was cold and dim.

I stared at the empty fireplace, my mouth open in disbelief. The grand structure with the runes carved into its stone was empty. There were no logs in it – there never were – the Eternal Flame needed no combustible fuel.

The Flame was inherently magical. There were rarely licks of anything as pedestrian as red and orange; it changed colour all the time, from the brightest white to emerald and purple. Sometimes I used to lose a whole afternoon watching it shift and swirl. But there were no flames changing colours now, just grey stone. The fireplace was cold and empty. Completely, utterly bare. Not a flicker of fire to be seen.

'How?' I turned to Maddie, eyes wide. 'What the hell happened?'

She wrung her hands. 'I didn't do anything,' she said quickly. 'I couldn't! You know that. You remember all the times we tried to put it out as kids...'

She was right. If you told three boisterous kids that something was impossible, you could bet your life they'd try to prove you wrong. In our case that impossible task was extinguishing the Eternal Flame. We'd tried buckets of water, buckets of ash, blowing really hard – yes, that one was stupid, but we were young and operating with the logic of children, which is to say no logic at all.

With hindsight, what we'd done was idiotic. If we'd somehow succeeded, we'd probably have been grounded for eternity.

We hadn't considered that the Flame's power helped maintain the most powerful wards in the village; I wasn't even sure if we'd understood that Witchlight Cove remained hidden *because* of the Flame. We wanted to prove we were stronger than this supposedly all-powerful magic. Spoiler alert: we weren't.

'When?' I stuttered, my brain still frozen with shock, guilt and horror because I was the freaking *guardian* and

I'd abandoned my post, and now the Flame was *gone*. 'When did it go out?' I still couldn't tear my eyes away from the fireplace. I must have looked into it a thousand times before and not once had it been this desolate.

'A week ago.' Maddie swallowed hard. 'I thought maybe it would come back. The wards around the village haven't dropped, so I thought it was a glitch.'

She was right: I'd felt the barrier as we'd arrived. Surely if it hadn't fallen, the Eternal Flame must be nearby? Could it have been stolen? But alarms would have been sent to all the covens if someone had tried to steal it, and that hadn't happened.

The Flame was supposedly impossible to extinguish, so what did that leave? I refused to accept that it had simply gone out.

Maddie continued. 'I kept waiting for it to come back of its own accord, but with Banks making his proposals to the council I started getting worried.'

At the sound of the developer's name, I turned to look at her. 'You think he had something to do with it?' I asked sharply, cogs finally whirring. 'If he wants to take over the place, maybe he wants to show that we're unfit to hold the guardianship.' At that moment it would have been hard to argue with him, even in my own head. 'The Guardian Who Abandoned Her Post and Let the Eternal Flame Mysteriously Vanish' wasn't exactly a glowing endorsement.

It had been a mistake to leave the Flame in Maddie's care. Even so, it wasn't her fault it was gone but mine. She wasn't a Stonehaven; I was.

I thought about the guilt and fear I'd felt from her; she'd been tying herself in knots over this for a full week. My own guilt deepened.

'I thought he might have something to do with it,' Maddie admitted slowly. 'But if he has, why hasn't he already gone to the council and told them? As far as I'm aware, he hasn't even been inside the house yet.'

'And now we definitely can't let him in!' I said, alarmed. 'No one can come into the house until we know what's going on.'

The relief that billowed from her was so strong it almost took my breath away. She was passing the torch back to me, so to speak, and her feeling was understandable. The unfamiliar responsibility settled over me like a stone shroud. 'Okay. We need a plan. Who else knows?' I asked. 'Have you told Yanni?'

Maddie shook her head. 'No. Nana has enough to deal with – she's basically running the police station on her own. She has Dove, but they're a two-woman team trying to police the whole village. The last thing I wanted to do was burden her with this.'

'True,' I agreed. 'And she'd probably let the covens know.' Yanni was a stickler for rules and regulations; she'd want to do the 'right' thing, which was to be open and transparent. I wanted neither; I wanted to be very opaque and secretive, thank you very much.

'Exactly. It can't get back to the covens,' Maddie said. 'You know how they are about me – they barely treat me as a real witch as it is. They'll start persecuting me immediately!'

I grimaced. 'You and me both.'

Our situations with the covens were very different, but neither of us was nestled into their bosoms. As a guardian, my mother – and subsequently me – had to stay impartial, much the same way Yanni had to be as the chief of police when she dealt with the different magical residents. As for Dad, I'd always thought he didn't care about being in a coven; despite being powerful he seemed to dislike using his magic and avoided it when he could. He didn't want a coven to increase his power when he didn't care about power in the slightest. Knowledge was his thing; he loved to learn and to teach.

Maddie's situation was stickier than mine. Both Yanni and her mum were shifters, but Maddie's dad was a merperson. Despite being only a quarter witch from her grandfather, she'd somehow ended up with a witch's alchemical powers but the covens didn't really consider her to be one of their own. They tolerated her because of Yanni, but they'd probably rather have had me join them than her, and that was saying something.

Unfortunately, the six covens were linked to every person in the village. Some had grandchildren who are half-werewolf or daughters-in-law who were sirens – but they'd all got a connection to the magical community.

'If the covens find out the Flame's gone out, there'll be panic. Riots,' I said quietly. The village took bad news poorly.

'I know. Who'd have thought it would have been a good thing for you and me to be ostracised?' Maddie gave a strained smile. We were lucky that the wards still seemed to be in working order – but that begged the question where on earth was the Flame if it was still doing its job? Because it sure as hell wasn't in the grate.

Maddie blew out a long breath. 'I think one of us needs to be here at all times to keep out intruders, to stop them from finding out the truth.'

The property had extensive wards at the best of times, but they ran on the Eternal Flame's energy and if it wasn't here we could well be sitting ducks. A lock would keep most people out, but we couldn't afford for anyone to find out about its absence until we had a plan to get it back. Right now we had sweet FA. 'I agree,' I said without hesitation.

'Great.' She checked her watch and grimaced. 'I need to be at the fayre in twenty minutes, at least for the first couple of hours.'

'So I'm on the first shift?'

Guilt washed over her again. 'I'm sorry to do this to you, Bea. I'll be back as soon as I can but, like I said, I know there are some mermaids waiting, and some shifter parents, too.'

'Shifter parents?' My eyebrows raised. 'Why do they want your help?'

'It's a long story,' she said. 'They're only small jobs, but every little helps, doesn't it?'

We were fifteen when Maddie had realised she had the rare ability to harness the power of the Eternal Flame to create wards; Dad had surmised that had happened because she'd spent her life around it. Her problem had been transporting power from the Flame to the person who needed it.

It was the rebellious teenagers in us that came up with the idea of magical tattoos. Maddie learned that she could use the Flame to create ink then tattoo the ward onto someone's skin; as long as it was visible, the magic worked.

Over time the tattoos faded and needed to be re-inked if someone wanted to keep them; that was a great marketing tool because she always had repeat business.

'You go,' I said firmly. 'Eva and I are—' I stopped mid-sentence as a thought struck me. 'Maddie, have you been making all your wards without the Eternal Flame?' My heart clenched. 'You haven't been...? You haven't been doing...?' I couldn't bring myself to finish the sentence.

As she stared at me, I knew she could tell exactly what I was thinking. Offering the most watery of smiles, she shook her head. 'Don't worry. No sorcery has taken place within these walls. I swear it.'

I exhaled in relief though I didn't entirely relax. 'So what *have* you been doing?' I asked.

'I've been giving the magic a bit more in return,' she said vaguely.

I frowned. 'What does that mean?'

'It means that I would never abuse magic and you should know that!' Her voice was sharp.

This time, the guilt I felt was solely my own. 'You're right. I'm sorry.' I reached out to touch her arm. 'I'm sorry.'

The tension eased from her frame. Given the rush she'd been in only a minute before, I assumed she was about to leave but she moved closer and wrapped her arms around me. It was the first time we'd hugged since I'd left Witchlight Cove a decade ago.

Tears pricked behind my eyes and I wasn't sure if they were happy or sad ones. All I knew was that I was never letting us go this long without seeing each other again.

We pulled apart. 'I'll stay in touch if I need anything,' she said briskly, surreptitiously dashing tears from her cheeks. 'The ward on the house should hold for a little while longer.' She smiled. 'I guess you should reacquaint yourself with the house.'

She looked down at Eva and her smile widened. My dog had already made herself very much at home: she'd climbed on the sofa, rolled around on the flowery fabric and now she was stretched out. A thin sheen of yellow fur was already coating the cushions. If the Eternal Flame ever did come back, it would probably have a layer of dog hair on it, too.

'Maddie,' I called as she reached the door. 'Bring back a pasty for me and Eva, will you?'

She winked. 'I'll see what I can do. You want anything else?'

I glanced at the cold, empty fireplace and exhaled slowly. 'Yeah. Bring back a bloody miracle while you're at it.'

Chapter Seven

Eva was dozing on the sofa, legs splayed in a most undignified fashion. If there had been a competition for 'least elegant nap position,' she would have taken gold. 'I need you,' I murmured to her. Her eyes snapped open and she tapped her tail once before she rose to her feet, stretched and came to stand next to me.

Her warm brown eyes looked into the heart of me and I stroked her head. 'Thank you.'

I needed Eva's support as I walked through the home I'd once known so well. I dreaded seeing how it had changed, yet as I explored each room I was surprised how little Maddie had done. I'd half-expected the place to have been taken over by tattoo ink and questionable spell ingredients.

The piano remained in the drawing room, though it was covered with a thick layer of dust; my dad had been the musical one, and without him there'd been no one to play it. I was grateful Maddie had kept it, though. The bookshelf housed all the same books, though unlike the piano these were clearly still being used.

There was now a slim dishwasher in the kitchen and the light fittings were new, but the cupboards were the same dark wood, and the heavy oak dining table in the centre of the room where I'd eaten hundreds of meals was unchanged.

I stepped outside to take a look at the garden, which was surprisingly well-ordered with its rows of herbs and flowers. There were almost no weeds; it was clear that Maddie had worked hard to keep everything in great shape. As I was about to go inside, I stopped when I spotted something that shouldn't be there. Nestled into the tree was a small patch of honey fungus.

I went cold.

Honey fungus is an invasive plant that grows beneath the soil as well as on top of it, and it devastates everything in its path. The yellow-hued growth appears in the non-magical community as well; it's a parasite that feeds on dying trees and hastens their decline. However, in the magical community its presence is strongly linked to black magic.

I shuddered to see it in my garden and I *knew* that it was my fault; I'd bet that the presence of the Eternal Flame had kept such things at bay but in its absence the honey fungus had flourished. No doubt the dark magic it grew from was an echo of my grandmothers' deadly sorcery.

Brilliant. I'd been back less than a day and my garden was already staging a rebellion.

I put the bad memories aside with an effort and returned to the cottage. Seizing my courage, I decided to explore upstairs. With every step, I felt my pulse rising but I tried to keep my breath steady. There was nothing here that could hurt me, and apart from that one – admittedly horrific – memory, my life here had been good. That was what I needed to focus on: the good. I wouldn't let *her* ruin this for me.

Maddie had taken over what was once the spare bedroom, which was no real surprise because she'd already been living there before I left. Now it was very much her space. Unlike me, Maddie preferred her clothes hung up neatly rather than scattered across the floor for easy access, but makeup was strewn across the dresser and bottles of coloured ink sat on the window ledges and mantlepiece. I couldn't decide whether the amount of tattoo ink she'd stockpiled was impressive or concerning. Possibly both.

As I stood outside my parents' room, I hesitated. I used to go in there a lot after they died, searching for something – clues, signs – anything that suggested I should have anticipated my grandmother's arrival. Or maybe something to reveal that they weren't dead at all, that it had all been some elaborate plan and I just had to find the right relic or spell to bring them back to me.

It had never happened.

As I stood there with my hand pressed against the wooden door, Eva nudged her nose into my leg and whined softly.

'I'm alright, girl,' I said. It was humbling when your one meagre empathic magical skill was outshone a hundred times by your totally untrained dog. If she ever figured out how to talk, I'd be out of a job.

It felt strange to push open the door to my parents' bedroom and switch on the lights. The room smelled of dust and old memories, possibly also of guilt, but I wasn't about to psychoanalyse myself just then.

When I was young, I'd loved to crawl into bed with them. When I was five, they'd become resigned to me still climbing into their bed in the middle of the night, so they got rid of the standard double and put in a super-king size instead. It dominated the room, nestled in the centre of an array of built-in wardrobes that wrapped around it.

At the other end of the room was my mum's dressing table for her makeup and moisturiser, complete with a mirror. She'd been fastidious about moisturising because she didn't want to look like a crone before her time. Truthfully, she'd barely had a chance to age at all.

The room felt incredibly empty and my heart ached all over again. Despite the musty smell, it was surprisingly clean, which meant that Maddie had made the effort to look after it. I was incredibly grateful; her kindness and compassion put mine to shame.

I took a deep breath and looked around. There were reminders of my parents everywhere: photos on the walls, Dad's books stacked on Mum's dresser. She'd always bitched about him taking up *her* space, but she'd never moved the ever-changing pile. A spare pair of Dad's glasses sat atop the books.

My eyes were hot, stinging. I wasn't sure whether I was grateful to Maddie and Yanni for leaving the room exactly as it was or if I wanted to curse them. It was more than a decade since Mum and Dad had died and it still cut me to the core. So much so that I'd run away to London, abandoned my post. Guilt swamped me.

'You're righting it now,' I whispered, wiping at tears I hadn't noticed were falling.

I took a shaky breath, left their room and went to my own room down the hall.

It was pretty much exactly as I had left it, with the same soft toys on the bed and pictures stuck to the wall. I picked up a teddy bear, whose gold fur was almost the exact same colour as Eva's, and pressed it against my nose, inhaling deeply before setting it gently back down.

Moving to my dresser, I found myself face-to-face with more memories I'd almost forgotten in the form of a pile of half-faded photos. With trembling fingers, I started to look through them all, reliving the moments as if they were only yesterday.

There was a photo of me on the beach with Maddie. I didn't know who'd done the spell, but purple waves were climbing up around us, sparkling like magic. Which they probably were.

Another photo was of Mum, Dad and me in the house, curled up on the floor in matching Christmas pyjamas, hot chocolate in our hands. Even in the photo, I could see that there were only pink marshmallows on top of mine; Mum must have picked them out especially to make sure I didn't have any of the white ones. I'd never liked white marshmallows because they always got mixed up with the cream and I couldn't see them, so she would have them instead.

Suddenly my throat felt thick. It was strange – I hadn't thought about that in so long.

As I stared at the wall, hit by the sudden urge for hot chocolate with pink marshmallows, Eva barked. I'd picked up some food for us at a service station en route, but she'd not had a proper meal since we'd left London. Given all the pasty aromas her dog nose must have picked up from the fayre, she was likely starving.

'Sorry,' I apologised, rubbing my eyes. 'I'm the worst puppy-mama ever, aren't I? Come on, girl, let's get you something to eat.'

She followed me downstairs and happily wolfed down some food. When she was done, she stopped and barked pointedly. A heartbeat later, there was a knock at the door.

Shit. I was not prepared for guests. I barely felt prepared for consciousness.

Chapter Eight

A flurry of nerves hit me. If someone could knock on the door, that meant they could see it – and that meant the ward Maddie had put on it had finally worn off. I shouldn't really have been surprised because we'd been back for more than an hour. Still, there would be no hiding for me now.

'You heard them coming, huh?' Eva was barking as an early-warning alarm. She gestured pointedly towards the door with her nose. 'Thanks.' I patted her head. 'Next time let's do a quick two-bark for visitors coming, okay?'

She barked twice in rapid succession.

'Oh, brilliant. Now you're fluent in sarcasm, too,' I muttered. 'But yes, like that.'

She wagged her tail once then looked at me expectantly, then at the door and then back at me. Yeah, yeah: she was waiting for me to open it. Obviously that was the sensible thing to do but my hands felt clammy and my heartbeat had picked up again.

What if it was Yanni, wanting to know why I wasn't down at the fayre? What if it was Helga and Volga, the elderly witches who lived down the road, who could never be more than six feet apart and who had never looked at me the same since my grandmother had shown up? What if it was someone who wanted to come in? They couldn't see that the Eternal Flame was absent!

Eva decided to bark again. Traitor.

'Shh, girl!' I whispered, pushing my finger to my lips as if that would reinforce my point. I reached out with my empathy skills and felt a wave of impatience from my would-be-visitor. Oops.

'I can hear you in there,' a deep male voice called from outside. 'You should know I'm not leaving until you speak to me. As a Witchlight resident, I have a right to view the Flame.'

Arrogant and entitled: ugh. I was pretty sure I knew who was speaking, but even so I edged towards the window to peer outside. The man had his back to me so all I could see was the dark-blue fabric of his sharply tailored suit. Men in Witchlight aren't known for their sartorial style – we're more a shorts and flips-flops place – so I was most likely looking at Fraser Banks.

I had two choices: ignore him until he went away and leave Maddie to deal with him, or try to get rid of him myself. Given that Maddie had been dealing with all the crap so far, it didn't seem fair to go with the first option. It was time to woman up.

'Look intimidating,' I ordered Eva. She instantly bared her teeth. I blinked. 'Dial it back a notch.' She hid the teeth but her body stayed tense. 'Perfect.'

I tried to cross my arms to match her intimidating vibe but then I had to uncross them to open the door. Damn: intimidation was hard when basic motor skills got in the way.

I took another steadying breath, opened the door – and then I gawped.

Yup, that's the only word for what I did. My jaw lost its ability to stay in place, while my lungs seemed to have forgotten that inhaling and exhaling were supposed to be automatic functions.

Fraser Banks was absolutely gorgeous. Why hadn't Maddie mentioned he was sex on a stick? Surely that was crucial information?

He was the type who dressed to impress. He really didn't need to because he'd look good in a dustbin bag – though admittedly the dark blue suit was a better fit. It matched perfectly with his deep purple shirt, which was open at the collar and giving the impression of effortless cool. His thick brown hair had a windswept look in a *good* way, and his facial hair was impressively manicured; it wasn't the type of designer stubble that came from three days of not bothering to shave. This was the type of stubble you went to the barber for.

As for his eyes? It didn't seem possible that they could be so blue, but they were like clear, cold water. And I wanted to drink them up. Or drown in them. Either worked.

'Who are you?' he asked, obviously taken aback. The surprise in his voice brought me back to the moment. This was not a man I was meant to be ogling; this was a man I had to keep away from the house whatever happened.

I folded my arms again, successfully this time. 'I think I should be the one asking that, don't you? Given that you're the one standing on *my* property.'

His head tilted to the side in a manner remarkably similar to Eva's when she was listening to me speak. '*Your* property?'

'*My* property. I'm the one with the lifetime ancestral tenancy. I'm Beatrix Stonehaven.'

I watched his pupils dilate and hide a fraction of those shimmering blue irises. 'Stonehaven? *You're* the generational guardian? But I thought ... I thought you didn't live here anymore.'

'Really?' I raised my eyebrows and gave him the most withering look I could muster. 'Why would you think that? I've been doing some travelling recently, but this is my home. This house and its guardianship have belonged to my ancestors for centuries.' I paused. 'And it's going to stay that way.'

His jaw tightened, though it didn't make him look any less attractive; if anything it added a brooding dimension to his look. I could do brooding for a night. Brooding was often very good fun for one night. And with those broad shoulders, he could definitely—

Stop it, Bea, I said to myself. This was not the time to fantasise about what I would see if I undid a couple more of those shirt buttons. He was the *enemy* and there was no sleeping with the enemy, no matter how good they looked.

'And you are?' I asked, even though I knew the answer.

'Banks. Fraser Banks.'

I wondered if he thought he sounded like James Bond. He didn't.

'The Eternal Flame is a gift to Witchlight Cove,' he continued sternly. 'All the residents should have the opportunity to benefit from its power.'

'And all the residents do have that,' I said coolly. 'The Eternal Flame has strengthened the wards protecting this village for centuries and kept us secret from the non-magical world. That's pretty much the biggest benefit people could ask for – not to mention the tonics and wards its power has created.'

'That's a small fraction of what it's capable of. If you knew what the Flame—'

'You're not about to mansplain the thing that I was literally born to protect, are you?' Anger rippled down my spine. Just because we'd lost the damn flame didn't mean I'd let some guy in a fancy suit talk to me like he knew better than I did. Because he didn't. Not a chance in hell.

'Trust me, I know exactly what the Eternal Flame is capable of,' I continued. 'And I also know exactly what people will do to get that power.'

His eyes narrowed. 'What are you accusing me of, Miss Stonehaven? Because I'm not the sort of man you want to get on the wrong side of.'

'I'm not accusing you of anything.' Yet. 'But most of the time, the people who talk about its amazing properties don't want to do pleasant things with it. In fact, they want to do very, very bad things. And if you want—'

My tirade was interrupted by a ringing sound coming from his pocket. I huffed and wished my arms were unfolded so I could fold them again. I'd just been getting into my stride. Bloody modern technology had ruined my soapbox moment.

Banks pursed his lips. 'Sorry... I need to take this.' To give him his due, he seemed mildly embarrassed at cutting me off.

'You go ahead,' I said. 'It's not like I'm going anywhere. I'm sure you're *very* important.'

He narrowed his eyes at my sarcasm then cleared his throat and answered his phone. I was about to walk away to give him a degree of privacy when his posture shifted and I felt tension ripple through him. Was it something to do with the house? Had he heard that the Flame was gone? I pricked up my ears and tried not to make it obvious that I was trying to eavesdrop.

'Poisoned? They're sure? Which contestants?' he demanded.

My stomach knotted. The call might not be about the house, but it obviously wasn't good news, not good news at all. Poisonings were *not* par for the course in Witchlight, and the mention of 'contestants' meant it had to be related to the pasty-eating contest. The contest that Ezra was supposedly taking part in.

Panicking a little, I took another step forward to listen in to his call.

Banks frowned. 'Amara Drakefield? No, I don't think I know that name.' The knot in my stomach became a matted rope; Banks might not know that name, but I definitely did.

He ended the call and opened his mouth, but I didn't give him a chance to speak. 'Has Mrs D been poisoned?' I asked urgently.

'Mrs D?'

'Mrs Drakefield,' I spat impatiently. 'Did you say she was poisoned?'

'They won't be a hundred percent positive until they've run more tests, but it looks like it.'

That was as good as a yes to me. 'Have you got a car?' I could walk because nothing in the village was that far away, but that would take time. I thought longingly of poor Rustbucket Rosie hundreds of miles away in London.

'Yes.' He nodded behind him.

I didn't even bother to look at his vehicle. Instead, I turned to Eva. 'You stay here. No one comes into the house. You understand, girl? You let *no one* in.'

She barked, gave me a little growl like she was showing me she knew how to stop people coming in, then she bared her teeth.

I patted her. 'You got it. Great,' I turned back to Banks. 'Let's go.'

'After you.' Once again, he gestured down the path.

I took one last look at Eva and the house I wasn't supposed to leave, then I strode forward.

Someone had poisoned Mrs D and that put them at the top of my shit list. And I was determined to find out exactly who it was.

Chapter Nine

I like to think that I'm not the type of person who cares about flashy cars and expensive accessories – but Banks' car was something special. Maybe it was the recent journey in Maddie's beat-up hatchback that influenced my opinion, but I swear that when my backside slipped onto the leather seats they felt like the softest, most comfortable place in the entire world. And the smell was divine. It was a far cry from poor old Rosie.

It was nice to have something else to think about, other than poor Mrs D. Anxiety churned in my stomach; I hoped she was okay.

I snapped on my seatbelt and tried to ignore the cool way the engine roared to life. Soft Celtic pipe music hummed through the car but Banks leaned forward and turned it off. Shame: I could have done with some soothing sounds right about then.

'So Mrs D was poisoned at the pasty contest?' I said into the silence.

'Apparently. Two of the contestants started vomiting a couple of minutes in. One of them is an acquaintance of mine – and obviously you know the other?'

'Amara Drakefield. Yes, I know her. *Knew* her. She was my form teacher in school.'

He smiled. 'A form teacher who does pasty-eating contests. I guess it's easy to understand why kids would get on with someone like that.'

I stayed silent as I gazed out of the car window, grateful that he let the silence fall. He must be as worried about the person he knew as I was about Mrs D.

When I'd been at school, she wasn't the sort of teacher who did pasty-eating contests; she was too busy arranging school trips, choir tours and debate teams, or organising breakfast clubs for the children she knew didn't get a proper meal at home. She was great with the problem kids, too, the ones who were always getting in trouble in other teachers' classes. She always did everything in her power to make sure everyone got every opportunity.

I had always respected her, even though I'd stayed off her radar for most of my school career. It wasn't until Grandmother Dearest had shown up that she'd become a more important figure in my life. Everyone had looked at me differently after that, including the teachers. It was as if they didn't know how to treat me; some of them acted like I was frail and about to fall apart at any minute, others were so scared of me I felt the fear radiating off them.

I was of my grandmother's blood and they had seen what she was capable of, so they thought I was capable of the same things. Ironically, I was about as much use as a soggy matchstick.

It's a strange thing that people in the magical community don't talk about their powers. Sometimes you can guess: if both parents are merpeople then the child will be a merperson too. But there are many others whose lineage is far more complicated than that, such as fifth-generation witches with a werewolf father.

Sometimes those mixed lineages strengthen the forms of magic, but sometimes there is a dominant strand that subdues the others, like with Maddie. And very occasionally, as in my case, for no apparent reason a person with an incredibly powerful witch mother and a pretty average witch father can be almost non-magical. But it wasn't the done thing to talk about our magic unless it was with our closest family and friends; it was an absolute no-no, on a par with talking about politics at the dinner table.

There were shifters in my class who could have been anything from beetles to bears for all I knew – and for all they were aware I was at home practising curses and black magic every spare minute to continue my grandmother's legacy.

But Mrs D was different. I wasn't sure what magic she had, though I knew she was a shifter of sorts. Apparently she'd married a non-magical man when she was young and, being a shifter, had aged far more slowly than him; she had already outlived him by decades. I didn't know if that was true, but something about the way she was with me after my parents' deaths made me believe it was. She had definitely suffered loss.

I'd gone back to school five weeks after my parents had been killed even though Yanni didn't want me to. The minute I arrived, I was sure I'd made a mistake. Then Mrs D strode toward me, all four feet five inches of her.

'Today won't be easy,' she'd said. 'Actually, it will probably be pretty awful, and I expect most days from now on are going to have a bit of awfulness in them. But I have several beanbags and a large tin of custard creams in my office at all times. You and your friends come and go as you need.'

It was the way she told the truth, that there was going to be a bit of awfulness in everything, that made me realise she was different. Even Yanni had tried to tell me that things would get better, that it would be hard and take time but they *would* get better. Mrs D said no such thing, probably because she knew it wasn't true.

She was also the one who'd told me it was okay to leave Witchlight Cove. 'You'll come back when you're ready,' she'd said. 'And the people who are meant to be in your life will still be here waiting for you.'

What she hadn't told me was that they would also be very pissed off with me. Then again, perhaps she hadn't expected me to bugger off for a whole decade.

Banks' voice interrupted my reminiscing. 'Where do you want to go? They said they were taking the two people who were sick to the hospital. Do you want to go there or to the fête?'

I snorted. 'It's a fayre, not a fête.'

'What's the difference?'

I shot him a look. 'One is right, and one is wrong. Take me to the hospital,' I said. 'Please,' I tacked on, because Mum had taught me my manners. 'Who did you say the other person was?'

He shot me an indecipherable look. 'I didn't.' He paused, evidently debating whether to share the information with me or not. 'Warren Storcrest,' he said finally. I guessed he thought it would be common knowledge soon enough and he was right; Witchlight

Cove was full of gossips. 'I take it you know the name?' Banks asked.

I gave a low whistle. Everyone knew Warren. He was a man who'd built himself up from nothing. Apparently his first ever job was as a deckhand for non-magical folk but now he owned all the charter boats on the waterfront. He wasn't one for keeping his wealth to himself and hoarding it like a squirrel with a pile of nuts; instead he took philanthropy to a whole new level. Yes, I knew the Storcrest name, everyone did. I also knew the man himself, though not intimately.

'I grew up in Witchlight so yes, I know the name,' I said drily. 'His business used to sponsor the girls' football team. And the boys. And the debate team tour.' Actually, he'd funded all the school teams.

Banks nodded. 'It sounds like two good people got hurt. Let's hope it's not serious.'

I grunted agreement and took out my phone. I fired off a quick message to Maddie to tell her I'd had to leave the house but Eva was standing guard. I hoped she wouldn't be mad that I'd left my post when I was only an hour into my Flame vigil. It wasn't exactly great going for a guardian. I really sucked at this.

Her message pinged back almost straight away: *I'll go back. Everything's closing down here anyway.*

I grimaced. Once again, Maddie was stepping up to my responsibilities.

'How long are you planning on staying in Witchlight?' Fraser Banks asked.

Suddenly everything got to me: the missing Flame, returning to the village, Mrs D, my constant feelings of guilt. Always the guilt.

Angry and frustrated and upset, I glared at him. 'Are you seriously trying to make small talk right now?'

He rubbed his forehead. 'I feel like I've offended you somehow.'

'Hm, I can't think why that might be. Oh right!' I snapped my fingers. 'Because you're trying to kick me and my friend out of my family's ancestral home?'

His hands tightened on the wheel. 'It's not quite as straightforward as that.'

'It is from where I'm sitting,' I said firmly. It was my turn to rub my forehead. I knew I wasn't being fair. 'Look, this isn't a great time to talk. Someone I care about was taken ill. How about some silence?'

'Sure.'

We didn't speak until he drove into one of the empty parking bays outside the hospital and cut the engine. 'I'll come with you,' he said, opening his door.

'I don't need a chaperone,' I shot back.

'I'm beginning to get that vibe,' he said wryly. 'But I'm guessing you're not family, and they might not let you in. I could put in a word for you.'

'You're saying you have sway in this village?' I scoffed.

'I do, actually.'

I rolled my eyes but there was no point telling him not to come. I got the impression he wanted to play the big protector even though I didn't need protecting. If it suited him to think his reputation in this area was more significant than mine, despite living here for less than a decade, then fine. Let him.

We marched through the double doors. 'Where is Mrs D?' I asked a nurse who was just inside them.

'I'm sorry,' she eyed me. 'Who are you?'

'Beatrix Stonehaven.'

I watched her eyes widen and the colour drain from her patchy cheeks. She took an involuntary step back. Charming. 'Stonehaven, as in...?'

'Stonehaven, yes.' I gave a long sigh. 'I assume your complexion is several shades whiter now than it was a second ago because you recognise the name. Is Mrs Drakefield here? She was brought in after the fayre. Can you find out where she is?'

'I'll... I'll... Wait there.' She scurried away.

Banks was studying me. 'It looks like your name has some weight, too.'

'No shit,' I snapped. 'Is there anything else about myself that you'd like to explain to me?'

He looked amused. 'You're not intimidated by me in the slightest, are you?'

'Oh, that is so sweet.' I gave him a flirty smile then immediately let it drop. 'It's *you* who should be intimidated by me.'

I was done waiting and that was a belter of a line to make an exit on. I turned on my heel and followed the nurse – whether she wanted me to or not.

Chapter
Ten

'Beatrix!' A voice said from behind me, one I hadn't heard from in three years but knew almost as well as my own. I started to turn but before I could complete the manoeuvre I found myself being squashed by a bear-shifter's muscley arms.

Yep, this was it. The day I died. Cause of death? Overenthusiastic bear hug.

'Yanni, I need to breathe!' I said tightly. It took a lot of self-restraint not to immediately get out of the hold, but flinging the chief of police onto the ground probably wouldn't go well for me. And what did it say about me that I immediately wanted to escape the hug? Probably something like 'has the emotional range of a teaspoon'. But at least I was self-aware.

I'd forgotten how much a hug from a brown-bear shifter could squeeze the life out of you. Growing up, there were several times when I genuinely thought Yanni had broken one of my bones, but somehow I'd never ended up with so much as a bruise.

For a split second her grip eased and I thought she was about to let me go, but she was only taking a breather. There was a short pause before the second round of attempted murder via affection and she started crushing me again. Something in me softened. She'd missed me. It was nice to be missed. God knows, I'd missed her.

Finally Yanni released me, stepped back and cupped my cheeks in her hands. She studied me and I gazed back at her. As a shifter, she aged a smidge slower than us humans so she still looked great for her age; there was a hint of laughter lines around her eyes, and her dark brown hair was liberally scattered with grey, but those were the only changes. Otherwise her broad, strong frame was the same, as was the uniform she almost always wore.

Her voice was soft. 'Look at you, Bea, all grown up! Oh, my goodness.' Her thick Cornish accent sounded like home, almost as much as the scenery and the smell of the salt water. I could see – and appreciate – that she was resisting the urge to pull me into yet another bone-crushing hug.

'Yanni,' I murmured, her name more than a moniker to me, but almost a title. It meant something similar to Nana, because that was the role she'd always played in my life. 'I'm so glad to see you,' I admitted, and my eyes welled with how much that was true. We'd spoken briefly in the last decade, but only fleetingly and she deserved so much more than I'd given her. 'I'm sorry,' I blurted. 'I'm so, so sorry.'

She couldn't resist that second hug and pulled me in again. She pressed a kiss to my forehead and it took everything I had not to dissolve into tears because all I felt from her was relief and love. Relief that I was home and abiding love; love I didn't feel I was worthy of. I was truly determined to earn it again.

'It's okay.' She pressed another kiss to my forehead. 'It was so much to deal with.'

'I dealt with it badly.'

'You were so young, Bea. So lost. It hurt to let you go, but I knew it was what you needed. I knew in my bones one day you'd be back, and here you are.' She gave me one last squeeze and released me.

I wiped the tears from my cheeks and tried to remember what the hell I was there for.

'I wasn't expecting to see you until tomorrow,' she went on. 'I'm ever so grateful you're taking over this job. I'm looking forward to seeing more of you. It's not the most exciting role, but I'm sure you can find a way to make it fun, can't you?'

Answering calls to the police station from people whining about their neighbours' fences being two inches too far to the left or someone playing music too loud on a Friday night didn't sound particularly wild. Maybe if I was lucky I'd get a case of a missing garden gnome. High stakes, thrilling stuff. Still, hopefully it meant I'd have time to dig up dirt on one Fraser Banks. I suddenly felt incredibly motivated to start work. Take that, Mr Mansplainer.

'Thank you for the job, Yanni. I'm grateful for the income while I find my feet.'

'Of course. I'm sure you'll be an asset.' Yanni studied me. 'What are you doing here, Bea?' she asked. 'Is everything alright?' I thought for a moment she meant what was I doing back in Witchlight Cove and I felt a surge of panic, then I realised she was talking about me being in the hospital.

'Right, Yes. No, I mean,' My cheeks warmed. Flawless sentence structure, an inspiration to linguists everywhere. I was so smooth. 'Yanni, is Mrs D okay?'

The chief of police sighed. 'You heard? I forgot you two were close. Yes, she's doing alright, a little better than Warren. By the looks of things, he got a bigger dose of whatever was in those pasties.' Her voice was grim.

Warren Storcrest had been the pasty-eating champion at least three years in a row when I'd lived in Witchlight, and

I suspected he'd lengthened his winning streak since then or at least got a couple more victories under his belt. No doubt he'd eaten more of the poison than Mrs D. He was the champion of pasty consumption, unbeatable – until someone poisoned them.

'Do you know what it was?' I asked. 'They weren't the only two in the competition, were they?'

'No, there were three others. One was a vampire – Sonny from the café. Do you know him?'

I shook my head. 'No, I don't. Who else was there?'

'A young warlock from the Barrows Estate, and a djinn – Runa Collek.'

I didn't recognise any of those names, but there was one thing about the list that stood out. 'The only ones who got ill were shifters? Is that what you're telling me? Someone was targeting shifters?'

'I don't know yet, but the evidence seems to point that way.'

I frowned. 'Ezra didn't compete?'

'There was a shifter matter he had to attend to otherwise I expect he would have been there.'

'Is there trouble with the shifter groups? Anyone who'd want to target them in particular?'

Yanni smiled. 'I heard you'd been working as a PI in the non-magical world. Why do I get the feeling you're going to dig into this even if I tell you not to?'

I didn't respond. I wasn't going to lie outright to her, not when I already had to keep the disappearance of the Eternal Flame from her. But I couldn't sit back if someone had targeted Mrs D.

After a moment's silence, Yanni sighed. 'There are no beefs with the shifters at the moment that I know of. But I'll do some digging. You can go in and see Amara if you want. I think the doc has finished giving her a once-over.'

I was about to thank her, then I hesitated. 'Are you sure she doesn't have any family she'd rather see?'

'No, she hasn't got any family and she insisted that we didn't make a fuss. But as you're here now, you might as well pop in. I'm sure she'd like that.'

'Thank you.'

'I'd better get off, but I'll see you bright and early and ready to start work tomorrow.'

Ugh. Bright and early. My nemesis.

Yanni was obviously preparing to leave – she no doubt had a tonne of police business to attend to – but I had a question I needed her to answer first. 'Yanni, about the job.' I tried to keep my voice as level as possible.

'Yes?' Her eyes narrowed. 'What about it?'

'How do you feel about me bringing a dog along?'

Her expression didn't change but I could practically hear her brain screeching to a halt. Her mouth hung open in surprise.

Was that a no, or… ?

Chapter Eleven

Yanni groaned, though a smile twitched the corner of her lips. 'I feel like this is the type of question I can't say no to,' she said.

'Well, I'm not saying I wouldn't try to sneak her in if you did, but... '

She chuckled and her smile widened. 'Fine – as long as she behaves herself.'

'She will,' I promised with a rush of relief. Probably. Hopefully. There was a chance Eva might eat a document or two, but that was a small price to pay for workplace morale.

I was so used to having Eva with me now that I'd hate to be without her, plus I wasn't sure how she'd cope with being left at home alone all day. What if she tore the place to shreds? Maddie would probably be there protecting the secret of the extinguished Flame *and* the furniture but even so... Eva and I had been joined at the hip for the last three years and I knew that I'd struggle without her.

Relieved that wasn't going to happen, I was about to say goodbye when Yanni spoke again. 'You're staying at your house with Maddie?' she asked.

'Yes, of course. Why?'

A hint of a frown crossed her features before she wiped it away. 'Could you keep an eye on her for me? She's been a bit short with me these last couple of weeks, though I'm sure it's only the stress of opening the tattoo shop.'

'She's opening a shop?' I tried to hide my surprise. It didn't work.

Yanni shook her head. 'You two have a lot to catch up on.'

I nodded sombrely. 'We do.'

For a moment, I thought she'd hug me again so I instinctively drew in a deep breath and steeled my muscles. Instead she leaned forward and kissed my cheek. 'Tell Amara to take it easy, okay?' Then she walked away with her characteristic swagger.

There had been a time in my life when I'd wanted to be like Yanni, full of self-belief, authority and rules, but as I grew up I came to appreciate that life was not always black and white. I was pretty sure authority was there to be defied, though I still wanted her self-belief, the confidence to say, 'No, officer, I did not see that traffic sign,' with absolute conviction.

As I walked down the corridor, I glanced through the windows into the rooms. In the first one there was a couple with a newborn that was constantly flicking from human to tabby kitten. Adorable. And slightly terrifying. But mostly adorable.

In the next room a teenager was scowling impressively as casts were being set around both their arms. Ouch. I guessed someone was allergic to the bone-healing potion. If that had been me, I'd have been a heck of a lot more careful than this kid evidently had been.

When I reached the third window, I slowed because I could see Warren Storcrest through the slats of the blinds. He was a brute of a man, only a couple of inches shorter than Yanni. If memory served me right, he was either a whale or a shark shifter, though he could have easily been some other great sea creature. He was *definitely* a water shifter, I knew that much.

I never remembered him looking so frail. His skin was pallid and his cheeks hollow, though he was forcing himself to smile at the young woman beside him. From the way he was sitting up and stroking her head like she was still a child, I assumed she was his daughter Jennifer. He was obviously alright; *she* was the one that needed soothing. I left them to it.

Fraser Banks was waiting patiently in the corridor; he was here to see Warren, but he'd clearly accepted that family should go first. He leant against the wall whilst he waited for Jennifer to leave.

He nodded as I walked past him. I nodded in return – fractionally – because mum didn't raise me to be rude.

The blinds were closed in the next room so I knocked on the door. 'Knock, knock,' I said, in that way people do when they want to make it clear who's there. 'Can I come in?'

'The door's open,' a voice called from inside.

I inched the door open. As soon as I saw the figure on the bed, I smiled. Despite her pallor, Mrs D looked identical to how she'd been all those years ago. Her hair was still the same soft, silvery blonde pinned at the base of her neck, and she was wearing a tweed suit that I'd bet good money was the same one she'd worn back when she was teaching me. I'd always suspected it was indestructible.

As I moved into the room, I felt a twinge of anxiety. What if she didn't remember me? After all, witches are one of the few magical creatures burdened with ageing, although a lot of them seem to linger unnaturally long at middle age and get very cagey if you ask how old they are.

I watched her frown before her jaw dropped in amazement. 'Oh my goodness, as I live and breathe!

Beatrix Stonehaven. How wonderful to see you!' She shuffled upright in her bed.

I found the glow that warmed her cheeks surprisingly humbling. 'Hey, Mrs D. I popped back to Witchlight for a visit and I heard you'd got yourself into some sort of trouble. How are you feeling?'

She shook her head, waving away my concern. 'I'm okay, honestly. Just came over a bit funny. But I must look terrible. Warren – he's alright, isn't he?'

'I saw him with his daughter.' I gave her a big smile. 'He looks okay.'

She bit down on her bottom lip and her brow furrowed. 'I don't know what happened. I don't— I don't—'

I stepped forward and placed my hand on her shoulder. 'Don't worry. Yanni is going to look into it.'

'Yanni is?'

'Yeah. Potential poisoning and all that.'

Her eyes widened so far they practically bulged from her skull. 'Poisoned? She doesn't think...? Oh my goodness, no. I'm sure it was just a funny reaction or something.'

'If it was a "funny reaction", it was one that only affected shifters and it could have easily taken out two of the village's most beloved characters. Someone needs to look into it,' I replied firmly.

'Oh. Yes, that makes sense.' She looked up at me and a deep pang of sympathy struck me. She might not have looked any older, but she was. And, if my suspicions were correct, she'd probably spent another decade alone apart from the kids she'd helped.

A wave of sadness and worry flowed through the air from her to me and I concentrated for a moment, trying to shore up my mental defences. After I'd strengthened my wards, I couldn't help yawning; I'd forgotten how draining it could be dealing with other people's emotions and keeping up shields strong enough to keep out magical emotions. I'd got into the habit of shielding again since I'd adopted Eva, but it was far easier in the human world where emotions didn't batter me.

'Are you alright, dear?' Mrs D said as I covered my mouth. A moment later, she echoed my yawn.

'You don't have to worry about me – you're the one in hospital!' I patted her hand. 'You must be tired too. But a question or two, if I may?' She nodded. 'Did you see anyone approach the pasties before the competition?'

She shook her head. 'No.'

'Anyone looking at you too intently from the crowd?'

She gave a helpless laugh. 'My dear, I was focused on the pasties! There were a lot of them – and I really wanted that £500 for the school.' She yawned again. 'Excuse me,' she muttered. 'It seems that poisoning really takes it out of you.'

'You don't say! Next you'll be telling me that jumping off a cliff leads to sore knees.'

Mrs D laughed and I was happy to have put the smile back on her face, if only for a minute or two. Now that I'd seen her for myself, I could relax. She might be ill, but she was miles away from death's door; that being the case, I could now focus on finding the fucker that thought poisoning Mrs D was okay.

'Anyway, I should go and let you get your rest,' I said. 'Besides, I've only been in Witchlight Cove a couple of hours so I should probably unpack. I'd like to meet up properly when you're out, though. Maybe we could catch up over a coffee?'

I lowered my shields a little. The gratitude and warmth that flowed from her was enough for me to know I'd made the right decision in leaving the house to visit her.

'Of course. It's been lovely to see you, Beatrix, really lovely. You go enjoy some of that Witchlight,' she winked. 'I bet you've missed it terribly. Such wonderful magic.'

Witchlight was a local term for the Eternal Flame. No one knew which one had been named first; it was a real chicken-and-egg situation.

'Yes, absolutely,' I forced out, keeping my face blank with effort. I was about to stand up when a thought struck me. 'Mrs D, you know most of the people in Witchlight Cove, don't you?'

She chuckled. 'Well, I should think so – I've taught most of them! I taught a lot of their parents and grandparents, too. But don't use that to try to work out my age.' She winked.

I smiled the way I knew she expected me to. 'Is there any chance you know of any witches who aren't in covens?' If Maddie and I were to retrieve the missing Eternal Flame, we needed someone who wasn't affiliated with the covens to help us.

Her smile dropped. 'Aren't in covens? You mean like your friend Maddie?'

'Yes. Just... I've got a few questions, but you know what it's like for me – and for her. The judgement. I wondered if there was anybody outside the general circle of things that I could talk to.'

She looked worried. 'Is everything alright, Beatrix? Do you need help? From me, I mean?'

I flashed her the easiest smile I could, grateful that I wasn't dealing with another empath because, without a doubt, she'd have felt my bull. 'It's fine, I promise. Just wondering, that's all.'

Mrs D gave a slight hum and pinched her brow as she thought. 'There's Old Jacobson at Shingle's End,' she said finally. 'You could try him, I suppose.'

'Shingle's End?' The only house that had been on Shingle's End when I'd lived here was an old, run-down shack where we may or may not have occasionally gone to smoke cigarettes. 'I didn't think anybody lived there.'

'He moved in a couple of years after you left. I only know because I was out for a walk one day and saw him. He very much keeps to himself. What type of magic he does – or if he'd be happy to speak to you – I can't say. I'm sorry I can't be of more use.'

'No, that's good to know. Thank you.' I patted her hand again. 'And don't you worry about the poisoning. I'm sure they'll work out whoever is behind it soon.'

Her smile was watery and I suspected that our conversation had worn her out, so I offered one last swift wave before I disappeared into the corridor.

The nurse who'd been horrified by my name was in reception when I left, and I felt her eyes follow me all the way out of the door. She wasn't scared of me, though, because I'd have felt it if she was. She was wary. Probably rightly so.

Back on the street, I turned to walk up the hill that led to the cottage but stopped after only a couple of steps.

From where I was standing, it was only a short walk to the cemetery.

A deep throbbing radiated from my chest. The feeling was always there, 24/7, but as the years had passed I'd got better at ignoring it. That was a lot harder to do now that I was back.

I drew in a deep breath and, for the first time in as long as I could remember, I didn't bother trying to quash the sensation. Maddie wasn't the only person who deserved an apology for me being away for so long. They did too.

And there was no time like the present.

Chapter Twelve

You'd think that someone who loved their parents as much as I loved mine would actually visit their grave more than once in a decade. And to be fair, I used to.

When they first died and I was still living in Witchlight Cove, I spent more time there than anywhere else. I could be found lying on the grass at almost any time of the day, staring at the grey headstone they shared, wishing they would respond. I even tried knocking once, just in case. Turns out graves are not doors to the afterlife, no matter how politely you rap on them.

I spent hours in front of that grave, praying that my parents understood how I felt. How I would've gladly taken their place and been the one my grandmother had killed. How I would've gone with her, the way she wanted me to, rather than having them lose their lives. God, I would have hunted her down and gone with her then and there if it would have brought them back. But there was nothing that could do that. They were gone.

Back in the here and now, I hesitated as I stood at the edge of the cemetery. I've conversed with a ghost a time or two, but my parents hadn't stayed behind as lost shades. If they have unfinished business to deal with, ghosts come back immediately after their death, then they hang around generally irritating the crap out of the living until their business is sorted. If it ever does get sorted. If it doesn't, they stick about, growing more and more annoying with every passing century, like that one relative who overstays their welcome at Christmas. Except ghosts are slightly more transparent and significantly less interested in the last of the mince pies.

The fact my parents hadn't come to me after they died – and trust me, I tried to make them – meant that they didn't have unfinished business. *I* wasn't unfinished business and that had hurt like hell. You'd think wanting to keep an eye on your only child would count as unfinished business, but apparently it didn't. Clearly they had more faith in my ability to function than I did. Love really is blind.

I was bitter about their absence for a good couple of years, but now I was older and wiser and I was *glad* that they hadn't felt their lives were half done. I had survived dear old fucking grandmama, and I had Maddie and Yanni; they knew I'd be okay. If you consider running away and ignoring all your responsibilities like I'd been doing is okay. Still, everyone's allowed a sabbatical, right?

As I walked through the gravestones, I found myself wishing I'd brought Eva. Part of that was for the moral support she offered, but the other part was me wanting her to meet my parents in the only form that was possible for her right now. If their spirits were there, I suspected she could sniff them out; if not, there were loads of squirrels in the cemetery and she'd love that too. A win-win situation – unless you were a squirrel.

I briefly contemplated going back to fetch her, then recognised I was using delaying tactics. My dog could come with me at any time. It wasn't like I was going back to London straight away, not until I'd found a way to find the Flame and get the absurdly attractive Fraser Banks out of our lives for good. And, whilst I was in Witchlight, it seemed like a good idea to look into whatever happened to Mrs D. We couldn't have a poisoner on the loose; our tourism industry would take a hammering, and we relied heavily on our supernatural tourists. We had to protect our brand: 'Witchlight Cove — Now With 100% Less Murder (Hopefully)'.

I was prevaricating again. Speaking to my parents, or at least to their headstone, was on me and me alone right now. Mustering courage I shouldn't have required, I continued on the path towards their grave.

I was still several feet away when I stopped. 'That's weird,' I muttered. There, beneath the headstone, were two wreaths. The first one was yellow calla lilies, and I suspected Maddie had placed it there.

Maddie knew they were my mother's favourite flowers; the house used to be filled with them, mainly because Maddie had begged Mum to whip them up out of nothing every time she visited and Mum had always obliged. When it became clear that Maddie's dominant magic wasn't aligned with shifting, I think my friend had hoped she'd turn out to be an earth witch, or at least master creating flowers with enough practice. As far as I was aware, that hadn't happened. Even so, everything about the yellow wreath screamed Maddie.

But it was the other bouquet that held my attention. It was placed a little to the right, directly in the centre of the shared grave. And it was a bunch of irises.

Iris, like my mother's name.

'Your mother is the only iris I will allow in this house,' my dad, Greg, would mutter when someone brought a bouquet that contained those vibrant blooms. He normally had the common sense to wait until the visitor had left before he spoke, but not always.

He hated their smell and the stamens with their bright yellow pollen that stained everything it touched. He once nearly threw a guest out of the house because they brought irises and – I quote – 'committed floral treason'.

'If I had my way, I'd ban all irises from the whole of Witchlight Cove,' he used to say. 'Honestly, they're the most revolting, pungent flowers. I don't care what they look like. They stink, they're a nightmare, and I don't want them in the house.' It always struck me as odd – and unfortunate – that he had such a strong reaction to the flowers that his wife was named after.

Why would somebody place a wreath of those flowers on their grave? It made no sense. Had it been a passing witch who saw my mother's name and did a quick spell to whip them up? It certainly couldn't have been anyone who actually *knew* my parents.

Knowing Dad would hate it, I picked up the wreath and went across to another grave. It was mottled and old, and it looked like it hadn't had any flowers placed on it for years. Sorry, random deceased stranger, but you inherited some very controversial foliage. Fingers crossed this person hadn't hated irises.

I placed the wreath down then moved back to my parents' grave. It was time I told them why I was back.

Chapter Thirteen

After I'd finished the conversation with Mum and Dad – most of which happened in my head in case someone was listening and overheard the issue about the Flame – I headed back to the house.

The moment I opened the door, Eva bounded over wagging her tail like she had missed me so much she'd barely coped. Honestly, the level of drama in that dog was unparalleled; if she could have thrown herself onto a chaise lounge and wept, she would have. I might have believed she'd been traumatised by my absence had it not been for the fur that covered Maddie's jumper. Clearly they'd been getting in some great cuddles. I was only a smidge envious.

'You can't leave Witchlight ever again,' Maddie said as she looked at me. 'I don't think I can live without this dog now. She's perfect. Do you know that she found my slippers and brought them to me?'

'Did you?' I glanced at my golden retriever, who tilted her head to the side. 'You never do that for me,' I accused. 'Mostly you just steal my keys.'

She tipped her head further and gave a slight whine, sinking into her shoulders at the same time as if she were shrugging and saying, 'I am totally innocent of all wild accusations.'

Maddie studied me, no doubt noting my red eyes that were the consequence of my chat to my parents. 'Are you okay? You're later than I thought you'd be.'

'Sorry. I went to visit Mum and Dad.' I smiled awkwardly. 'Thanks so much for the calla lilies.'

'You're welcome. Just so you know, they're not a spell – I get them at the florist every month. I spell them then to make sure they last until the next month, but I know how much your mum loved *real* flowers.'

'That's sweet of you.'

As I dropped down to stroke Eva, Maddie continued. 'Nana rang and told me you went to see Mrs D. Is she alright? I can't believe she was poisoned. It's crazy.'

'She's pretty shaken up.'

'I bet. Claude is a complete mess. I saw him clearing everything up when I was on my way home.' Claude was a three-foot brownie who, like the rest of his family, had run the bakery for decades; he'd made all the pasties. 'He was devastated. He said he's never had anything like this happen before.'

I frowned. 'I don't think the food was to blame. If there was something wrong with his pasties, surely everyone would've got sick?'

'True, but you know how ridiculous people can be when something unexpected happens. They scare easily. Especially people in our community.' She rolled her eyes.

She was right: Witchlight excelled at mass hysteria. We could probably win awards if there was ever a 'World's Most Overdramatic Village' competition. I knew that from personal experience.

Silence settled between us and I suspected Maddie was thinking about the Eternal Flame. People would definitely be scared if they knew that it was missing.

'Mrs D gave me a name of someone who might help us,' I said finally. 'Old Jacobson who lives down at Shingle's End. She reckons he's a witch but apparently one who doesn't mix with the others. He might help us work out how you can make your inks and tattoos without the Flame – without telling him it's gone, obviously.'

'I know the guy you mean, but I didn't even know he was a witch. He really keeps to himself. I thought he was an ogre or something.'

My eyebrows rose. 'Wow, he really is reclusive then.'

'Yeah. I've seen him at Sonny's once or twice but he doesn't really speak to anybody there.'

'Sonny's?' I asked.

Maddie sighed dramatically. 'My God, I can't believe you've been gone so long that you don't even know Sonny's. It's a coffeehouse – Insomnia Coffee – but everyone calls it Sonny's. He's the owner and he makes the most amazing coffee. He's a seriously cranky vampire. I do his sunlight tattoos so you'd think he'd give me a discount on my coffee, but no. He is the most miserable guy *ever* – even for a vamp. But he roasts the beans himself and the coffee is divine. We should get one tomorrow. Which reminds me – Nana said she's expecting to see you at the station at eight.'

'Eight in the morning?' I asked, horrified. Yanni hadn't been kidding about the bright and early thing.

One of the joys of being self-employed is that I get to pick my own hours and before Eva had arrived, that generally meant nothing before midday. Since I've had her, I can only stay in bed until she starts whining and needs to be let out. Even so, she's a true queen; she knows her owner loves to sleep, so she tries to give me until 9.00 or 10.00am. The thought of not only being up at eight but dressed, awake and ready to deal with the public was a little daunting.

'In that case I guess I need to get an early night.' I yawned and at the same time realised I hadn't eaten since the service station stop that morning. Tired as I might be, I was also starving and food always takes priority in my book. 'How do you feel about ordering in pizza?' I asked. I didn't know what Maddie's cooking skills were like nowadays, but standing over a hob or chopping up food was more than I had in me.

She grinned. 'Pizza sounds perfect. Let me get the number.'

As she flipped open her phone, I remembered there was something else I needed to tell her. 'I meant to say – Fraser Banks came by.'

Maddie's gaze narrowed on me. 'Of course he did. He probably knew I'd be at the fayre and was using the opportunity to sneak in. Ass wipe. You didn't let him inside, did you?'

'Of course I didn't! Though you didn't tell me he was *that* good-looking.'

'Really?' Maddie chuckled. 'Oh sure, I mean if you go for that obviously attractive, well-groomed thing. But that man is toxic, I'm sure of it. You need to stay clear of him.' She wagged her finger at me.

'Don't worry, I'm not going to mix business with pleasure.'

A smirk lilted her lips. 'And speaking of pleasure, I saw Ezra at the fayre before it all went to pot. He got very excited when I mentioned you were back.'

'I heard he had to do a shifter thing and couldn't take part.'

She nodded. 'Yeah. He was too late to enter but we watched the contest together.' She sent me a sideways glance. 'I thought maybe we could all go to Shady's one night and catch a drink.'

I could tell from the way her eyes glinted that she obviously had visions of me and Ezra hooking up, which was not going to happen. Once we had the Flame back, I'd be hightailing it back to London and I had no intention of hurting one of my oldest friends by doing so. *Hurting them more,* I amended mentally.

'Shady's?' I asked, not rising to her bait.

'That's what they've renamed the club. It's run by Sonny's brother.'

'Another vampire business? I guess the pair of them are taking over the village.'

She laughed. 'Rumour has it they don't get on at all. But Shady's has damn good cocktails and Ezra promised to get the first round. So what do you reckon? Friday night?'

I knew she wanted me to say yes, but I'd only just got back to Witchlight Cove. I already had a new job to deal with, plus three investigations to look into if I included Mrs D alongside Fraser Banks and the missing Eternal Flame. I wasn't sure I had the mental capacity to deal with people asking me questions about what I'd been up to for the last ten years when the truthful answer was, 'Not much, but I got a dog.'

'Are you okay if we wait and see how I'm feeling?' I asked Maddie. 'I don't want to agree and then be knackered and not able to go out. I'd feel like I was letting people down then.'

'Sure. Ezra's not going anywhere. I'm pretty sure he's already waited ten years for you to come back,' Maddie drawled, but the mischief in her tone was unmistakable.

I sighed, reached for my phone to place the order – and it buzzed in my hand with a message. From Ezra.

My stomach twisted.

Maddie grinned. 'Told you so.'

Chapter Fourteen

Ezra's text was a simple one, welcoming me home and saying he was looking forward to seeing me. Nothing salacious, much to Maddie's disappointment. She'd sighed so dramatically that I was surprised the house didn't collapse under the weight of her crushed expectations.

After the pizza we mulled over what could have happened to the Eternal Flame, but the truth was we didn't have a clue. There had to be a reason it had disappeared: a *cause*. And if there was a cause we could undo it, damn it. What was weird was the fact that the wards were still intact; wherever it was, it hadn't gone far.

We spent the rest of the night renewing our friendship. Our easy camaraderie had clicked back into place like no time had passed but we still had a decade to catch up on – and it was clear that Maddie still resented me for my absence, for which I didn't blame her a jot.

I told her about teaching self-defence, and she shared details of her 'minimalist' dating life – which appeared to be her choosing a series of 'bad boys'. There was a clear pattern of her dating guys who wanted her to tattoo them and their friends for free before they lost interest – until a full moon was near or their current ward was fading. I didn't point that out; I suspect she already knew she was making bad choices.

'Maybe you should be the one thinking about dating Ezra,' I suggested lightly.

Maddie looked faintly green, like she'd imagined licking a troll. 'Eww. He's like a brother to me. Don't get me wrong, he's been my first port of call since you left – but no. There's nothing romantic between us and there never will be.' She hesitated then sipped her drink; letting slide whatever she'd been about to tell me.

Curiosity gnawed at me but I didn't press. She wasn't a suspect to interrogate, she was my friend and I needed to respect her lines in the sand. I wanted to get to know her properly again, to show her how much her friendship did truly matter to me.

'Wine?' I suggested.

'Sure,' she agreed easily. 'I have a bottle of Oy Bay in the fridge.'

I couldn't help but smile. It had always been our drink of choice, while Ezra was mainlining real ales.

'Perfect.'

Maddie poured us each a glass of wine and we settled on the sofa. I took a sip, liquid heaven. 'So,' I said, 'tell me about your plans for a tattoo shop.'

She lit up as she gushed excitedly about finally having enough clients to justify opening her own office premises. She talked about equipment, overheads and her bottom line; she sounded so unlike the ditzy girl I'd once known who hadn't understood the difference between gross and net income.

'I'm so proud of you,' I said, the thought slipping from me before I could stop it. 'You're going to crush it.'

Her bright smile faded. 'Without the Witchlight...' She trailed off, shaking her head. 'Without the Eternal Flame, my dreams are dead in the water.'

'We'll get it back,' I promised fiercely. 'Of course we will.'

'I've missed that Stonehaven bullishness,' she laughed.

'We will,' I repeated. We had to.

Maddie's passion about her business had burned through our entire bottle of wine and the time was waaaay later than I'd intended to go to bed. I gave a yawn so wide that my jaw clicked. Maddie chucked a cushion at my head. 'Go to bed! We need you in Nana's office so you can dig up dirt on Fraser,' she ordered. 'We can't afford you being late on your first day. You know Nana hates it when people are tardy. Go. Sleep. Now.'

'Yes, Mum,' I sassed, as I stood up.

I let Eva out for a wee, then we went up to my old bedroom. I set my phone alarm for the obscenely early hour of 7.00am and settled into my old bed.

Thankfully Eva was by my side and she chased my memories – and nightmares – away.

When the alarm went off at the crack of dawn, I hit snooze. I did so repeatedly until I clawed my eyes open enough to see it was 7.30am. Fuck!

I had no time for a shower so I hastily brushed my teeth and hair, chucked on some clean clothes. Eva had done her favourite trick of hiding my keys, so it took a fraught five minutes to find them, then Eva and I jogged to the police station. We arrived, panting, at 7.55am. Perfect timing, and I wasn't even sweating *that* much.

I sat in the waiting room for all of two seconds before Yanni barrelled out of her office. 'You're here!' she said, her tone reflecting pleasant surprise.

'Of course I am,' I replied, as if affronted. I tried to make sure my breathing didn't give away my last-minute sprint. Eva, meanwhile, flopped onto the floor like she'd climbed Everest.

'Oh well,' Yanni sounded slightly apologetic. 'I expected you to be late. You were never an early bird.' She smiled. 'More of a permanently grumpy pigeon.' Her words were warm and teasing. 'Come on in.'

She led me through a door to the right of the reception area into the bowels of the police station. We went into a room with a few desks in it. Filing cabinets lined the walls but didn't appear to be in use because there was paperwork *everywhere.* Yeesh: they didn't need someone to answer the phones, they needed someone to sort out this shit.

'The phone is here.' Yanni gestured to a desk piled with paperwork but with no visible phone. She frowned. 'No, wait. It *was* here but I moved it last week. Hold on. I need to move a couple more of these. I promise I've been meaning to tidy this lot up.'

She shuffled a stack of papers from one side of the desk to the other before picking it all up and dumping it on the floor next to a massive heap of folders – and more paperwork. That was some filing system. Organised chaos? More like chaotic chaos.

I sat and waited as Yanni tried to find the phone I was supposed to be manning. After a solid ten minutes had passed, I broke into her mutterings. 'Yanni, don't take this the wrong way but it seriously looks like you need help.'

She grinned suddenly. 'What gave it away? The mountains of paperwork or the missing phone?' She sobered. 'I know – I know we need help,' she said. 'But it's so tricky to find someone to do the job. You've got to be impartial if you're working for the magical police, and it's difficult to find someone like that around here. We've got covens, clans, shifter groups –people feel like they're being disloyal to their own sect if they take a job with me.'

'Rather than thinking their loyalty should extend to all types of magic folk and helping the whole community?' I said incredulously.

'I know. It's ridiculous, but that's the way it is. I've got a couple of years till I retire and I'm sure I can find somebody to get this place shipshape before then. Dove is coming along wonderfully – you'll like her. She's on leave for the next day or two, but she'll need some help when I go.' She eyeballed me pointedly.

'Yanni, I'm here to earn some money and help you out, but this won't be my forever job. I'm laying that out for you now. I'm a PI – that's what I do. I set my own hours,

I take the cases that I want. I'm not made for nine-to-five work.'

She sighed. 'Well, I appreciate you stepping into the breach for now. And I appreciate your honesty, though I can definitely say there is nothing nine to five about this job. I'm on call the whole time.'

'That must be hard.'

She beamed. 'I love it. Retirement's the thing that will be hard for me. A few years more yet,' she said firmly. 'I'm not ready to slow down.'

Yanni may have liked her job, but she clearly didn't like the paperwork. I'm an untidy soul, but the state of this room was making me itch to start filing. How could she find *anything* in this mess?

'Oh, there it is!' she said triumphantly, pulling out a heavy, outdated piece of technology that I half expected to be steam-powered. It was a large plastic phone with several lights labelled *Line 1*, *Line 2*, *Line 3*, and *Line 4*. Considering there was only one other office in the station, I couldn't imagine where those lines went unless they had telephones in the interview room and cells, though that didn't seem likely.

Yanni found a clear space to put it down. 'All you need to do is answer it and find out the issue. Most of the time it will be people wanting reassurance, like old Mr

Margate who lives on his own by Wheatsheaf Grove. He's convinced that banshees keep announcing his death. He'll probably ring up, tell you it happened last night and we should get ready to make arrangements.'

'Is that something we have to deal with?' I asked. 'Someone's death being foretold?'

'It's his *own* death and it hasn't been foretold at all,' she said. 'According to him, they've been predicting his death every week for the last decade. No, it's all fuss and nonsense. Another thing, we've had a bit of a problem with young water shifters leaving puddles with fish on people's doorsteps. It's hardly the worst type of criminal activity, but it's worth keeping an eye on in case it starts getting out of hand. If there are some repeat offenders, we'll speak to their parents.'

'Sounds good,' I said. 'And the rest of the time, when I'm not answering the phone?'

'Up to you, I suppose. I'm sure you've got things to keep you busy.'

'Yes. Yes, I have.' My mind went straight to Fraser Banks – and the way his broad shoulders filled out the top of his shirt *perfectly*.

I hurriedly brushed aside the image and remembered why I was meant to be thinking about him. 'Yanni, is it possible for me to access some of the police files online?

That way, if names come up on calls I can check if they're repeat offenders. It'd save time going back and forth and bothering you.' I looked at her, wide eyed and innocent.

She looked back at me cynically. 'That look didn't fool me when you were a teen and it doesn't fool me now.' She studied me. 'It's important?' I nodded. 'You want to tell me about it?'

I grimaced. 'I can't. Not yet, anyway.'

She sighed. 'Okay. Well, I trust you and one day soon I hope you'll trust me too. Dig into whatever you need, Bea. I'll give you general access.'

'Thank you. And I do trust you, Yanni. I really do.'

'Come to me when you're ready,' she said. 'Whatever it is, I can help.'

Her words made me feel both warmed and incredibly guilty. I *did* trust Yanni, but she was one for the rule book and I didn't want to put her in an invidious position by telling her about the Eternal Flame's absence. Being between me and the covens would be one heck of a hard place.

She cleared her throat. 'Alright, let me sort out those logins for you. You make yourself comfy.'

Given the mess, making myself comfy was easier said than done. I pulled out the wheelie desk chair, only to discover it was also covered in papers. I'd just leaned down to pick them up when I heard the door creak open. A moment later, someone cleared their throat.

'Hey, Trixie.' The voice was deep and husky, like a whisky-soaked promise of trouble. 'Did you miss me?'

Chapter Fifteen

I immediately recognised the voice and a smile crept onto my face. As I stood and faced him, my breath hitched. Maddie hadn't been kidding: Ezra had grown up *good*.

Yanni huffed. 'Just let yourself into the office,' she grumbled to Ezra.

He blew her a cheeky kiss then turned his attention to me again. 'So you're back and you still haven't come to say hi. You're making me hunt you down and do the hard work like always.'

'Ezra.' I smiled and shook my head. 'Ezra Bentley. You look ... different.'

'Yeah. I grew up a bit.' He grinned.

Ezra had absolutely grown up a bit – well, a lot. He was easily six foot six, and any jokes about being the runt of the werewolf litter were very much in the past. In fact, if he got any taller he could rent out his forehead as a billboard. He had a scar through his right eyebrow that gave him a "tough guy" vibe, and I wondered how he'd gotten it.

As I stood there struggling to find my voice, I couldn't help thinking back to when we were kids and I'd used him as my sparring partner. With his quick werewolf healing, Mum didn't feel too bad when I'd thrown him across the floor and, on more than one occasion, broken his nose.

I wasn't so sure I'd get the best of him so easily now. He was dressed in a plain black T-shirt that hugged his torso, hinting at the chiselled abs underneath. Not that I was looking. Much. Just scientifically observing for the sake of research. He had a paper under his arm and he was holding two paper cups.

'Here,' he said, passing me a drink. 'Maddie mentioned you'd had an early start after a late night. She didn't think you'd had time to grab a coffee, so I thought I'd bring you one.'

'Thank you.' I reached out and took the cup, not realising until the smell wafted under my nose that I was desperate for a caffeine hit. I took a long sip. 'Oh my God, this is divine.'

'And where's mine?' Yanni complained. Without missing a beat, Ezra offered her the other cup. She sighed. 'It's fine. I don't actually want to steal your coffee.'

'I had mine in the shop,' he promised. 'I really did bring this for you.'

She eyed him dubiously but took him at his word and accepted the hot drink. 'I'll leave you two to catch up. Bea, I'll be in my office if you need me.' She went through a plain wooden door to the right and shut it behind her.

I looked after her then turned back to the fibbing werewolf. 'You *totally* forgot about Yanni.'

'I did. I never could get anything past you.' He shrugged. 'I'll grab another one later.'

I finished one gulp of coffee and promptly took another. 'What the hell is in this? It's amazing!'

'Sonny's special brew. If the guy didn't hate witches, I swear he'd had one put a spell on the beans.'

'He hates witches?' I asked, my interest piqued. Anyone who hated witches might want to do something to screw with them. Like stealing the Eternal Flame.

'Sonny hates everyone,' Ezra clarified. 'His motto is "customer service is for those with shit products" and I think he genuinely believes it. Anyway, he has reason to be grumpy. It's pretty well known in the village that he's been all but disowned by the other vampires, including his older brother, because apparently selling coffee and pastries is below a vamp.'

'Hmm.' I took a mental note. Sonny might have beef with a lot of people, but that wasn't a reason to wipe him off my list of those who'd want to steal the Witchlight.

Ezra went on, 'Maddie mentioned you might be up for a drink at Shady's on Friday night.'

Damn it, Maddie! 'I'm not sure what my shifts here will be,' I said. 'Or if I'm going to have the energy to head out, if I'm honest.'

Ezra's face dropped a fraction before it reformed into a perfect smirk. 'I'll ask Yanni for you. She has a soft spot for me – she'll give you the time off. She knows we need a proper catch-up.'

I could already tell there was no way I was going to get out of it. Still, catching up and having a drink wouldn't be the worst thing in the world. After all, if Shady's cocktails were half as good as his brother's coffee, it would be worth it.

I rolled my eyes. 'We both know she likes me more than you. *I'll* ask.'

His grin faded slowly and he looked at me as if truly seeing to the heart of me. 'You've changed, Beatrix Stonehaven.'

'We all have. A decade is a long time.'

'It is,' he agreed solemnly. 'But no matter the length of time, it's still the Three Amigos together forever.'

I smiled, but he didn't. 'You owe Maddie an apology, Bea. You cut her off without a backward glance. I know you were hurting, but so was she. We *all* were. Losing you on top of everything else...' He shook his head then fixed me with a firm look I'd never seen from him before. 'If you're going to leave again, just know that there won't be any fixing what's broken after that.'

Guilt swelled, thick enough to choke on. I managed to nod because I knew he was right. 'I'm sorry.'

'It's not me you should be apologising to, it's Maddie. She's the one who's been tied to the house guarding your inheritance for you.'

'I've apologised to her and I will again, but you deserve an apology too. Don't think I don't know it. I'm sorry, Ezra, I didn't mean to ever imply by thought, deed or action that you weren't important to me. You were. You still are.'

His eyes softened. 'Then let's start over, Beatrix Stonehaven, and see where this road takes us.'

'Deal.'

'Deal. Well, I'd better get off.'

As he took the paper from under his arm, I caught a glimpse of the cover and leaned forward, holding out a hand to stop him from leaving. 'Is that a photo from the pasty eating contest?' I asked.

Ezra glanced at it and nodded. 'Yeah – before it all went to pot. Mrs D actually looked like she was in with a chance of second place. Not that you get anything for second other than bragging rights.'

I stared at the photo for a minute. Mrs D was there with a single pasty in her hand, while next to her Warren had his nose buried in a mass of them like he was a bear shifter, not a water one. Next to them the other contestants were using their own methods of getting the food down their gullets, but they were certainly being daintier than Warren who was totally going for it.

My eyes kept going back to Mrs D. Something about the photo didn't feel right; then again, maybe it was simply that I would never have expected her to do something like take part in a pasty-eating contest.

'I can leave it here if you want.' Ezra's voice broke into my reverie and made me realise I was still staring at his paper. 'Although I'm pretty sure the station gets its own delivered.'

'Sorry, no. It's fine, thank you,' I said. 'And thanks for the coffee.'

'No problem. You can pay me back with a drink on Friday night.' He winked. Just like that, *my* Ezra was back, persistent and cheeky. Maybe Ezra hadn't changed all that much because he'd always had a stubborn streak a mile wide.

Several minutes after he'd left, I was still thinking about the photograph. What had bothered me about it? I wished I'd taken up Ezra's offer to leave it because my subconscious was buzzing away, telling me I'd missed something – something important. Maybe there was someone in the background, someone my brain hadn't latched onto at the time? I'd have to look at the article again.

Knowing I wouldn't rest until I did, I opened up my laptop and a new YouTube page. As well as all the physical wards around Witchlight to stop non-magical people stumbling on the village, there was a hefty array of other safeguards.

One of the covens, which specialised in elemental magic, had found ways to disrupt electromagnetic signals so that anything posted online inside the barrier couldn't be viewed outside of it. Even if someone accidentally typed in the correct link, all they'd find would be a video of cute otters playing in the snow. From what I heard, the otter shifters were pretty mad about it but, hey, village safety came first.

I typed in Witchlight Cove followed by the date and finished up with the words 'pasty contest'.

More than a dozen videos pinged up. The first one had a deliberately click-bait title about the contest ending in disaster; exactly the kind of thing I was looking for.

The video was three minutes long and started at the very beginning of the contest. The contestants were announced one by one and walked down to take their places. Mrs D was up first – and the old woman looked terrified; she certainly didn't look like she was doing it for fun. In fact, she was so confounded by what was going on that she sat in the wrong seat and picked up one of the pasties straight away, like she was going to start eating then and there.

Claude nearly had a fit. He jumped in before she could take a bite, made her put the pasty down and move up to the place with her name on it. After her, Warren came in followed by the others. Claude gave his spiel about how this was the oldest pasty shop in the country and thanked everyone for coming while mentioning the cash prize at least a dozen times. It wasn't until someone from the crowd called 'Get on with it!' that he finally huffed and moved across to the buzzer.

Was the heckler keen to get started because they didn't want their poison or potion to wear off? It was possible.

When the buzzer sounded, the contestants threw themselves into the competition – literally, in one case.

The woman on the end, a redhead about my age, tipped herself into the bowl. Okay, maybe Warren *hadn't* been the messiest one. It was hard to draw my eyes away from her – it was like watching a car crash – but she wasn't my focus so I restarted the video and concentrated on Mrs D and Warren.

Ezra hadn't been joking. Mrs D was funnelling those pasties into her mouth like a professional, but even so she wasn't a patch on Warren. For every bite the old woman took, he had three – until he suddenly stopped.

The whites of his eyes bulged and he started rocking from side to side. A minute later, the pasties made their reappearance and that was when Mrs D started looking peaky, too. She lifted her gloved hand to her head and wiped her brow before she started retching. It was only when she was doubled over the bowl clutching her stomach that the other contestants finally looked up and stopped eating.

I paused the video; I didn't need to see any more. It made sense that Warren would have had a stronger reaction given how many more pasties he'd eaten, but there was something that didn't make sense.

I stood up from my desk, went to Yanni's office and knocked on the door. 'Everything alright?' she asked. 'You haven't had a call already, have you? I didn't hear anything.'

'No, it's not that. I wondered what time my lunch break would be.'

Her lips parted in surprise and I realised it sounded like I was trying to get out of the job before it had even started. 'I wanted to pop out and see Mrs D,' I added.

Relief flowed over Yanni's face as she realised she hadn't employed the world's laziest person. 'Oh, right. It's supposed to be at half past one but I can be flexible. Mrs D left the hospital yesterday, though, and I'm sure she's fine. They wouldn't have let her go otherwise.'

'That's great news. Even so, I have a couple of questions for her.'

Yanni's brow furrowed. 'Anything you fancy sharing with the chief inspector?' she asked.

Maybe it was the PI part of me, but I wasn't ready to spill any ideas yet, not even with Yanni. Not when they could be so far off the mark. But I wasn't a PI now; my job was answering calls in the police station and this was official police business. I was likely to get myself into a heap of trouble if she found out I was snooping into an official investigation. Besides, I already felt bad enough not telling her about the Eternal Flame. The last thing I wanted to do was add even more to my burden of guilt.

'There was something in a video I watched,' I said. 'Mrs D sat in Warren's seat first and picked up one of his pasties.

I think that might have transferred the poison from the pasties to her glove. If she still has the glove, we could confirm it.'

'That would explain why she got a smaller dose,' Yanni mused. 'Are you sure you want to talk to her about this?'

'I think so. I mean, I work for the police now.'

Yanni arched an eyebrow. 'Tentatively.' She sounded a little amused. 'But okay. Just let me know what you find out.'

'Of course.'

This was it: my first bit of official police business while simultaneously helping out an old friend. Maybe this temp position wasn't the worst. Even if I hadn't actually answered the phone yet.

Chapter Sixteen

My lunch break wasn't until half-past one, and before that I received three telephone calls. The first was a complaint about someone littering and ruining the village's aesthetic. They hadn't seen the culprit so there was pretty much nothing I – or Yanni – could do about it. I promptly filed my notes on that call into the bin: no need to add to the various paper piles. Efficiency is my middle name. Actually my middle name is Elizabeth, but Efficiency sounds cool and starts with the same letter.

The next call was from a mermaid who complained that someone kept sailing their yacht out to sea and disrupting her by playing music too loudly above the kelp forest. Given that Yanni had given me access to the police database, I did a quick search while the caller was still on the line. This complaint had been made before with a repeat comment in the response logs: *There are no boundaries in the kelp forest.*

'Unfortunately,' I repeated, 'there are no official boundaries in the water. Meaning they are within their rights to do that.'

'That's ridiculous! It's practically my home!'

I felt for her, I really did, but I couldn't see a way around it. 'Sorry,' I apologised. She rang off in a huff and I imagined her flipping her tail dramatically before swimming off in a swirl of indignation. I didn't really blame her.

The final phone call was, as Yanni had already predicted, from Mr Margate complaining that the banshees had once again announced his imminent death. I told him how sorry I was and assured him we would prepare accordingly, though I didn't know what preparations he expected us to do. Throw a farewell party? Order him a coffin in his favourite colour? I did neither of those things.

When half-past one rolled around, I grabbed my stuff and headed straight to Mrs D's. Halfway there I wondered if I should have checked she still lived in the same place; it had been years since I'd visited her and she could easily have moved house.

I dismissed the idea when I saw all the catmint in the garden; Mrs D still lived in the same place. We'd been pretty sure she was some kind of feline shifter, though what type I had never found out – and today wasn't the day I was going to ask. It felt rude to greet someone with, 'Hey, are you part housecat, lynx, or an ancient tiger goddess?'

After knocking on the door I waited patiently, but there was no response from inside the house. Instead it came from behind me. 'Can I help you?' I turned around to find myself facing Mrs D.

With her walking boots, thick coat and a bit of colour in her cheeks, she looked substantially better than the previous day. 'Oh my goodness, Beatrix!' Her wrinkled face beamed. 'Twice in two days? This is a lovely surprise. Come in. Come in.'

She shuffled past me to open the door then beckoned me in. 'To what do I owe the pleasure?' she asked as she removed her boots.

I did the same before I followed her inside. 'Hi, Mrs D, I hope you don't mind but I wanted to ask you a couple of questions about what happened yesterday.'

'Really?' Her eye twitched slightly, possibly because of the light drizzle that covered her skin. 'I'd heard you'd become a bit of a detective out there on the outside.'

'I'm a private investigator,' I told her. 'But yes, I wanted to look into it, find out what happened. For your sake.'

She patted my arm. 'That's kind of you but I'm sure Yanni will get to it when she has time. You don't need to worry yourself.'

'Unfortunately Yanni having time is a bit of a rarity,' I pointed out. 'I'm working at the police station now on the phones. But I've only got a few questions, and they won't take a minute.'

Mrs D scratched behind her ear and her left eye twitched again. I got the impression she didn't really want to talk about it. I wasn't surprised: she'd never been one to like any fuss. Being on the front page of the newspaper was probably her worst nightmare.

'Warren's still alright, isn't he?' she asked.

'I haven't heard otherwise.'

'Well, I'm okay too so I don't think the matter requires looking into.'

'It definitely does, Mrs D. Imagine if somebody tries the same thing again – and uses more poison. We have to get to the bottom of this. Now, I noticed that at the start of the contest you sat in Warren's seat first and you picked up one of his pasties with your glove. And you were only wearing a glove on one hand, right?'

'Yes. Yes. I think I was.' The twitch was non-stop now, and not only in her left eye but her right one, too. It looked like she was trying to communicate in Morse code. 'Please, dear, I don't know why we need to go through all this if everyone is okay. Can't we forget about it?'

'You can't really want to do that, Mrs D. Look, I have a theory that perhaps Warren was the target, and when you picked up his pasty with your glove—'

'It was me, okay! It was *me*!' Her voice shot across me, rendering me silent.

'You?' I said, unsure I had heard her correctly.

'It was me, Beatrix. I'm sorry.' She was trembling and then she started wringing her hands. 'I'm not cut out for a life of crime.' That much was clear considering she'd cracked faster than a cheap biscuit. 'I didn't think it would make anyone ill – it was only meant to taste horrible, to slow him down a bit so I had a chance of winning.'

'You tried to *poison* Warren?'

The old woman sniffled and big, ugly tears dripped down her cheeks. 'I didn't mean to hurt him,' she reiterated. 'Warren has cut off funding for the underprivileged children's trip to the museum in London – and that is his prerogative,' she added hastily. 'But I needed the funds for the kids. Five hundred pounds would cover it. I didn't mean to hurt him, I really didn't. It was a type of chilli that should have made his throat burn and stop him from eating all the pasties. That was all I wanted. He was my only real competition. I'd already done so much damage to those children by losing his funding. It must have been my fault he stopped supporting us – I must have done something wrong because he's been a stalwart supporter for years.' She was so upset she could barely breathe. 'You must think I'm a horrible person.'

I patted her hand. 'I could never think that, Mrs D. You know that.'

'But you'll have to tell Yanni, won't you?'

I nodded reluctantly. Yanni had to know if for no other reason than to stop the investigation and avoid wasting any more police time. 'Look, from what I know of Warren he's a pretty generous guy. I'm sure he'll understand that this was a mistake.'

'So generous that he stopped our payments without a word and hasn't replied to any of my emails? That's not exactly a charitable man, is it?' she responded bitterly. 'I'm sorry, I'm sorry. I know it's his money, but I don't know what to do. We rely on him so much.'

'Can't you ask the parents to pay?' I asked.

She shook her head. 'With clubs and uniforms and the cost of living being so high, we can't. A lot of families are already struggling – good people in good jobs.' She pressed her lips together. 'We'll have to stop a lot of our out-of-school activities. It's heartbreaking that this will be my final legacy.'

'Your legacy is in the generations you've taught and helped. You can't be blamed for this situation.'

She ignored my words of comfort. 'Will I go to prison?' she asked. 'Only I promised my class I'd take them to a camp-out for the homeless in Edinburgh next month. Some of the young water shifters have been a bit adrift – they need to see how tough life can get and how we can help. Do you think I could still go? One last hurrah?'

The guilt and anxiety rolling off her was so strong that all I wanted to wrap my arms around her and tell her everything would be okay. But that wasn't something I could do. 'I'll talk to Yanni,' I said instead. 'I'll make her understand it was an accident. I'm sure it won't be as bad as you think.'

My stomach knotted as the words left my lips. Fingers crossed I wasn't lying.

Chapter Seventeen

'Mrs D was responsible for the poisoning?' Yanni shook her head in disbelief and pressed her fingers to her temples. 'God, who'd have thought it?'

'She really didn't think she was poisoning him,' I insisted. I'd already told her exactly what had happened, but I felt the need to reinforce that point again. Mrs D had made a very poor decision but she'd never intended it to be a deadly one.

In my absence Eva had claimed the large chair that was meant to be for people waiting to see Yanni; given that it now had a soft blue blanket on it, I guessed my boss was okay with that. 'She seemed absolutely desperate,' I continued. 'She wanted to get the money for the trip, for the kids.'

Yanni sighed. 'I believe her. She'd do anything for those kids.' She frowned. 'It's strange that Warren has cancelled his financial support for the school. He always credits his success to the education he had there – and recently the profits from his charter company have been the highest ever.'

'Do you think it's personal?' I suggested. 'Could he have some sort of issue with Mrs D, or the direction the school is taking? Maybe he feels like his money is being frittered away.'

Yanni shrugged. 'Your guess is as good as mine, but I should go and talk to him, let him know we found out what happened and that he's not being targeted by any dangerous criminal elements.'

'Could I come?' I asked. 'I know I'm not a police officer but this is about Mrs D. If he gets mad, I'd kind of like to be her voice.'

'Being police is about being impartial, Bea,' Yanni said sternly. 'You can't let your opinions cloud how you handle a situation.'

'I'm not. I don't. It's ... she was really upset. That's all I want him to know. She was really broken.'

Yanni drew a breath then exhaled with a sigh. 'Fine. You can come with me – but *I'll* do the talking.'

I gave her a mock salute and mimed zipping my lips shut. I'd let her take the lead – but that was another reason I knew this job was only a short-term fix: I relished asking the questions and solving the mystery myself. After you've been self-employed it's hard to go back to having your actions dictated by someone else rather than by your own whims. Still, I could help Yanni for a couple of weeks and at least then I could still pay rent on my flat in London.

I expected a yearning for home to hit me when I thought of my apartment but it didn't. Witchlight Cove was, and always would be, my *true* home. Perhaps it was the ten years I'd been away, but it didn't hurt to be back, not like it had before when every shop or road carried a memory of Mum and Dad that cut me to the core. Now those reminders were bittersweet and they made me smile as I remembered our lives together. It had been good – far, far too short but really good. I'd been raised in a loving home and, in that sense, I'd been lucky.

Eva lifted her eyes, tipped her ears forward and gave a slight grumble. She was used to being my wingdog and she wanted to come with us to speak to Warren.

'Fine,' Yanni groaned. 'You can come too.'

We piled into the police car and set off. Warren lived on the expensive side of the village where the roads were all freshly tarmacked and the wide pavements were lined with trees even older than the oldest inhabitant of Witchlight Cove – and that was saying something.

I sat in the passenger seat as we drove past big houses guarded by high walls and electric gates with intercom systems that only allowed entrance to the most honoured guests. When we reached Warren's house, Yanni parked outside and pressed on the buzzer. 'It's Police Chief Yanni Greenridge from the local police station,' she said into the speaker. 'We'd like to speak to Mr Storcrest regarding the incident at the weekend.'

She let the button go but there was no response. 'Strange,' she murmured, her frown lines deepening.

As she peered through the gates, I stepped out of the car with Eva close on my heels and looked down the drive. My breath tightened at the sight of the luxury cars parked on the gravel; they were a far cry from my own Rosie Rustbucket, though to be fair Rosie had character. And a tendency to make ominous noises every time I hit 40mph.

I knew that the vehicles out front were nothing compared to the ones out back on the water where Warren Storcrest kept his private boats. When I'd lived here, they had included a 120-foot yacht and two speedboats, though I suspected his collection had increased since then if he'd been making such healthy profits.

'Mr Storcrest,' Yanni called out, though with the distance between us and the house I wasn't sure that anyone inside would hear us. She stepped back and pressed the button again.

Nothing.

'I guess he's not in,' I said. I didn't know if I was pleased or not; it gave me more time to work out how to plead Mrs D's case – if Yanni let me get in a word –, but I also knew that Mrs D would be turning herself inside out with worry as she waited to learn her fate.

'We'll have to come back later,' Yanni said.

As we turned to leave, Eva gave a loud bark. I frowned at her. 'Come on, we'll come back later.' I tapped my thigh, which was normally all I needed to do for her to come to my side, but she refused to budge. She looked into the property again and barked pointedly.

'Eva! Eva, come on,' I called.

She barked again. 'She thinks someone's in there,' I said to Yanni. 'Someone or something she wants us to pay attention to.'

'Is this normal behaviour for her?'

I thought back to when I'd first met Eva and the way she'd stubbornly refused to let the puppy thief get away. That hadn't been the only time she'd alerted me to something, though it was normally when I was on a stake out and our suspect had appeared while I'd drifted off to sleep. 'Occasionally,' I replied. 'And she's always right.'

Yanni bit her bottom lip. 'Alright. Let's go around the back, see if we can find another entrance.'

Before I could answer, Eva took off from the gate and started running towards the waterfront. 'Eva! Hold on, wait for us!' I yelled, exasperated. That damn dog!

She glanced back over her shoulder but she didn't stop until she reached a little wooden gate that led directly into the back of the property.

We followed. Yanni rapped on the wood loudly. 'Maybe they're in the garden,' she said and called again. When there was no reply, Eva barked again and nudged the gate firmly with her nose.

'We get it,' I murmured to her.

Yanni nodded. 'Fine, let's go in.' She pushed open the gate and stepped inside.

It was an incredible property. To the left was the three-storey house with the entire back wall made of glass. Manicured lawns, which included a vegetable patch and a fountain, were in front of us and to the right the ground sloped down towards soft sand and glittering blue water. A wooden jetty jutted into the sea where four large boats bobbed lazily on the tide.

Eva darted ahead of us straight for the jetty. I broke into a run as I tried to keep up. 'Eva, calm down. What is it? What's got into you?'

She raced across the wooden slats, only stopping when she reached the largest boat. She lifted her paws up against the ladder and whined, then looked back at us with sad, soulful eyes. 'This doesn't feel good,' Yanni said, striding to keep up.

I climbed the ladder, unsure which way to go next on the massive boat. The decision was made for me because I spotted immediately what had caught Eva's attention. A person was lying unmoving on the deck only a few feet away from me.

It was Warren Storcrest.

And he was definitely dead.

Chapter Eighteen

Yanni called in backup, which came in the form of Dove, a petite bird shifter who'd been a couple of years below me at school, and a coroner who looked at least three hundred years old. He may very well have been.

'Hi.' Dove gave me a friendly smile and offered me her hand to shake. 'Nice to meet you, Beatrix! I'd actually made you some cupcakes as a "welcome to the team" gift, but they're back at the office.' She grimaced. 'No one wants cupcakes with a side order of dead body.'

I smiled. 'That was the right decision. And I'll totally eat some later when my stomach has stopped roiling.'

Dove nodded. 'I hear you. Dead bodies always make my tummy feel wobbly.'

'Yeah. They're not my favourite thing.' There was so much blood, and the corpse had me flashing back to the still forms of my parents. No, dead bodies did not make me happy.

'A single bullet wound to the back of the head,' Yanni muttered. 'With a silver bullet. Whoever did this either sneaked in so Warren didn't see them, or it was someone he trusted enough to turn his back on.'

'I can't believe there's been a *murder* in Witchlight Cove.' Dove let out her breath in a sharp whistle. 'Usually the dead bodies we go to are the old dears who've passed in their sleep. And after the goings-on yesterday at the fayre, too! It feels like the place is going to pot – I dread to think what might happen next.'

'We don't need to think about what happens next, we need to deal with what we've got now,' Yanni barked reproachfully. 'We need to comb the area, see if there are any clues.'

By now we were all wearing bootees over our shoes and had snapped on gloves. We'd tied back our hair, and Yanni had asked Eva to move away from the scene so it wasn't contaminated with the golden strands that frequently fell from her coat. Reluctantly, Eva had agreed.

'It looks like there was a party here,' I said as I moved towards the front of the boat. I was sure it had a proper name like hull, or deck, or something like that but I'm not – and never will be – a boaty person. But this was clearly where someone had been entertaining: there were several empty bottles of wine and glasses littered about.

'The murderer's fingerprints could be on one of those, couldn't they?' I asked.

'Yes – along with those of half the other people in the village. Including mine,' Dove replied with a grimace.

My eyebrows rose in surprise.

'Warren always holds a big party on the night of the fayre,' she explained. 'I was at school with his daughter, Jennifer, so I usually get an invitation. I didn't stay for long, though – I was too busy and Samuel isn't good with crowds. He's my husband,' she added.

'Warren held a party even though he'd been taken into hospital?' I asked incredulously.

'He'd already paid for the caterers and entertainers,' Dove said. 'He's really sensible with his money. There's no way he would have been happy letting all that go to waste.'

'I don't think we should assume the murderer was one of the partygoers,' the coroner said as he examined the body. 'This happened recently.'

'How recently?' Yanni asked.

'An hour ago, tops. He's still warm.'

A chill ran down my spine: we must have just missed the killer! At least we didn't have to bag up all the glasses and bottles for fingerprint testing, though. That would have taken hours.

'We need to find out who had an axe to grind with Mr Storcrest,' Dove commented.

My pulse rocketed as a thought occurred to me and I turned to Yanni in panic. 'You can't be considering that Mrs D did this!' I said firmly.

'All I'm interested in is what the evidence tells us,' Yanni said. 'And right now, we know that Mrs Drakefield had already tried to harm our victim. Like it or not, that makes her a prime suspect.'

Refusing to accept what she was saying, I shook my head. 'Mrs D wouldn't do this – she wouldn't murder someone. The poisoning was an accident. And why would she confess to poisoning Storcrest and then kill him? That would make her the worst murderer ever!'

'I know it's hard to believe, but I've seen a lot of idiocy in my day. The fact that it's foolish doesn't rule her out, Bea.' Despite her words, Yanni's tone was gentle. 'You think you know her but you don't. You haven't known her for a decade, and before that you knew her as a child knows a teacher, through rose-tinted glasses. She's lived a very long life and we don't know what that has involved.'

I knew everything she was saying was true but my gut refused to accept that Mrs D could possibly be the killer. I was a PI; I had good gut instincts – and I bloody well *knew* that Mrs D wouldn't do something like that.

We were still talking when Eva barked loudly. We all looked at my retriever, who was looking pointedly inland. 'There's someone up at the house.' Dove pointed to a silhouette in one of the windows.

'Go see who that is,' Yanni said to me. 'And tell them they can't come down here. It's a crime scene.'

Eva had been sitting on the jetty guarding us the entire time; given how much she liked to doze, I was impressed she'd stayed awake for so long. 'Come on, girl,' I told her. 'You can help me.'

Tail wagging, she jumped up to follow me as I moved across the lawn towards the house and the mysterious intruder.

Chapter Nineteen

I was still a good twenty feet away when I realised who it was. My stomach gave an annoying somersault. Ugh.

'You,' I said, as Fraser Banks joined me next to the fountain.

'It would appear so,' he replied.

I wouldn't have thought it possible, but Banks looked even more attractive. His collar was still undone, but now there was no jacket and his shirt sleeves were rolled up above his elbows as though they couldn't go any further because of his biceps stretching the fabric. Honestly, did he buy his shirts from the children's section to show off those muscular arms?

A flutter of attraction rippled through me, and for a split second I could have sworn I felt the same attraction rolling from him into me. But that couldn't be right: there was no way I was reading Fraser Bank's emotions. My lousy empath skills were the only powers I'd inherited from my parents, and even they were pathetic. What was the point of being able to feel that someone's upset when you could already see the tears in their eyes?

'What's going on?' he asked. 'I saw the police car outside. Is this to do with yesterday?'

'I'm not at liberty to divulge details,' I said. I'd already mastered sounding official from my PI days.

'Is everything alright?' he asked. 'Is Warren okay?'

'What are you doing here?' I demanded instead of replying. 'Are you and Warren friends?'

'I wouldn't go so far as to say we're friends, but we're part of the same sect.' Banks' tone was casual, relaxed, but the investigator part of me felt there was something I could dig into more deeply. If he and Warren had issues, that would push Banks up the suspect list and reduce the pressure on Mrs D. It could also help me get him away from my house and the missing Eternal Flame – two birds with one stone.

I hoped like hell that he *was* our killer. Killers always returned to the scene of the crime, didn't they? Not that I had much experience with murder, I was more of an affairs-of-the-heart PI than a murder one.

'What does that mean?' I probed. 'You're here at his house, but you're not his friend?'

He quirked an eyebrow. 'Is this an interrogation?'

'No, it's a question. Answer it. Please.'

His eyes narrowed. Much as I didn't want to, I felt my pulse tick up under the scrutiny of that icy blue gaze. 'I brought the minutes for him,' he said finally.

'Minutes?'

'Yes. I'm the second in command for the water shifters, under Lorenz. Warren's a polar bear. He didn't turn up at the morning meeting, which a couple of us thought was strange, so I volunteered to bring the minutes to him and check he was okay. He's normally quite fastidious about going through them.' He lifted up the folder in his hands to prove his point.

'Couldn't you have emailed them?'

'I could, but it was pretty odd for him to miss a meeting. And after yesterday, tensions are pretty high so I thought I'd swing by. Anyway, Warren likes to have the minutes printed out – he's a stickler for seeing things dated and signed in case someone tries to change them.'

'Have they been altered before?'

He shook his head. 'Not that I know of, but he's donated large sums of money to various good causes so it makes sense that he'd want to keep the paperwork organised and filed away. He enjoys his paperwork.'

Uh-huh: nothing said excitement like an evening spent filing minutes of a meeting. Maybe Yanni should have hired Warren to sort out the mess at the office.

'I'll take them.' I held out my hand and after a beat he released the folder.

'For Yanni's eyes only,' he said pointedly.

I nodded. She'd let me know if there was anything relevant in them.

Banks looked over my shoulder. 'So is Warren okay? Can I speak to him?'

I took a long breath. Sooner or later it would get out that Warren was dead. Lorenz would be one of our first ports of call, but we needed to notify the family first. 'Wait here,' I said brusquely, before heading back to the boat to find Yanni.

'Fraser Banks is here looking for Warren,' I told her, handing over the folder. 'What do I say to him? He keeps asking if he's okay. Apparently he missed a water-shifter meeting today and they're all concerned. Banks is their second in command.'

There was a good chance that Yanni already knew Fraser's position in the group, but it seemed relevant. Hierarchies are important in magical communities and it means something when someone rises to that height so quickly. Especially when they're not even from Witchlight Cove. Whether it meant something good or bad in this case, I couldn't say.

Yanni sighed and scratched her head. 'Well, it's gonna get out soon enough. I don't know much about Banks but I've never heard anything bad about him. Take his number, tell him what's happened, but make it clear that he's not allowed to inform the other shifters until we've spoken to the family. Is that okay?'

I nodded, taking a moment to digest what she'd said. Maddie seemed to think Fraser was the devil but Yanni clearly didn't, and she wasn't someone who could easily have the wool pulled over her eyes. He'd obviously gone to some effort to cover his tracks, whatever he was doing; either that or Maddie had got it wrong – but as he'd shown up at the house yesterday, I was inclined to agree with her assessment.

'Sorry to keep you waiting,' I said as I returned to Banks. 'What I'm about to tell you can't be disclosed to anybody, not until we give you permission. Is that understood?'

His expression clouded. 'This is serious, isn't it?' he said tightly.

'Did you hear what I said?' I repeated. 'You can't tell anybody – not even Lorenz – until the family has been informed.'

His jaw dropped. 'Oh God. Is Warren dead?'

It riled me that he was smart enough to deduce that, but it was probably my own fault for mentioning Storcrest's family. 'Yes. We haven't told the family yet, so you need to keep this contained until we've done so,' I reiterated.

'They're going to be heartbroken. His daughter, Jennifer... They're so close. And he's got two boys too – I think one of them is still in school.'

I was struck by a wave of sympathy and sadness that I knew wasn't my own. Just like the attraction I'd felt earlier, it was very real and it was coming from him. I was feeling what Fraser Banks was feeling, and I had no idea how I could feel it so clearly when my shields were up so high.

I stepped back, confused. I normally only feel emotions when they are incredibly strong, like Mrs D's guilt about accidentally poisoning Warren, or when they're coming from someone I'm close to such as Maddie or Yanni. Despite that, I could get a good read on the nuances of his emotions and it made me uncomfortable.

I tightened my mental shields still further. 'Can I take your number, please?' I asked, focusing on the job Yanni had asked me to do. 'The police station will contact you when it's okay to release the news.'

He took my phone and typed in his number. 'If there's anything we can do – the water shifters or me personally – you'll let us know, won't you?'

'For now, just keep it to yourself.'

Fraser Banks turned to leave, but then he stopped and I was hit by another wave of emotion. Hope, perhaps? 'It would be nice to see you under more pleasant circumstances at some point, Beatrix,' he said with a smile.

I gave him a flat look. 'This is a crime scene.' This was *not* the place to flirt with me. Besides, my romantic life was already full. Of stress, caffeine and poor decisions.

But why did the thought of him flirting with me make the butterflies in my stomach wake up and take flight? He was the *enemy,* damn it.

And I wouldn't forget that again.

Chapter Twenty

When Yanni and I got into the car, I felt the anxiety radiating from her. I should have realised that we weren't going straight back to the police station, but it wasn't until we'd been travelling for several minutes in the opposite direction that it finally sank in where we were actually heading. 'We're going to speak to Storcrest's family, aren't we?' I asked.

Yanni nodded grimly; this part of the job evidently wasn't her favourite thing. 'His daughter Jennifer lives on Sugar Lane. They were very close.'

'Sugar Lane?' I was surprised. Back when I'd been growing up, that had been the rough end of the village and I couldn't imagine Warren Storcrest's daughter choosing to live there. I guessed gentrification happened everywhere; maybe Sugar Lane wasn't so bad now.

'I saw them together yesterday,' I admitted. 'In the hospital.'

'She works there, although yesterday was her day off. She's one of the head nurses – she does a wonderful job.'

My eyebrows climbed upwards. I'd expected Jennifer to be a high-society nepo baby, spending her days taking photos to post on the 'Gram. If the daughter was grounded, though, it made more sense that Dove liked her. I didn't know much about my new colleague yet, but I already had the impression that she was down to earth. Plus she baked, and that ticked a box in my plus column.

'We'll speak to Jennifer first, then she can decide if she wants to tell her brothers or let us do it.' I felt Yanni's trepidation; she knew and liked Jennifer so this would be hell for her. I was relieved I wasn't delivering the news.

Sugar Lane looked much nicer than it had back in the day, but it was still a long way down from the grandeur of Warren's area. Jennifer's neat little cottage had two small windows upstairs, two downstairs, and it was well kept. Assuming she had inherited her father's skills, I was surprised she didn't live near the water; water shifters love to be near the water.

Thinking of water shifters tipped my thoughts back to Fraser Banks. He was part of the water shifters, so whatever his magic was I would've assumed he'd want to buy property by the sea rather than sniffing around *my* house, which was near the forest. But other houses didn't come with the Eternal Flame. Well, tough shit. Mine didn't either.

'Maybe you can make a cup of tea,' Yanni suggested as we got out of the car. 'Stay quiet and give her space to take in the news. Sometimes people need to yell or shout. Sometimes they don't say anything at all. Everybody reacts differently.'

'Sure.' I was happy to follow her lead. I'd never had to deal with family bereavement as a PI, something I was grateful for.

'I think you'd better stay in the car for this one,' Yanni added to Eva, giving her fur a quick ruffle. 'We'll try not to be long, okay?'

Half a day in and my dog had already cemented herself into Yanni's life; it was impressive going. Eva wagged her tail and stretched out on the back seat. Yanni cracked the windows to give her fresh air, but the weather was mild so she'd be fine there even if we were inside for hours.

When the front door opened, it was the same young woman I'd seen in the hospital with Warren the day before. Her hair was blonde and wavy, streaked with pink, and she wore a pair of denim dungarees with a ripped T-shirt underneath.

'Jennifer... ' Yanni started.

Finding the chief of police on her doorstep, she blinked. 'Chief? Is everything okay?'

'I wondered if I could come in and talk to you for a moment? It's about your father.'

I watched – and felt – the fear flood through the young woman. She froze. 'Is it bad news?' she asked faintly. 'Because if it is, I need my brothers here.' Her voice cracked.

'You go ahead and call them,' Yanni said sympathetically.

Jennifer's eyes slid shut and she gave a low moan before she leaned against the door frame and took a few deep breaths. 'I don't understand. He was recovering well from the food poisoning. I saw him myself.'

'If we can come in?' Yanni pressed. 'And you call your brothers?'

'Come in and I'll do that. They won't be too long – Rory's on school holidays and Gilbert works on the boats.'

She stepped back and let us into her living room, then went into the kitchen to have some privacy whilst she called her siblings. I sat quietly, wishing there was something I could do or say.

'Should I make you a cup of tea?' I offered when she was done on the phone. 'Or hot chocolate?' Hot chocolate had always been the comfort food in our house. It felt silly to suggest it, but it was something my mum always did to make me feel better.

Jennifer shook her head. 'No, it's fine. I ... I'll wait outside for them. Is that okay?'

'Of course.'

Yanni and I sat in silence, preparing to destroy this family's whole world.

Chapter Twenty-one

Five minutes later, a car pulled into the driveway and two young guys joined us. The oldest looked stiff, visibly braced for bad news after Jennifer's warning. They sat either side of their sister and she reached out to grasp their hands, her knuckles white.

'I am so sorry,' Yanni started. 'We found your father dead this morning. It wasn't the poison,' she went on, forestalling the inevitable question. 'He had a silver bullet wound to the back of his head. If it is any consolation, he didn't see it coming. He wasn't scared.'

Jennifer let out a sob. Rory stared forward, looking numb. Gilbert's jaw worked then he put an arm around his sister, pulling her into him as her crying gained momentum. 'The poisoner at the fayre came back to finish the job,' he snarled. He was tall and gangly with narrow features; assuming he was a water shifter too, the only sea creature he reminded me of was an eel. Not a comparison to voice aloud.

'We don't think so.' I jumped in before Yanni could say anything damning. The last thing I wanted was Mrs D being implicated for a murder. My boss shot me a glare, telling me to shut the hell up. There may even have been an expletive in it. She'd told me to stay quiet and let her do the talking but I couldn't help myself.

'I know this is a very difficult time for you all,' she said, 'but we need to ask you some questions if you're up to it.'

Jennifer wiped the tears from her face. 'Of course,' she sniffed. 'We want to do everything possible to help catch this son of a bitch! Ask away, Yanni.'

'Is there's anyone you can think of who might do this to your father? Any enemies he had?'

Jennifer shook her head. 'He's well-loved within the community. No one that knows him would harm him.'

Gilbert scoffed, 'Well-loved people are always the most well-hated, too. Depends on which circles you move in.'

'What do you mean by that?' I asked, intrigued that his response was so different to his sister's.

'Dad was generous but some people didn't like that. Take Sonny at the coffee shop – Dad was always pestering him to show that same spirit – you know, help with charity events, donate a few free coffees, that sort of thing – but he wouldn't do it. Dad made others feel bad about their lack of philanthropy.'

Rory shook his head. 'Sonny isn't going to kill Dad for pestering him to donate free coffee.'

'I agree,' Jennifer interrupted. 'That's a stretch. Sonny complained about Dad, sure, but it was good natured. It's not like they ever fought.'

'Is there anyone your dad *did* fight with?' I pressed.

At my question, the two older siblings went quiet and their gaze shifted to their younger brother. 'Rory?' Jennifer said softly.

Rory folded his arms. 'No way. You can't be serious.' He was far shorter and stockier than Gilbert, dressed in ripped jeans, and he looked like he was in the throes of teenage angst. If he hadn't been before, he certainly would be now. Losing a parent would do that to a kid. I knew it all too well.

'I'm sorry to press,' Yanni interrupted. 'Can you give me a name? Someone who fought with your father?'

'No.'

'Yes.'

'Yes.'

The siblings spoke over each other but only Rory went red in the cheeks. I'd tried to get a reading on the emotions in the room but there were so many ping-ponging around that I couldn't untangle them and they threatened to overwhelm me. I hastily drew my shields back up again.

Rory sighed. 'They're talking about my mum, Angelica – their stepmum,' he said finally. 'And yes, she and Dad fought a lot, but usually through lawyers. They're still in the midst of their divorce and they barely see each other these days.' Under his breath he muttered, '*I* barely see her.'

I felt a sharp pang of sympathy; his father was dead and his mother was absent. He had it tough.

'Have you seen her recently?' Yanni asked.

He shook his head. 'It's been a couple of weeks.'

'She doesn't live locally?'

'Oh, she lives locally.' Jennifer's lips were pressed together tightly in disapproval. 'The lazy bitch lives about ten minutes down the road.'

Rory scowled but didn't object and the ache within me deepened. If my mum could have been with me, she'd have been there in a heartbeat. The idea of a mother living so close to her children but not caring enough to see them...

'Mum would never hurt Dad,' Rory interrupted. 'I promise. Look, I'm not her biggest fan – but no. I can't imagine her doing that.'

'You know she's tried to squeeze Dad for every penny he had,' Gilbert said. 'Maybe he wouldn't be squeezed any longer.'

Rory's scowl deepened. 'He's her source of money and you don't kill the golden goose, do you? Besides, she couldn't be behind it. You said Dad was shot today, right? Mum isn't even here. She goes into Southampton for her dance classes on Tuesdays, she's there all day and normally stays overnight with some non-magical friends. She'll be back tomorrow morning.'

It sounded like a too-perfect alibi. Apparently my dubious expression betrayed my thoughts because Rory looked at me and continued. 'I promise. Look, she sends me videos of her at the lesson – she does that every week. It's basically the only communication we have. She never askes after me or my life, but she sends these videos of her looking young and beautiful, dancing perfectly.'

Jennifer rubbed his arm sympathetically as he pulled out his phone and passed it to me. 'She sent one from this morning's class about fifteen minutes ago. See?'

After a nod from Yanni, I pressed play. The video showed a beautiful woman in her mid-fifties dancing with a gentleman half her age. She had a full face of makeup and hair that was dyed a startling white with streaks of icy blue through it.

I couldn't take my eyes off her. Her feet were gliding across the dance floor so smoothly it was as if she were skating on ice. As the light glinted off the floor, I realised that was exactly what she was doing. 'Your mum's an elemental witch,' I observed. 'Ice magic.' Okay, maybe she'd come by the icy hair honestly.

'An elemental who's seriously into younger men,' Gilbert commented.

Rory shot a glare at his half-brother and snatched back the phone. 'She got chucked out of magical dance classes because she kept using the ice to her advantage. And she likes younger dancers because they can do the moves more easily.'

'*All* the moves,' Gilbert said, waggling his eyebrows.

We all shot him a glare and he flushed with embarrassment. Apparently he'd forgotten for a moment that they were there because their dad was dead.

Rory took a long breath and flashed a reluctant glance at his half-sister. 'Look, if we're going to talk about people Dad had a fight with, we need to mention Toby, don't we?'

'That's out of order!' Jennifer snapped instantly. 'He would never harm anyone!'

'You don't know that!' Rory shot back. 'If Mum is a suspect we have to consider Toby!'

'Sorry, who is Toby?' I interrupted.

Yanni's lips pursed; clearly, that was a question she'd been about to ask. I was supposed to be a *silent* observer but I was too used to asking the questions.

I sent her an apologetic glance; I wasn't *trying* to piss her off, it was wholly accidental. I would have to keep my mouth shut or she wouldn't let me ride shotgun again and I didn't want that to happen. The PI side of me much preferred talking and interviewing people to looking for information online.

Which reminded me: I still needed to dig into Fraser Banks. Hopefully when I did there would be more dirt on him than you could buy in a garden centre.

'Toby is my ex-boyfriend,' Jennifer said finally. 'Toby Brown.'

I held my tongue with effort.

'And he and your dad didn't get on?' Yanni asked.

'Well, they used to...'

'Until Toby went psycho,' Gilbert interrupted. 'It was bad enough that he was a land shifter!'

'Psycho?' I asked, the question slipping out before I could stifle it.

'No.' Jennifer shook her head firmly. 'He was not a psycho and he never *went* psycho. He was protective, that's all. There was a merman who tried it on with me one night at Shady's – *really* tried it on. He was a water shifter and he thought he had more of a right to me than Toby did. Toby didn't take kindly to *anyone* thinking they had rights over me, himself included. It got a bit ... heated.'

'They had to split up afterwards,' Rory said. 'Dad was pretty insistent.'

'Is that right?' Yanni asked Jennifer gently. 'That must have been hard for you.'

Tears welled in Jennifer's eyes. 'Yeah. Dad was on the water shifters' council and it didn't look good for my boyfriend to attack one of them. And the merman... He was pretty powerful too. It was making the political landscape difficult for Dad and he asked me to break up with Toby – *told* me to,' she admitted.

'But that was months ago,' she went on. 'Toby wouldn't hurt Dad – he's a teddy bear. Literally. That incident was a one-off. Ask his family, ask him, ask anyone who knows him. There's no sweeter guy than Toby in the world, I promise you.' The way she was speaking about him wasn't the way people generally spoke about an ex. Not in my experience, anyway.

'Don't worry,' Yanni said. 'We'll look into everything. Now, could you give me the addresses for your stepmother and for Toby? We'll be in touch as soon as we know more.'

Jennifer nodded and scribbled a note on a scrap of paper. The room stayed thick with tension, grief pressing down like a weighted shroud, and beneath it that gnawing guilt. It was the kind of guilt that whispered, '*you should have been there'* or, even worse, *'it should have been you instead'.* I knew it only too well.

Yanni shot me a pointed glance and rose. We were done for now.

The worst part was over. Now came the hard part – finding the killer.

Chapter Twenty-Two

Yanni sighed as she closed the car door. Eva jumped up and gave her a hello lick designed to make her feel better. It was the canine equivalent of a motivational speech: short, effective and slightly damp. It worked, because a small smile tipped up Yanni's lips.

'Good to see you too, Eva,' she murmured. As she put the key in the ignition and Eva sat back down again I was only a little jealous that I hadn't got the same greeting.

Yanni's gaze shifted to me. 'If you're gonna spend all day out with me, we'll have to sort a mobile line from the station so calls come to you wherever you are. Otherwise I'm in no better situation than I was before.'

She gave a half-hearted chuckle. It was already nearly six in the evening and I could see how much the day had taken out of her. I imagined that no matter how many times you had to tell someone that a loved one was dead, it didn't get any easier – not that you'd make that kind of call very often in a place like Witchlight Cove. Other than after my grandmother arrived, I couldn't recall a time something like this had happened. And it didn't look like the crime rate had soared during my absence or Yanni would definitely have recruited more support.

I thought about the phone issue and grimaced internally. I really did want to help Yanni; I owed her so much. 'I'll make some calls tomorrow,' I promised, wanting to take some of the weight off her shoulders. 'See if there's someone who can sort the phone for me.'

She patted my hand. 'Don't worry. Dove's husband Samuel tends to deal with any practical issues like that. It keeps the station costs down. He'll know a way to divert the calls.' A yawn escaped her but she immediately shook it off. 'Do you want me to drop you home?' she asked. 'You don't need to come with me for the other interviews.'

'It's okay – I'm happy to come. It's not like Eva is pining for me at home.'

Eva barked; it was the unmistakable equivalent of a dog rolling its eyes. 'We don't want to leave you on your own,' I told Yanni firmly. The last thing I wanted was to go home and tell Maddie that I'd let her grandmother work an unreasonably long shift alone after such an emotionally taxing day. 'So where are we going? The stepmum or Toby?'

Yanni didn't ponder the question for very long. 'There's no reason not to believe Rory about the dance classes because those messages seemed in order. We'll go find Toby, see what we can get out of him, then visit the stepmum in the morning when she should be back.'

'Do you think one of them did it?' I asked nosily.

She shrugged. 'I don't know yet. We need more evidence before I have any thoughts either way. Using a bullet doesn't seem like the easiest way for an elemental witch or a bear shifter to kill someone. Then again, if they were trying to keep what they were about to do hidden from Warren, a gun might have been the quickest and easiest option.'

'You said before that it was likely someone he trusted enough to turn his back to them,' I said. 'Would Warren have trusted both of those two?'

'Maybe.' She tapped her fingers on the steering wheel as she thought.

'Do you know the Browns?' I probed. Jennifer had said Toby was a teddy bear, and Gilbert had said he was a land shifter. Yanni was a bear shifter so I wondered if they ran in the same circles.

'Not especially,' Yanni admitted. 'I have to keep myself separate so I don't socialise with any of the sects.'

A pang of loneliness hit me and I realised with horror that it was from her. Yanni was lonely? I'd never got that vibe from her before; her police chief poker face was hiding more than I'd realised. 'That must be hard for you,' I said softly.

She shrugged, her face showing none of the emotion that I could feel. 'You get used to it, and I have Maddie.'

I kept my face blank with effort. 'What about your amateur dramatics group?'

'I don't do it any more – I don't have the energy I used to. I still go and watch the shows, and I heckle supportively,' she added with a smirk.

Silence fell, and for me it was filled with gnawing guilt for abandoning Yanni and Maddie for so long. 'You have me too,' I blurted.

She kept her eyes on the road. 'Until you go back to London.'

Ouch. Direct hit. If guilt had a physical form, it would be punching me in the kidneys right about now. 'I'll stay in touch this time,' I promised.

'You said that last time.' Her tone was matter of fact rather than accusing.

'I was a self-involved teenager last time. I'll do better,' I promised.

Yanni lifted a hand from the wheel and patted my arm. 'You were grieving. You don't have to explain yourself to me.'

'Maybe I don't need to but I *want* to. I'm sorry, Yanni. I didn't mean to hurt you.'

She squeezed my arm before returning her hand to the wheel. She didn't contradict me, though, and that made me feel even worse. 'You've already apologised, Beatrix, you don't need to keep doing so. It's in the past. Now, let's focus on the present.'

She was right, I needed to get my head in the game. Toby lived further away from the coast in an area of Witchlight Cove I knew well. It was only a couple of miles from the border barrier, and I'd spent a lot of time playing there when I was a kid with Ezra and some of the other wolf shifters.

Whilst Mum always ensured I did at least a couple of hours' training most days, once or twice a year she gave me a whole day off. I spent several of them around here, climbing trees, messing around, building forts, normal kid things.

Even then I'd known something about my magic wasn't quite right. Maddie's powers had been growing stronger and stronger with every passing moon, and the wolves were growing more and more formidable. Me? I'd stayed the same, the stunted runt of the litter. Even so, neither Maddie nor Ezra ever did anything to make me feel bad about myself.

'You're at a different stage,' they had always said to me. 'It'll happen.' And then as the years passed, the refrain had changed to, 'You don't need more magic. You're perfect the way you are.' They had said it so often that I knew they'd come up with that party line together. Their care made me feel loved, but I still despised my own ineptitude.

I should have had more magic because my mother was incredibly strong. I'd kept hoping that one day it would come, but at twenty-eight I'd finally learned to stop wishing for something that was clearly never going to happen.

It had taken a couple of decades, but now I could accept it. I was a magical dud.

Chapter Twenty-Three

It was only when Yanni stopped the car that I realised I'd drifted away into my own thoughts. 'We're here,' she said. 'Do you want to bring Eva in with us?'

Eva had spent most of the day as a guard dog, first outside Warren's yacht and then Jennifer's cottage. Knowing her, she was in desperate need of some human interaction even if it was only listening to more questioning and getting the occasional pat.

'Yeah, why not? She can be disarming. A dog helps settle people, which sometimes mean they reveal more than they mean to.'

Yanni looked impressed. 'Maybe I should get one,' she mused. 'For the office,' she added hastily.

'If you do, don't forget to increase the snack budget. And add some extra money for baby wipes – they're handy to clean up the drool.' Eva shot me an outraged look, which we both knew wasn't warranted. When she was waiting for treats she drooled like she'd turned on a tap. It was gross, but I loved her anyway.

'Come on, girl,' I said and she jumped out behind us. I didn't tell her to be quiet; she already knew that. She'd been my wingdog during many an interview and she knew her role well: disarm, charm and calm.

When Yanni knocked on the door, it was answered promptly by a stout woman with an amazing head of deep brown curls. Her eyes glinted with a smile that flickered slightly when she saw Yanni standing there. 'Oh, hello,' she said.

'I'm Police Chief Greenridge,' Yanni introduced herself. 'We're looking for Toby Brown. Is he in?'

'I'm his mother, Selena.' The woman's face tightened. 'What do you need him for?'

Yanni smiled broadly, though I could feel the tension in her body. 'We actually need to speak to your son directly. It's in connection with one of our investigations.'

Eva stepped forward and put her puppy-dog eyes to work. Instinctively Selena crouched down, held out her hand and let my dog sniff her before patting her head. Perfect: she was a dog person.

'Investigation?' Selena asked. 'What sort of Investigation?' Her lips pressed into a tight line. 'If it's poaching, then he's *not* poaching. That land out back is for all the shifters – it's in the original agreements, the ones that date back as far as the Witchlight.'

'No, it's not about poaching.' Yanni's tone grew more serious. 'It's a bit more than that. It's a murder investigation.'

Selena froze mid-pat and her eyes shot up to meet Yanni's. 'What? A *murder*?' She'd gone pale. 'You'd better come in.' She straightened and held open the door for us.

She led us into her lounge, a small room painted sage green with worn sofas and a well-loved rug. When we sat down, Eva jumped up, snuggled next to Selena and laid her huge head on the woman's lap. Instantly Selena tangled her hands into Eva's long golden fur.

Finally she asked the question she'd been building up the courage to ask. 'Who's been killed?'

'Warren Storcrest.'

Selena's mouth dropped open. 'Oh, good God. The poor man. Oh poor Jennifer. She must be devastated.' Tears filled her eyes and she clutched a hand to her heart.

I lowered my shields and her emotions clobbered me over the head: shock and sadness. The punch of them was so strong that I struggled to breathe for a second then hastily tried to pull my walls back up. It took effort and I sagged a little in the chair. Damn it, I'd forgotten how strongly a supernatural's emotions could hit me; it was so much stronger than being around humans all the time. I'd need to use my magic sparingly because Selina's impact had instantly left me with a pounding headache.

'You know Jennifer well, I take it?' Yanni asked, and I tuned back into the here and now.

'Oh yes, absolutely. She's a lovely girl. Jennifer and Toby were so well matched, though unfortunately her family didn't see it that way.' Selena grimaced. 'Especially not after the incident with the merman.'

'I heard about that,' Yanni said pointedly. 'So, is Toby in?'

Selena's eyes widened. 'No, he's out, but you can't think he had something to do with this! He wouldn't—'

'We need to talk to him, that's all,' Yanni interjected smoothly. 'To ascertain his whereabouts for the last day or so. It's simply procedure.'

'He was with me all of last night and most of today. He only went out hunting – I don't know – an hour ago? I could try ringing him but he doesn't get much of a signal in the woods. Oh God, I wish his father was here! This is terrible.'

'Honestly, it's fine,' Yanni reassured her. 'He's not being arrested; we're just trying to follow up all the leads we can.'

'I bet it was Jennifer's brothers pointing fingers, wasn't it? Of course it was. They're the ones that had a real problem with Jennifer dating Toby. The youngest brother particularly – but then, that one's had it rough. His mother isn't much of a mother, if you see what I mean, but Warren has tried his hardest with all of them. He's a great role model, teaching them the real values in life, making them work like he did. Gosh, poor Jennifer. I can't imagine how she's coping with this.' She sighed. 'You know, I was sure she and Toby would get back together once the anger about that merperson incident had died away.'

It was a lot of things to share in one breath but somehow Selena had done it.

'The thing is, we still need to talk to Toby,' Yanni said gently. 'Just to confirm where he was.'

'I already told you he was with me last night and this morning. I can prove it to you. I've got video tapes, security around the house, you know.'

'You have security cameras?' I interjected, surprised. Why on earth would she have cameras in a cosy little seaside village? I bit my lip immediately after the question left me. I'd managed to stay silent, but that little titbit had got me. After all, it was a tiny house and it didn't look like it had much worth stealing.

'Nothing elaborate – it's an old system,' Selena said. 'I had it put in after Toby was born when that sorceress tried stealing that teenager. You might have been too young to remember the incident,' she said to me.

Blood rushed in my ears. I remembered it all too well.

Yanni looked at me sympathetically, but I gave Selena my best bland smile and did my best not to reveal how much the comment bothered me. 'Yes, I remember it,' I said as evenly as I could.

'None of us felt safe after that dreadful incident. So many deaths.' She clutched a hand to her heart again. 'A lot of us were scared for our kids so we put in additional safety measures.'

'We'll need to check the footage,' Yanni said. 'Can you let us know when Toby gets back? If it's late tonight, ringing the station tomorrow morning will be fine. Beatrix will answer the phone,' she added pointedly, implying I'd actually have to do the job I'd been employed to do at some point. Outrageous.

'Toby is going to be so upset for Jennifer.' Selina took a deep breath. 'He usually heads out to work with his dad about nine, so it'll be before then.'

Yanni nodded. 'That would be great.'

Damn, I thought grumpily. There went any chance of a later start tomorrow, then. I despised early starts.

This job was temporary, but it was really chafing at me not to be running my own business. I appreciated Maddie sorting me out with an income whilst I sorted out the Eternal Flame situation, but if I stayed here much longer I'd have to think seriously about advertising my PI services in the local paper, *The Cove Chronicle*.

'Thank you for your time,' Yanni said, standing to leave.

Eva nuzzled Selena Brown pointedly, and a small smile crept onto her face, 'Aren't you a dear,' she murmured, giving her a quick hug. It might be wrong to trust a dog's reaction but Eva had taken so well to Toby's mum that it made me think her son probably wasn't involved in the murder. Still, Yanni was right: we had to follow the evidence.

Selena agreed to get her husband, Darren, to bring us the footage from the security cameras first thing tomorrow. As we left the house, I did a quick scout around. Now that I was looking for them, I found the two cameras mounted on the house easily, one at the front, one at the back. The problem was that their coverage wasn't complete; there were a few blind spots. If Toby had been determined to sneak away unspotted by the cameras, I reckoned he could have done so.

Eva stayed hot on my heels. I opened the car door for her to jump in, then hesitated. Yanni was done for the day but

I wasn't, not quite. I looked at Eva and closed the car door again. She sat down at my feet.

'Yanni,' I said casually, 'we're not far from Shingle's End, are we?' That was where Old Jacobson's lived, the hermit witch that Mrs D had told me about. The one who might be able to help Maddie and me.

'Shingle's End?' Yanni sounded surprised. 'Well, no – you're on the right side of the village. Probably half an hour's walk. Why?'

'Oh, I fancied going for a bit of a stroll. You know, reminiscing about my time here,' I lied.

She frowned at me. 'Are you sure? It's a bit of a trek back home.'

'Eva could use a proper walk. I think I owe her at least an hour or so.' Eva thumped her tail in agreement.

'Okay, I'll leave you here,' Yanni said. 'See you at the office bright and early tomorrow.' Her words had an edge; she knew how well I did with early starts.

I hid a wince. 'Absolutely. See you at the office bright and early,' I repeated.

I watched her drive away then figuratively rolled up my sleeves. It was time to look into one of my other investigations – namely, getting back the Eternal Flame.

Chapter Twenty-Four

The sky was grey and from the way the leaves were flurrying from the trees, a breeze was picking up. It was probably quite chilly but I didn't feel cold; I never tended to feel the cold that much. I sometimes wondered if it was a side effect of growing up in a house with an Eternal Flame; maybe it had left me forever warm.

On the magical front, I was feeling pretty tired. It had been a long time since I'd felt so many strong emotions cascading into me and it was tough. That was more than enough to remind me why I'd left all those years ago. I'd been working hard on my shields for a long time, and I was grateful for that now, but the shields still didn't stop the pounding in my head. I pushed the pain aside with effort.

'So, what do you think?' I asked Eva as we walked. 'Will this Jacobson guy talk to us about the Eternal Flame?' She trotted beside me, tail wagging faintly. 'Do you think he even knows anything about the Eternal Flames?' I added with a grimace.

Eva did not respond, not in words, though she snorted in a way that implied she thought my optimism was laughable. I was getting judged by a dog. Again.

Old Jacobson might know nothing about the Flames, and even if he did he might not know there was one in Witchlight Cove. Witchlight was a local term for the Eternal Flame, so the name of the village wasn't a huge giveaway to other supernaturals.

From the books I'd read and the lessons I'd learned from my mother – sandwiched between my fighting training – I'd discovered the Flames' history. There were twelve of them, each one hidden in a town or village, though the exact locations were unknown. The general regions were well documented, and I knew they were spread across the continents, but that was it. If I'd wanted to, I could have narrowed it down a bit; after all, there were far fewer magical communities in the world than non-magical ones. But I'd only become interested in them when I'd wanted to remove myself from the magical community altogether.

If Old Jacobson kept to himself, maybe he knew nothing. Divulging the existence of the Eternal Flame wasn't exactly the first thing the community did to newcomers.

Shingle's End was exactly as its name described, at the far edge of the village where the beach changed from soft, white sands to harsh shingle stones. 'Let's walk up on the bank,' I said to Eva, wanting to spare her paws. She moved to my right, onto the soft bank.

The sun was sinking on the horizon and I took a moment to soak in the view. There was something inherently magical in watching the sun disappear from the world. Those stunning hues of red and orange made it look like the sky was on fire, and all the while the sea was lapping on the beach, soothing me like nothing else with its rolling rush and roar.

This was home. This moment lived within me like thousands of the other sunsets I'd witnessed in my lifetime here. Like she knew that I needed it, Eva sat next to me and together we watched the sun take its final dip into the sea.

When it was finally gone, I walked on. It was only a dozen more paces until a small cottage came into view: the haunted house of Shingle's End.

Given that Witchlight Cove is a magical village, it had always struck me as faintly ridiculous that anyone would call a house 'haunted'. Here ghosts were a part of life – or death; we didn't call houses with ghosts in them 'haunted', we simply called them houses. Although to be fair, 'The

House With the Screaming Apparition Who Won't Stop Singing Off-Key' was a bit of a mouthful.

I remember playing Cherry-Knocking, or Knock Down Ginger as they called it in London, knocking on a door and running away before you could be seen. Trying to act brave, Ezra had always insisted on doing it, though his short, timid knocks barely made a sound before he bolted away.

Maddie was the braver one, pounding her small fist against the door before dashing off. We'd knocked on this particular door plenty of times and sometimes we'd sworn we heard music or voices; looking back now, I realised it was probably kids using the cottage to drink or smoke.

Either way, it had never looked lived in, and with all the beautiful homes nearby I couldn't imagine someone choosing this particular ramshackle place to live in. They obviously had, however, because a light was glowing inside.

'Ready for this?' I asked Eva. 'Just to warn you, I'm not sure if this witch is as friendly as Maddie and me. If I even count as a witch,' I added wryly.

Eva pressed close to my leg and I swear she shuddered. I grimaced. 'Honestly, your trembling doesn't make me feel great.' Apparently my dog was not a fan of haunted houses. Crime scenes and murder investigations? Absolutely fine.

This was a far cry from when she'd happily bolted away from me at Warren's house even though a murder had taken place there. If Eva was nervous, there was probably good reason. She shuddered again and looked up at me as if to ask if I really wanted to do this.

'I have to,' I said. 'We need to figure out what's happened to the Flame. Time for some bravery, Eva. We mustn't give up.'

Taking a few steadying breaths, I walked towards the door. The guy wasn't a green witch, that was for sure because his garden was completely overgrown. Most of the weeds were waist-high and their stalks were brown and brittle. I hated to imagine what the back garden looked like if the front was this bad.

I heard music coming from inside the house – a piano – then it stopped abruptly. The old man knew I was there so there was no point in prevaricating. I knocked on the door. My instinct to run was strong but I told myself it was a reaction from my childhood, not a legitimate gut warning.

I held my breath, unsure why I was so worried. I doubted Old Jacobson had much magic because even witches with the most basic skills made their houses look decent and filled the garden with herbs and flowers to use in spells. This desolation was a show of strength. If I used that as a benchmark, he had no power at all.

I waited, my heart pounding. Finally, the door creaked open. 'Mr Jacobson?' I said. 'Hi, my name is—'

'How dare you disturb me!' he snapped, before his eyes locked on mine and the blood drained from his face. He shook his head. 'No!'

Oh-kay then. I stepped back and held up my hands. 'I'm sorry, I wanted to ask you a couple of questions—'

'No! No, you can't be here! You can't be here!'

Shields or not, his panic hit me like a sledgehammer to the gut and I staggered back. He was shaking, his grey beard trembling as his face quivered. The despair and anguish radiating from him was so intense that I felt it seeping into my very bones.

'I'm sorry. I didn't mean to upset you,' I said desperately. 'I wanted to ask if you knew anything about the Eternal—'

The door slammed shut and with it came a shockwave of green magic so strong that it flung me across the garden. Terrific: I love spontaneous flights.

Eva was caught in the blast too, hurled back by the same pale green ripples of light that had struck me and made the very earth tremble. She landed with a thud and gave a sharp whimper.

'Eva!' I scrambled to my feet as she staggered to hers then threw myself down next to her, desperately checking her for signs of injury. She yipped softly and licked my face to reassure me.

'You're okay,' I panted in relief. She nudged at me pointedly. 'I'm okay, too,' I reassured her as I stood up again and brushed myself down. Fucking hell. The back of my head and neck hurt like hell.

As my vision cleared, I stared at the house. So much for thinking the old man was a weak witch; that ward would throw out a hundred witches, never mind just me and Eva. That was some serious freaking magic.

The good news was that with power like that, maybe Mr Jacobson did know something about the Flame or had something that could help us.

The bad news? He didn't seem willing to share.

Chapter Twenty-Five

I felt like I'd been hurtled twenty feet through the air and landed on a bush – which, of course, I had been. Walking back home would be slow going. There used to be a taxi firm in the village, and I was sure there still was, but I didn't have its number. Besides, I wasn't convinced a driver would be okay allowing a dog and a woman covered in leaves and twigs in their car.

I swallowed my pride and rang Maddie. When she promised to come straight over, something in me eased. It was nice having someone to call on. I'd missed that, in London.

Her car rocked up with my bestie behind the wheel dressed in her pyjamas. I opened the rear door for Eva then hopped into the passenger seat. 'This is a change for you,' I said gesturing at her attire. 'What happened to the girl who didn't like to go out until nine o'clock at night?'

She rolled her eyes. 'Just feeling shattered, that's all,' she said. 'Don't worry, I'll be up for going out on Friday. Ezra told me he'd spoken to you.'

I slid her an accusing look. 'Of course he did because you totally told him to go and get me a coffee.'

'Maybe.' She smirked. 'So?'

'So what?'

'He looks good, doesn't he?' She waggled her eyebrows.

A half-laugh, half-huff escaped me. 'He's grown up,' I admitted. 'But I'm not going there, Maddie.'

'Why not? He's a really good guy – he's funny and you two always got on really well.'

'When we were *seventeen*. But people change. He's not my type now.'

'No? So what is your type?'

A picture flashed into my mind: someone in a smart shirt, sleeves rolled up over bulging muscles, brooding eyes that I could lose myself in for hours. I pushed the unwanted image away forcefully. Nope. I was *not* going there, either.

'Regardless of my taste in men, at the minute I don't have time for one,' I said primly. 'I've got enough to sort out. I think Mr Jacobson might be the one we need to speak to.'

'That's great!' Her excitement and relief were palpable and I hated to quash it, but I needed to tell her the truth.

'Yeah ... but it's complicated. I think perhaps you were right in thinking he's an ogre.'

Her face crinkled with confusion. 'But I thought he was a witch?'

'I mean he really doesn't like people. He didn't like me, anyway. I'm not sure how we'll get him to talk to us. I think he might have a screw loose.'

'Screw loose, or screw missing entirely and held together with hope and duct tape?'

I grimaced. 'The latter.'

'You'll think of something. You have to. *We* have to,' she said grimly. Her words didn't make me feel great.

With effort, she dredged up a smile and tried to dispel the grim atmosphere that had descended. 'So how was the first day on the job?' she asked. 'Did you have time to dig up stuff on Banks?'

'Actually, it was pretty manic.' I told her everything that had happened.

'Shut *up*!' she said finally. 'I can't believe someone killed Warren. That's insane. I've seen Toby in passing and met him a couple of times socially but I could never imagine he'd do something like that. But the stepmum...?' She paused. 'Well, Yanni's not her biggest fan.'

'Is she not?' I hadn't got that impression from Yanni at all, then I realised that was the whole point: she had one heck of a poker face. I knew that from that wash of loneliness I would never have guessed at.

I'd have to do something about that too, but one problem at a time. 'If you're planning on going to bed when you get in, I can do a little digging from home,' I suggested.

'Sounds good,' she said. 'Although the Wi-Fi can be patchy.'

'I'm sure it'll be fine.'

Maddie nodded. A companionable silence was beginning to fall between us when she spoke again. 'I know it's not the best of circumstances,' she said softly, 'but it's really, really good having you back. It's a bit like you've never been away.'

'I feel the same.' I squeezed her arm. 'And I'm so damned grateful for it. Grateful for you.'

I was genuinely shocked by how much her friendship still meant to me; I'd honestly believed that I'd let her fade into my past, but now that I was here that ache that lived in my heart had finally gone. Until that had happened, I hadn't realised just how crippling it had been.

Back home, I bid a yawning Maddie goodnight. I grabbed my laptop and sat down in the cold living room, the empty fireplace taunting me. Maddie wasn't the only thing I'd missed, and when she had persuaded me to come home, I'd been looking forward to basking in the Witchlight. That it was gone left me more than a little depressed. The Eternal Flame was my inheritance, and I had failed it miserably. Well, I was done failing. I was going to find it, and restore it, and that was all there was to it.

I opened my laptop and navigated my way to the dark web, then opened up pages on some of the websites I frequently used as a PI. One of the most useful things I'd ever done in London was pay a magical hacker called Donovan a ridiculous price to get me banking access codes and encryption keys; using the portal he'd created for me, I could pretty much log into any bank I wanted from anywhere in the world.

So that's what I did.

I thought I'd have to search half a dozen Fraser Banks to find the one I was looking for but when I narrowed down the search parameters to Cornwall there was only one person with that name and an English bank account. Or rather several English bank accounts.

As I opened the first one, my jaw dropped. The numbers were massive; we were talking my annual martial arts earnings plus my PI fees multiplied by ten, *per month*.

'Banks, indeed,' I muttered. 'This man could open one himself with all that money. Crikey.' I wasn't even *that* jealous. Uh-huh.

I scanned down. Some debits were for mundane things – internet, bills, rental on property – and there were large amounts going to building firms. Judging by what I knew of Banks, that wasn't a surprise; as a property developer he'd gotta develop.

Halfway down the page something caught my eye. Two hundred thousand pounds had gone out of the account but there was no name listed for the recipient, just an address. That didn't feel right.

I typed the address into a search engine but nothing came up. I tried changing my servers and using one on the dark web. Still nothing. My first lead and I'd hit a dead end. But that wasn't the last of my options. I pulled open my phone and scrolled down to a name: Donovan.

There was a reason I had used him before: when it came to finances, he was the absolute best if you wanted to stop payments to somebody or wanted full disclosure. But this wasn't a case of accessing bank statements, which I could already do thanks to his portal. Donovan was better than that: he could trace the money from source to final destination going back years. He also had systems linked to public CCTV cameras that could track where high levels of cash were spent, not only in the UK but overseas as well.

When I pressed on his number, he answered within two rings. 'Beatrix Stonehaven. Long time, no see – or hear. How can I help? Unless you're ringing for my stimulating conversation?'

'Not much time for conversation today. Sorry. Could you do me a favour?'

'Depends on what it is and what you'll pay me for it.' He sounded amused.

'I was hoping for a discount this time based on my charming personality and the fact that I once saved a cat from a tree.'

He let the silence hang. That was a no, then. I sighed. 'I'm on a case. There's a payment to a bank account. I've got the associated address and number but no name. Any chance you could track that down for me? And to be honest, I'm not sure the address is legit.'

'You need me to do some deep digging?'

'Possibly. Probably.'

He grunted before he spoke again. 'Payment will be the usual,' he warned.

I gritted my teeth. Donovan wasn't cheap and I didn't know what Yanni was going to pay me, but it wasn't like I had a choice. If we could get some dirt on Banks, we could stop him dead in his tracks, stop him getting anywhere near my house. When it came to my home, money was no object. I had credit cards. I'd use them.

'All right. I'll transfer it to you now with all the information that I have.'

'I'll get onto it as soon as I have time. Pleasure doing business with you,' he said. A click. The line went dead.

I shoved my phone back into my pocket. One step closer.

Now all I had to do was hope that Donovan's 'deep digging' didn't put us both in a hole too deep to climb out of.

Chapter Twenty-Six

Next morning, Eva woke me at seven by repeatedly licking my face. Apparently she thought that dog breath was the best way to stop me oversleeping and being late for work. She wasn't wrong; it was like being waterboarded, but affectionately.

As I stretched, there was a knock on the door and Maddie poked her head around it. 'Great, you're up.'

'I wouldn't go as far as "up",' I groaned. 'Stretching barely counts as awake.'

'Let's go get a coffee.' She was annoyingly chirpy. 'After last night I really need one. Maybe a double shot.'

'Is this the same coffee Ezra bought me?' I opened one eye a fraction.

'The very same. You're going to love it.'

My mouth watered with the memories of the intense creamy caffeine hit. Some things were worth getting out of bed for. 'In that case, give me two minutes. I'll be there.'

Having lived in London for so long, I'd seen plenty of cafés and coffee shops with queues outside them. There were restaurants where you had to wait on the street three times longer than it took to eat brunch, and where you had to book a year in advance for a dinner reservation. I'd never seen anything like that in Witchlight Cove. Sure, Claude's bakery could get busy, particularly when he pulled out some of his seasonal specials like his spiced pumpkin pasty at Halloween, but as far as I was aware this was just a normal day.

Even so, a queue was already snaking down the street outside the little door on the unassuming building with the large sign that said *Insomnia Coffee*. A smaller sign simply read *Sonny's*. 'Wow, people here love their coffee these days,' I muttered.

'No, they love *Sonny's* coffee,' Maddie corrected. 'And wait until you've tried his mocha. It's out of this world.' She rubbed her hands together in anticipation.

'Is that a review or a prophecy?' I asked. 'Because if I'm going to have some kind of mystical awakening after one sip, I want a warning first.'

She snorted.

We slipped into the queue. I was surprised by the way my nerves were fluttering. I was in a queue in full view of half the village – okay, not quite half, but it felt that way. Did they know who I was? *What* I was? A lapsed guardian?

A woman a few places ahead offered me a wave and I reciprocated with a vague smile. 'That's Pepper Polter,' Maddie murmured. 'Ezra's cousin. She was a year below us at school. She married a vampire.'

'Huh.' I didn't know what surprised me more, that a werewolf would marry a vampire, or that someone a year younger than me was already married. I'd thought I was being mature by committing to my dog for the next ten to twelve years; to agree to be with someone for life was a whole different matter.

I spotted Helga and Volga ahead of me. Both had matching blue rinses, though Helga's hair was long and curly whilst Volga's was short and straight. The two old ladies lived together in the cottage next to mine, and until that moment I'd always assumed they were just good friends. Watching the way Helga's arm snaked around Volga's waist, though, I suddenly realised that they were probably lovers.

'Hey,' I whispered to Maddie, 'are Helga and Volga *together?*'

Maddie grinned. 'You're just now realising huh?'

I blinked. 'I just thought they were friends, like us. We always said if we didn't find love by thirty we'd move in together.'

She snorted. 'As if thirty is old enough. Let's amend the pact to forty.'

I laughed. 'Deal.'

As I looked down the queue, I was surprised how many faces I recognised even if I didn't know their names. I guess it's a small-town thing – people tend not to leave, and even if they do they often migrate back at some point like particularly stubborn swallows who've decided city life isn't for them.

I supposed I was in the latter group, though I refused to admit it. This wasn't a migration; it was a temporary stopover like when you end up crashing at a mate's place after a night out because the buses have stopped running. I was in Witchlight until I'd sorted out the house issue and that was it. No nesting, no putting down roots. And definitely no getting attached. I looked at Maddie standing next to me and grimaced. The roots were already taking hold.

Despite receiving some surreptitious glances, Pepper was the only person who actually waved. That made sense; if she was Ezra's cousin, she'd probably heard what had actually happened rather than the dark gossip people had bandied around.

When we finally reached the front of the queue, I stared at the barista. I couldn't help it. There was no disguising that he was a vampire, not with his fangs fully visible and perching over his bottom lip.

Eva whimpered beside me and I sympathised. I'd always thought there was no reason to be more scared of vampires than other magical creatures. Yes, they could kill you, but that death could come with a side dish of eternal life that you didn't get if you were killed by a werewolf or a witch. There was the whole blood-draining thing, but I'd been willing to overlook that.

'I thought vampire fangs only came out when they were hungry,' I whispered to Maddie. 'Or angry.'

'And there's your answer,' she whispered back. 'Sonny is *always* angry.'

'Fantastic,' I muttered. 'A grumpy vampire with unlimited access to hot liquids. What could possibly go wrong?'

The customer in front of us snagged his drink and moved out of the way. 'Hey, Sonny,' Maddie smiled at his scowling face. 'How are you doing? That tattoo looks like it's only got a week or so left. Do you want me to book you in for another appointment?'

I saw what she meant: the ward she'd placed on his skin was only faintly visible. No wonder he was totally covered up and wearing a flat cap and sunglasses. 'I'll make an appointment when I need an appointment,' he snarled in a deep New York drawl.

Well, if that wasn't customer service, I wasn't sure what was. I half-expected him to chuck my coffee at me and charge extra for the trauma.

'So?' he said, shifting his gaze to me.

'So?' I asked, a little taken aback.

'What do you want to drink? I assume that's why you're standing here.'

Wow. Polite. He was a New Yorker through and through: busy, direct and brusque. 'Can we get two cappuccinos, please?' I said, trying my most charming smile. It didn't seem to impress him.

With a grunt, he moved to the coffee machine. As he filled the filter with freshly ground beans, a commotion started near the door. 'In the police car? You're sure?' someone asked loudly.

'Absolutely. In the back of the car. They've arrested her.'

I turned my attention away from the counter to listen. 'Sorry?' I said, tapping the shoulder of the person next to me. 'What was that?'

The man squinted as if he recognised me but then shook his head. 'Mrs D. The old schoolteacher. She was in the back of a police car. It looks like she's been arrested.'

Chapter Twenty-Seven

I didn't wait to hear any more. With Eva hot on my heels, I pushed my way out of the shop. Maddie called my name, but I didn't bother looking back to see if she was following me. If Mrs D had been arrested, did that mean that Yanni had found more evidence? No way did Mrs D murder Warren Storcrest! It had to be a mistake.

When I reached the station, Dove was sitting behind her desk. 'What the hell is going on?' I demanded.

'Bea,' Dove began. 'I was about to call you. Mrs D was—'

'It's okay, Dove, I'll take this. Beatrix.' Yanni's voice was firm and controlled. I turned and saw she was standing in front of her office door, hands on her hips.

I realised I was trembling. The strength of my reaction surprised me, but then again I knew what it was like when everyone thought you were guilty of a crime you hadn't committed. 'You arrested her?' I said brokenly. 'She's innocent, Yanni, and you paraded her in front of everybody!'

Her eyes were sympathetic: she knew me too well. 'I did *not* arrest Mrs D,' she responded calmly. 'And I most certainly did not *parade* her anywhere. I brought her in for questioning, which I'm entitled to do – and which I need to do. This is a murder case and we have reason to suspect her.'

'You can't be serious! It's Mrs D!'

Yanni studied me. 'Tell me this, Bea. Before yesterday, would you have expected Mrs D could poison someone?'

I didn't reply because I couldn't, not without proving her point.

'Exactly,' she said, taking my silence as the answer she wanted. 'Now, I understand she didn't mean to poison someone but she *did* intend to rig a competition so that she won. You wouldn't have thought she was capable of cheating, either, would you? Would you have thought Mrs D could cheat to win money?'

I remained silent and my shoulders slumped. There was no point replying. Yanni knew she had me.

Her voice softened still further. 'I'm not doing this to be cruel, Bea. The last thing I want is to find that Mrs D is guilty. She taught Maddie too, remember? And

Maddie's mum and dad – she taught all my kids and all the kids around here. I *get it*. But right now, I need to question her because she had a motive and she has form, albeit accidental. Plus, she might know other people who had similar motives and were willing to take it a little further. You can't let your personal feelings affect this investigation.'

I ground my back teeth. I loved Yanni, I understood it was her job, and from her perspective I was being unreasonable. But I couldn't help it: my emotions were too high. 'You put her in the back of the police car,' I said accusingly.

'Because she was more comfortable there. I offered her the front seat but she wanted to stretch out a bit because she has arthritis in her shoulders. It was her choice to go in the back, like it was her choice to come down to the station rather than have me question her at home. Fingers crossed she can give us an alibi for Warren's time of death and we'll move on with the investigation.'

'And if she can't?'

Yanni didn't reply. I sucked in a sharp breath. I needed to clear Mrs D and that meant I had to *think*, dammit. 'Do we have an official time of death?'

Yanni's gaze didn't waver. 'Yes. The coroner placed it between thirty minutes to an hour before we got there.'

As I thought about those times, a thought struck me. 'We went to Storcrest's house after I'd seen Mrs D, so it can't possibly be her. *I'm* her alibi.' I shot Yanni a triumphant smile.

'Beatrix,' she said evenly, 'you were with her for all of twenty minutes and after that you came back to the station. That doesn't give her an alibi. If anything, knowing we were onto her could have been the reason she finished him off.'

'That doesn't make sense,' I protested.

'Doesn't it?' Yanni raised an eyebrow. 'You also said she'd been for a walk when you arrived at the house. Am I remembering that correctly?'

She was right. 'Yes.'

'And would you agree it's within walking distance from Amara's place to Warren's?'

'Yes, but—'

'It's not about the "but", Beatrix. We don't deal with "buts" in this job, we place the evidence where it stands – and right now it stands against her.' She sighed wearily. 'Look, I need to go question Mrs D.'

'I want to be there,' I said firmly.

'Not a chance.' She shook her head. 'You can sit in the other room and watch through the one-way mirror,' she conceded.

I wanted to object; after all, shouldn't Mrs D have a lawyer present? But I suspected she'd already refused that right and there was no point in making more fuss. Pushing Yanni any further could result in her kicking me off the case and I couldn't let that happen. Especially as I wasn't officially on it.

'Okay,' I said begrudgingly. 'Thanks. I'll sit in the other room and watch.'

'Good. And bring the phone with you in case it rings. That's your actual *job*, remember?'

I grabbed the phone off the desk and turned towards the hall, then I paused. 'You know, in all the years I spent imagining myself in an interrogation room, I always pictured myself on the other side of the glass.'

Yanni snorted. 'Yeah? In handcuffs or as the detective?'

'You'll never know,' I said airily, and walked towards the viewing room.

It was time to find out what Mrs D had to say for herself and, more importantly, whether I had accidentally vouched for a murderer.

Chapter Twenty-Eight

Yanni and Dove sat at the table opposite Mrs D while I was banished with Eva to the room behind the mirror. In another situation, I'd probably have been excited to be in the type of room that featured so heavily in the crime shows I loved to watch, but at that moment I couldn't see any positives at all.

In all the years I'd known her, I couldn't remember seeing Mrs D look so fragile. Yes, she had always been old, but she'd never been frail. As I sat down I found myself absently rubbing Eva's fur. I needed something to occupy my hands and distract my thoughts.

Yanni cleared her throat slightly, making Mrs D jump as though a gun had been fired next to her. 'Amara,' she said gently. 'I assume you know why we're here.'

'It's true, then? He's actually dead?'

Yanni nodded. 'I'm afraid he is.'

'Oh God. I'm so sorry. It wasn't ... it wasn't the chili peppers, was it?' Mrs D looked close to tears.

Yanni smiled. 'No, it wasn't the chili peppers.'

'Oh, thank goodness.' Relief flooded Mrs D and she sagged into the chair, clutching at the pearls around her neck. The gesture was so classic, I half-expected her to start fanning herself and calling for smelling salts. That anyone in their right mind could think Mrs D was guilty was beyond belief.

'But you understand the predicament we're in, don't you?' Dove said, taking over the questioning. 'You can see how this looks? And why we have to ask you a few questions – questions that might not be comfortable? We'll try and make it as quick and painless as possible.'

The only professional environment I'd seen Dove in was at the crime scene on the boat. Now I was impressed by how well she handled herself, how she'd mastered that voice of firm, caring command like Yanni's.

Mrs D wrung her hands. 'Of course I understand. But you have to know I wouldn't do something like this. I didn't want to hurt him – that wasn't my intention. I needed to raise the money so the children could go on the trip to London. That's the only holiday some of them get every year.'

'We understand,' Yanni said. 'Do you know why Warren stopped giving you the money?'

Mrs D shook her head. 'I don't have a clue. The news came out of nowhere – he sent me an email saying he would no longer be supporting any of my charities or clubs. He didn't even sign it in the way he normally does, with a little smiley face and a "W". There was just his name at the bottom. It was so impersonal! I tried emailing back, but I guess he'd blocked my email or something. I wanted to speak to him at the fayre. I'd decided I would only use the chilies if I couldn't get him to see sense, but he was so busy and he seemed to be ignoring me. I didn't feel like I had any choice.'

I watched Yanni and Dove exchange a look. Surely they could see something suspicious was going on here? If Warren hadn't signed his email in his usual way, maybe he hadn't sent it.

'Can you tell us what you were doing yesterday at about eleven o'clock?' Yanni asked.

'I went for a walk – I always go for a walk, just around the seafront. I like to feed the birds when I'm in my human form.' She hesitated. 'I may have plucked off one or two – you know, when I've transformed – but I always feel a bit guilty about it so I take some homemade seed balls for them. As an apology.'

I couldn't imagine Mrs D in any form plucking off living creatures. Yanni had been right: I didn't know everything about my old teacher, no matter how much I wanted to believe that I did.

'Did anybody see you?' Dove asked.

'I don't think so. I try to go at quiet times in case my instincts get the better of me and I fancy a snack. That's not something I'd want any of my students – past or present – to see me do.' She looked flustered.

'So you have no witnesses. And you have a motive,' Dove said.

Mrs D nodded. Tears started to trickle down her cheeks. 'I know.'

'I'm afraid this doesn't look good,' Yanni said. 'I think it's best that we keep you in for further questioning.'

'Keep me in?' Mrs D looked horrified. 'Does that mean I'm officially a suspect?'

My stomach twisted. That was it – I was done listening to this! I swivelled around, ready to march out of the door and into the interview room, only for Eva to block my path. 'I need to go in there,' I said.

She tipped her head to the side then made a quiet noise that was something between a bark and a squeak. I thought I knew what she was trying to tell me: this was an official police investigation and I had no business sticking my nose in. After all, if Mrs D was innocent as I was sure she was, the evidence would point to that, wouldn't it?

But I wasn't so sure. How many crime dramas had I watched in the non-magical world where false evidence was planted to bring an innocent person down?

Yanni walked out of the interview room and came through to me.

'You have to be joking!' I snapped. 'You said it was questioning!'

'It *was* questioning,' she replied evenly. 'And the questioning leads us to believe that she could've done it. She had a motive, priors and no alibi.'

'But it's Mrs D!'

'I understand that you're mad.' Yanni's voice was calm but firm. 'But I've got the council on my back – and not just the shifters. Everybody is freaked out by what's happened. This is the first murder we've had in Witchlight since ... since—'

'Since my grandmother came in and killed everyone,' I finished for her. And I had shouldered a lot of ill-feeling about it because my grandmother had come here for *me*.

'You must understand why everyone's on edge. You might not remember, but it started with a murder back then, too.'

'I remember.' My voice was sharp. 'My parents were among the dead.'

Yanni shook her head. 'No, before their deaths, Bea. Your grandmother killed a shifter and took his power so she could get through the ward.'

'*What*?' I shook my head, struggling to take in her words. 'She could take a shifter's power?'

'She could take whatever power she wanted. After she'd tracked you and your father down, she needed to get past the wards that were intended to keep people out. She waited. When a fox shifter went too far one night and travelled beyond the barrier, she killed him and transformed into his body to disguise herself. That's how she got through.'

I sank into a chair. 'I ... I didn't know any of that. Why didn't anyone tell me?'

'Because we were trying to protect you.'

None of it made sense. I thought I knew everything about my grandmother and what she'd done but apparently I *still* didn't.

'But this isn't the same,' I said. I couldn't change what my grandmother had done but I wouldn't let Mrs D go down as a scapegoat for a scared community. 'Magic didn't kill Warren. It was a gunshot.'

'I know, but we need people to see that we're taking action, that we're keeping them safe.'

'And you're doing that by arresting a little old woman?' I snorted.

'We're doing that by arresting the person that the evidence points to. Mrs D knows that. If you can find someone else, please do because I don't want this any more than you do. But right now, it's the right thing to do.'

'What about Toby? What about the stepmum, Angelica?' I insisted.

'We'll talk to them. Just because we have Mrs D in custody doesn't mean the investigation has stopped. But Toby sounds like he has a solid alibi, and from what I saw of Rory's message Angelica's alibi seems good, too. Regular dance classes in the non-magical world where she can cheat and use her powers? That sounds exactly like the type of thing Angelica would do. We're speaking to her today. It's on my to-do list.'

As she spoke, the phone started buzzing. 'You need to answer that,' she said. 'That's your official job, remember? And if you're not careful, it'll be your *only* job.'

I gave a frustrated huff and picked up the phone. 'Witchlight Police Station,' I said.

'Beatrix? That is Beatrix, isn't it?'

'Yes, this is she. Who is this?'

'It's Selena Brown, Toby's mother.'

'Hello, Mrs Brown, is everything all right?'

'No. It's not all right.' Her voice wobbled. 'Toby didn't come home last night.'

Oh, shit. Just what we needed. Should I schedule a village-wide panic for later, or were we already booked up?

Chapter Twenty-Nine

Yanni didn't bother telling me I couldn't go with her because I was standing next to the police car with Eva at my heels before she'd even picked up the keys. 'Just let me do the questioning, okay?' she said, sounding resigned.

'Absolutely.' I paused. 'But you have to admit this makes him look guilty. Toby had to end his affair with the woman he loved because her father said so. Who wouldn't be angry about that? And then, when he knew we were onto him, he fled. That's what's happened here.'

'We have no idea what's happened here apart from a woman's son going missing. Can you remember that, please?'

I thought back to my initial impressions of Mrs Brown, how warm she'd been and how I'd assumed her son would be the same. Had I jumped to conclusions back then and misjudged her? Or was I jumping to them now simply because I wanted to clear Mrs D's name?

Annoyingly, I knew the answer: it had also been naïve of me to think that the measure of the mother made the son. Apples could fall far from the tree, and sometimes they rotted right next to it – usually when you were hoping for cider. I needed to put my emotions aside.

When we pulled up at the Browns' house Selena was waiting outside, her eyes red-rimmed and bloodshot. 'This isn't like him,' she said. 'I've been calling him all morning, and he's not responded. I mean, he's had some late nights before – he's a young lad and he enjoys a drink or two at Shady's, and he used to stay over at Jennifer's cottage when they were together. But he's never missed work with his dad. Not once.'

Yanni rested a hand on her shoulder. 'When was the last time you heard from him?'

'Last night, after you left. He got my message saying you wanted to speak to him and he texted back that he'd ring you in the morning before work. He was going for a drink. He even sent me a picture of his kill – two hares with only a bow and arrow.'

'Bow and arrow?' I frowned. 'I thought Toby was a bear shifter.'

'Oh, he is. He has no problem catching game in his shifted form, none of the shifters do. That's why he chooses the bow and arrow – it shows he has a bit more skill than the average shifter out there.' She smile weakly.

Ah yes, the old 'look how competent I am at murder' tactic. Classic.

I connected the dots. Bows and arrows, guns – both were man-made weapons. Even so, it was a big leap to make from one to the other.

'Can I see that photo, please, Mrs Brown?' Yanni asked.

Selena handed over her phone. The photo showed a young man with a bow and a sheaf of arrows slung over his shoulder and two hares in his hand. He was a good-looking lad, dressed in a red plaid shirt; he and Jennifer must have made an attractive couple. His face was split by a broad, carefree smile. I didn't immediately look at him and think '*killer*'. Then again, I hadn't thought that when I'd met Grandma, and she was as deadly as they come.

Rather than looking at Toby, Yanni was focused on the trees in the background. I realised that, as a shifter, she was more likely to recognise the woodland location than I was. 'I don't recognise the coppice,' she muttered, as much to herself as to me or Mrs Brown. 'I don't suppose you know exactly where he went?'

Selena shook her head and took her phone back. 'I don't know exactly where but it would be inside the barrier. That was my only condition. If he was hunting on his own, he had to be inside the barrier, but other than that I don't know where he was. I'm sorry. I should have asked him. I should have, I should—' She dissolved into tears.

'I know this is difficult.' I tried to use the same calm compassion I'd seen Dove demonstrate when she was talking to Mrs D. 'But right now, he hasn't even been missing for twelve hours. You weren't expecting him back until late last night, were you?'

Selena nodded reluctantly and Yanni shot me an approving smile. Apparently, I'd done that right. She took over. 'Which means he hasn't been gone long. I'll put out notices, see if we can get any sightings of him, okay?'

Selena nodded again as she continued to sniff and wipe away her tears. 'Warren was a shifter, too. I know he was a water shifter, but even so... Do you think someone's going after shifters?'

'No good comes from jumping to conclusions,' Yanni chastened gently, the same way she'd spoken to me about doing exactly that, but this time I could hear the tightness in her voice.

She'd been telling me the truth when she'd said that people were scared. They were scared because they automatically recalled what my grandmother had done. If Selena and her family still had a security camera on their property ten years after that incident, the memories were still there.

I felt like I needed to say something more. 'You have our number. If you hear anything, call us. We'll do the same. We promise.'

Selena sniffed again. 'Thank you.'

As we got back into the car, Yanni glanced at me. 'What are your thoughts now?' she asked. 'Still think Toby's the murderer and he's done a runner?'

'I don't know,' I admitted. 'But we've still got the stepmum, Angelica, to question. We could always head there now.'

Yanni looked pleased, and for a moment I got the impression that she liked working with me. 'That's exactly what I was thinking, too,' she said. 'Let's see if we can't find some more evidence to follow.'

I pulled on my seatbelt. Angelica might have answers or she might have more secrets. Either way, we were about to find out.

Chapter
Thirty

As we drove through the village, I leaned my head against the window and closed my eyes. I'd not had the best of sleeps last night with the echoes of the day's high emotions rippling through me, and I still hadn't had my early morning coffee fix.

I didn't realise quite how much I needed caffeine until the days when I didn't get it and my temples started pounding and my eyes needed matchsticks to hold them up. If coffee ever became sentient, I would immediately pledge my allegiance and fight for its cause. But there was no chance I was going to ask Yanni if we could swing by Sonny's to pick up a takeaway; time was of the essence and Mrs D was still locked up.

As the police car rumbled down the lanes, I thought about all the other tasks that I still had to do. I was no closer to solving the original problems Maddie had asked me to return to Witchlight for. Other than getting thrown out of Old Jacobson's house and realising he had a serious amount of magic, plus learning Fraser Banks was ludicrously rich, and handing over that mysterious bank account number to Donovan, I was treading water and moving nowhere fast.

The reminder spurred me to send Donovan a quick text: *This is urgent. Please update when you can. Also, if you have any miraculous investigative breakthroughs, now would be an excellent time to share.*

With that done, I closed my eyes and took a deep breath. Much as I wanted to focus on the Flame, finding Warren's murderer had to take priority. Hopefully his ex-wife would give us some much-needed clues.

Angelica Loren, formerly Storcrest, lived in an exclusive development on the edge of the village: twelve luxury houses that, according to the large sign outside the gated community, came with open-plan living areas, hot tubs in the gardens and prestigious views. It hadn't existed when I'd lived here and I was surprised the council had given permission for buildings of that size, but I supposed needs must. Magical people needed somewhere to live and Witchlight Cove was one of the loveliest places for them to do that. Big houses also meant that these magical residents had money. I wondered if Banks had built the development.

'Come on,' I said to Eva as I opened the car door. 'Let's go.' Immediately, she pointed her nose toward the house and gave a low growl. 'Hey, what's got into you?' I asked. She didn't move and growled again.

'Is she a trained police dog?' Yanni asked, eyeing Eva with the same curious caution as me.

'She's come with me on a lot of cases, but nothing formal,' I replied.

Yanni nodded grimly. 'Well, I don't like that reaction and I trust her after she found Warren. Stay behind me, will you?' She pulled out her revolver, holding it ready as we approached the front door.

I felt pretty useless: I wasn't carrying a gun and I regretted having next to no magical skill. That was a regret that stayed with me regardless of the situation, together with many others like not studying for a practical degree. Wearing shoes that pinched my toes. That time I'd once waved back at someone who wasn't waving at me. Still, I let Yanni take point. This was her gig, after all.

She knocked once. Although it wasn't the most forceful of knocks, the door swung inwards. She looked at me and I knew we were both thinking the same thing: an unlocked front door wasn't a great sign.

'Hello? Mrs Loren?' Yanni called. 'Witchlight Police. We'd like to ask you some questions.'

Eva growled again and tried to push in front of me. 'No. Stay back, girl,' I said firmly.

I might only have minimal magic but if something happened I was more likely to survive than Eva was.

'Stay close,' Yanni murmured to us as we stepped inside.

The house seemed to pulse with tension. 'Mrs Loren?' Yanni called again. Nothing. Not a sound.

The house epitomised fashionable minimalism: white marble floors, whitewashed walls, a couple of bright art prints, a clean white kitchen island and a large white sofa. It was the kind of place that screamed 'wealth' but also whispered, 'No one is allowed to have sex on the sofa.' It didn't exactly give off a homely vibe – and it didn't offer many places for someone to hide. At that moment, that was something I was grateful for.

'Upstairs?' I whispered. Yanni nodded.

As we crept up the stairs, we continued calling Angelica's name. I tried to home in on any emotions because I assumed that if a murderer was hiding somewhere, their emotions would be strong enough for me to feel even without any connection. But there was nothing. Either they could cloak their emotions or we were alone in the house.

We cleared the rooms one by one. 'She's not here,' I said unnecessarily. 'Do you think she hasn't come back from her dance class yet?'

Yanni shook her head. 'The front door was open. So was the back.'

I hadn't even noticed that, I'd been too busy sweeping outwards in search of feelings. 'She went out the back when we came to the front door?' I queried. If she had, that *smacked* of guilt.

Yanni didn't respond; even when evidence was staring her in the face, she seemed reluctant to speculate. 'Come on, let's go back downstairs,' she said finally.

As we passed the last room before the stairs, I hesitated. It was a small office with a dark wooden desk and a laptop. That was what had caught my eye. 'The screen is still on,' I said. Normally, if you left a laptop for a while it went to sleep but this screen was still active. Had someone been typing a few minutes ago then heard our car pull in and fled? Unless the owner had turned off the screensaver, but what kind of fool did that?

'Yanni,' I said, moving toward the computer. 'Come and look at this.'

'What is it?' She came in to look over my shoulder.

'She left her emails open,' I said.

Yanni's brow furrowed as she studied the screen. 'No. That's Warren's email account. The address is W. Storcrest.'

I stared at the email address at the top of the page. She was right. 'Why would his *ex*-wife have access to his emails?' I asked slowly.

'I'm not sure.'

Mrs D's words echoed in my mind, how the emails cancelling Warren's donations hadn't sounded like him. 'What if Warren didn't write the email to Mrs D? What if Angelica cancelled his donations so that she could siphon off some extra money?' I couldn't contain the flutter of excitement in my chest. 'That would give her a motive for murder, wouldn't it?'

Yanni pursed her lips. 'It's pure speculation, Beatrix. That's all it is.'

But I wasn't so sure. I finally had something to go on that suggested Mrs D wasn't to blame for Warren's murder. And I was going to prove it.

One way or another, Angelica was about to realise that secrets don't stay buried forever – and neither do guilty consciences.

Chapter Thirty-One

It was only when my stomach growled that I realised I hadn't had any breakfast. We'd planned on grabbing a muffin or something at Sonny's with our coffees, but that hadn't happened. My belly was so loud that Yanni heard it, too.

'I'll drop you at the coffee shop.' She shot me an amused glance. 'You can pick me up a cappuccino while you're there. Then perhaps this afternoon you'll sit at the desk and answer telephone calls.' She paused and we both laughed.

When we stopped snickering I felt the need to defend myself a smidge. 'I did answer Mrs Brown's call.'

'Oh yes. Sorry, I forgot that one. It's been rather chaotic having you back but it *has* been lovely. You've been missed.'

'By you and Maddie?'

'Do you need anyone else to miss you?' She raised an eyebrow.

'I guess not.' I smiled faintly. 'I'm sorry I stayed away for so long.' I thought that there'd be a silence, one of those moments where no-one really knows what to say, but I should have known Yanni better than that. Somehow she always had the right words.

'You did what you had to do, Bea. Enough apologies now. We understood that, even though it was hard to see you go. Maybe now you'll consider staying a little longer? You've definitely got a flair for investigative work and there are plenty of mysteries in a place like this – tracking down lost relatives, finding lost heirlooms – that type of thing. We don't have the manpower to deal with them all. You could be a PI here just as easily as in London,' she suggested. 'Just think about it, Bea. For me.'

'I will,' I promised before stepping out of the car towards the siren lure of coffee.

Thankfully the café was substantially quieter than it had been earlier, with only one person ahead of me in the queue. Another vampire was clearing the tables of the detritus from the earlier rush; the badge on her T-shirt told me her name was Kaz. She flashed me a friendly smile and I wished she was serving me instead of Sonny.

I turned to the grouchy vampire. 'Two cappuccinos, please.' I offered him my most winning smile.

To my surprise, he reciprocated – or at least something close. As his lips stretched, not only were his two pointy canines on show but his entire top row of pearly white teeth. The smile had a distinctly sinister edge to it, though, and I had a funny feeling he was about to spit in my coffee.

Almost immediately, he placed two cups in front of me. The service was way too fast, but on the upside he hadn't had time to spit in them. I frowned as I picked them up. 'Hey! These are stone cold!' I objected.

'Yes. Those are the ones you ordered this morning then left without paying for. I assume those are what you want.' His smile crept closer to a snarl.

I balked. 'That was a police emergency!'

'Well, emergencies don't pay my bills.' His tone suggested he wished they did – preferably in gold bullion and firstborn children. He really was the grumpiest near-human I'd ever met. Why on earth had he chosen a career that involved working with the public? It was a good job his coffee was so damn good because people sure as hell weren't coming for the warm, welcoming environment.

Now I understood what Ezra said about Sonny's motto: customer service was for those with a shit product.

'It's alright, Sonny,' a familiar voice cut in. 'I'll cover the cost of these. And can I get another two, please?'

The way my stomach flipped was a sure sign of who it was, but I forced myself not to jump straight around to check. Instead, I turned as slowly as possible.

There he was, standing behind me, and somehow he looked even more attractive. His hair was tousled, his stubble *perfectly* rugged. My hands twitched as if my fingers were begging to run through it. *What is wrong with you, Beatrix?* I cursed internally. *Fraser Banks is* evil. *He probably dines with Satan on a regular basis. Just* no.

'You don't need to do that,' I said tightly. 'I can afford my own coffee.' Or the police department could.

'Yes, but I'd like to pay,' Banks replied. 'And anyway, I've got a tab here.' His voice dropped to a whisper. 'And a discount, too.' There was something about his lowered tone that was so primal I felt it reverberate all the way through to my bones. And other fun places. Uh oh, spaghettio.

'Sonny gives you a discount?' I blurted, thinking of Maddie's remark about how he was still rude to her even though she did his ward tattoos.

Banks shrugged. 'I guess he likes me.' The smile he flashed me was so bright it sent my stomach into yet another somersault, this one combined with a backflip and a handspring. At this rate, I'd qualify for the Olympics gymnastics team.

'Well, thank you for the offer, but—' My words trailed off as I caught sight of someone else, someone staring at me from across the coffee shop. 'Thank you. Yes, you can pay for those coffees,' I said quickly and walked away from him towards Old Jacobson.

There was no doubt he'd been staring at me; that was clear from the way he became flustered and shuffled the paper in front of him as I approached. He coughed a couple of times, not to clear his throat but a full-on, chesty cough. His weak old man act was convincing and I might've bought it if I hadn't known better. But I knew what he could do beneath the fake nervous shuffle: he could throw me across the room, out of the window and probably as far as the sea if he wanted to.

I tried to catch wind of his emotions but there were too many people in the café and instead I was hit with an onslaught that was too tangled to parse.

'Do you mind?' I said as I pulled out the chair opposite him.

His head shook almost imperceptibly. It could've been a refusal but I took it as permission and sat down. Eva placed herself squarely between us under the table.

'You're not her,' he said, his voice trembling.

'I'm not who?'

'The sorceress. You look like the sorceress. Just like her.'

The blood drained from my face; if there was ever something I didn't want to hear, it was *that*. 'I don't know what you're talking about,' I said faintly.

'Yes, you do. I can feel it. You know her.' His eyes widened. 'Are you...? Are you the girl?' His voice rose. 'Oh, good God! It's you. It's you. You're *her!* I ... I wasn't meant to do that. I wasn't meant to do that to you.'

He wasn't talking now, he was virtually shouting, rambling in panic and horror. Tears welled in his eyes as he covered his mouth and shuffled his seat back. The skin on his face was so white it was nearly translucent.

'I'm not her.' I stood up and backed away from him. 'My name is Beatrix, Beatrix Stonehaven.'

He moaned pitifully and covered his eyes with a trembling hand. 'I'm sorry. I'm sorry. I didn't know. I'm sorry.'

'Is everything okay here?' Fraser appeared beside us and placed a hand on Jacobson's shoulder.

'I can't. I can't,' Jacobson stammered. Now I could feel his emotions whether I wanted to or not; he was paralysed with horror and it was mounting as he started to lose control.

'Fraser, get back,' I instructed sharply, realising what was about to happen an instant before it did.

The property developer didn't move in time; instead, he put himself between Jacobson and me. Before I could push him out of the way, a flash of magic shot out from the old man and struck Banks square in the chest. He flew back and hit the coffee counter with a sickening thud.

Chapter Thirty-Two

I spun in a circle, not sure where I was supposed to go. Eva was growling, her teeth bared as she faced Jacobson, but my eyes were on Banks. However much I needed to work out what the hell was wrong with the old man, Banks had been hurt because of me. He had to be my priority.

With my decision made, I moved. A collective gasp rang out from the customers. Simultaneously, Eva's growling stopped.

Old Jacobson had disappeared. His low-magic witch act had now been officially rumbled.

Knowing that I needed to focus on Banks made it far easier as I raced across the room and dropped to the ground next to him.

'Wow, what a punch,' he said, sitting up and rubbing his head.

'Are you okay?'

'I've felt better,' he admitted then a smile tipped his lips. 'Hey, you called me Fraser.'

I blinked. Had I? 'Sorry. Banks,' I said gruffly.

'Oh no, I liked it.'

'Don't tell me – Banks was your father's name?' I said drily.

'My mum's actually,' he said mildly. 'But no, it reminds me of *Mary Poppins*. I hadn't watched the film when I made the name change, but now ... *Mary Poppins*. Everyone calls me Fraser and I'd prefer it if you did too.'

I stared at him. This man had been thrown across a room and was now having a crisis over a fictional nanny? Still, given that he'd been thrown across a room for *me*, it seemed churlish to refuse. 'Sure. I can do that.'

He grinned like I'd agreed to go on a date, which I absolutely hadn't. Next to him, Eva wrangled her way in and started licking his hand. He turned to her, his eyes soft. 'I'm okay, little lady,' he murmured. 'Thanks for asking.'

Her tail wagged with such fierceness she nearly wagged it right off. I eyed her. Traitor.

I looked at Banks again – Fraser. 'I'm really sorry about the whole—' I gestured aimlessly. 'I don't know what happened. I wanted to talk to Jacobson but he totally flipped out.'

'Yeah. I'm going out on a limb here, but I'd say he's not the type of guy who's big on conversation.' Despite the light-hearted comment, Fraser frowned at where the old man had been.

'Shame, that was why I liked him,' Sonny grumbled as he moved past us and started picking up the tables and chairs that had toppled over in the drama.

Fraser offered me a smile to show he was alright, but it didn't ease my guilt. Seeing someone get hurt like that – hit with magic – brought back memories I had no desire to relive. 'Any chance you can give me a hand up?' he asked, reaching for me.

I had absolutely no doubt he could get himself up quite easily, but considering it was my fault he was lying on the floor it was the least I could do. As I took his outstretched hand, a warm shock wave ran through me. From the way his eyes widened as he looked at me, he'd felt it, too.

Oh boy. This wasn't good. Obviously I'd been physically attracted to guys before, and I'd felt the release of finally giving in to that attraction. The first kiss that led to a late-night fumble was like setting off a wind-up toy.

There was no way that could happen with Fraser, and yet each time I saw him I was conscious of that spring inside me winding tighter and tighter. Maybe that was why I could sense it burning from him because we were both feeling the same. Even when he was on his feet, our hands remained clasped, our eyes locked on each other.

My throat was dry. I needed to say something or at least move away from him, to do anything that would break this moment between us because it felt wild. Dangerous.

Sonny cleared his throat and I stepped back, my cheeks flushing. I assumed his interruption was intended to stop us from doing anything ridiculous, like ripping off each other's clothes in broad daylight in his café. That was when I became fully aware of my surroundings, like I taught my students in my classes to be.

Every single person in the café had abandoned their drinks and was looking straight at me. Not at Fraser and me, just me. Ah yes, my favourite pastime, being stared at like the main act in a magical freak show.

Near silence had replaced the normal hubbub of the eatery. A beat later, hands came up to mouths and the whispering started.

'Beatrix Stonehaven,' someone murmured.

'Stonehaven. Do you think...? It has to be her,' came another voice.

'Are we safe if she's here? You know what her grandmother did!' That voice had an edge of hysteria. Charming.

As I scanned the faces, a mother pulled her daughter closer as if I might throw the child across the room the same way Jacobson had done with Fraser. I didn't need to lower my shields to feel the fear in the room.

'Are you okay?' Fraser's voice was laced with concern.

'Fine,' I spat. The next moment I'd spun on my heels and stalked out, putting the lie to the word I'd spoken. 'Eva!' I snarled. 'Come!' She sprang to my side and, bless her heart, she bared her teeth at the customers and swung her head in a general warning. She let out a menacing growl at the people who had upset me. It was throwing gas on the fire but she didn't know that.

Hot tears were stinging my eyes but I blinked rapidly and refused to let them fall. I didn't know where I was going, only that I needed to get away from the coffee shop and as far from those stares as possible. I didn't care that Yanni had asked me to be back within half an hour, or that I'd forgotten the coffees for a second time and Sonny would hate me even more now. None of that mattered.

I didn't have to check that Eva was still beside me because I knew she was. I kept walking, my eyes forward and my pulse drumming. Only when I reached the waterfront did I stop. As I gazed at the white-crested waves, I felt the pressure of her body pressing against my side.

A moment later, a gentle hand grabbed my arm. 'Beatrix.' Fraser coaxed me around to face him. 'Hey, what happened back there?'

Damn him for following me. I'd held the tears back for as long as I could and now they were tumbling down my cheeks. The last thing I wanted to do was cry, especially not in front of Fraser. I'd spent the last decade closing off my heart, training myself not to feel, but now I was back in Witchlight Cove and it was as though the last ten years had meant nothing.

I struggled to bottle up the tears back to where they damned well belonged: inside me.

Fraser ran his tongue over his lips then bit down slightly before he spoke. 'I don't know why people reacted to you like that, but I saw the whole thing. You didn't do anything wrong. You *know* that you didn't do anything wrong.'

He thought the reaction in the café was due to Old Jacobson because he didn't know my sordid history. Was that better or worse? If he knew my history – and possibly my future – the attraction between us would fizzle and die. Which wouldn't be a bad thing, I told myself firmly.

'I shouldn't have come back.' The words spilled from my lips before I could stop them.

'Okay,' he said slowly. 'We're not talking about Old Jacobson, are we?'

I shook my head.

'I won't pretend to know what happened, but whatever it was is in your past. No doubt it took a lot of guts for you to come back here, and I admire that.'

'You don't know anything about me. You don't know what happened.'

'I know a little,' he admitted. 'I know your parents died, and you were only seventeen when you were appointed guardian of the Eternal Flame.'

There was no pretence in his voice, just sympathy, and I could feel the warmth and compassion radiating from him. It was tempting to lower my shields and wrap myself up in it, let myself feel that everything would be okay.

I met his eyes and my heart skipped a beat. I knew that if I leaned forward, he'd wrap me in his arms and I could lose myself in his scent and his presence.

Just as I considered succumbing to my desire and letting myself fall into Fraser's arms, my phone buzzed in my pocket. The moment broke our eye contact. I stepped back and pulled out the phone, expecting to see Yanni's name flash up but it was Donovan's.

'I'm sorry, I have to take this,' I said, my tone back to being businesslike.

'Of course. If you need me, I live down there.' Fraser pointed towards a house perched over the water. Glass, wood and sleek modern beauty: it looked like something out of a luxury magazine.

'You live there?' I asked, raising an eyebrow.

He smiled. 'Yes. Just turn up if you need me. The spare key's under the doormat.'

I shook my head. 'A water shifter has been murdered so maybe don't tell that to all and sundry.'

His smile widened. 'You're not all and sundry, Beatrix Stonehaven. You're something else, and you have a standing invitation.'

He turned and walked towards his house and I'm damned if I didn't watch the way his jeans hugged his backside.

Irritated with myself, I swiped up to answer the call.

Chapter Thirty-Three

'Donovan,' I said briskly. 'What do you have for me?' I hoped he'd say something that would help me forget about Fraser Banks, though it suddenly seemed unlikely.

'Well, your friend's got a lot of money,' he replied. 'He is crazy rich.'

'I already know that,' I lowered my voice. Fraser was still walking away and I couldn't be too careful. The shifters I knew didn't have exceptional hearing while they were in human form, but I didn't know what type of shifter Fraser was. He could have powers I'd not come across.

I moved in the opposite direction as I cupped the phone and whispered, 'What about those outgoing payments? That one was nearly a quarter of a million.'

'It took some digging to get a name for the account you gave. The address it corresponds to is a business that belongs to a shell company, which is obviously a front.'

'You didn't get a name?' I said, trying to speed things along.

'Now that's not what I said!' He sounded affronted. 'I'm trying to make you see that this person he's giving his money doesn't want to be found.'

'Who is it?' I could hear the impatience in my voice but it had already been a very long day. I'd paid Donovan more than enough to get a straight answer.

'The account belongs to a Ms Fatima Crawley,' he said finally. 'And that's not the only money he's sent her. In the last five years, he's sent her nearly two million.'

'Two million pounds?' I whistled. 'All to this same person? This Fatima Crawley?'

'Yes. Does the name mean anything to you?'

'No,' I admitted. 'It doesn't.' I hadn't actually expected it to. A link to some of Witchlight Cove's dodgy dealers would have been great, but I'd known it was unlikely. Well, at least with a name, I could start to some proper digging. Preferably the kind that didn't require a shovel or a body bag.

'Alright. That's all I can give you for now. Hope it helps.'

'It will. Thanks.' I hung up on him – I didn't have the headspace to deal with pleasantries.

I glanced down the beach at Fraser's silhouette disappearing into the distance and I thought of his offer for me to take his key and let myself into his home. Had he been waiting for the offer to be reciprocated? It hadn't felt like that at the time but it would make sense; it would be a way to get his claws into the Flame – metaphorically, at least. That *had* to be why he'd made the offer, because the only other reason was that his personality was as attractive as the rest of him and there was no way I could handle that right now.

When I arrived back at the station, Dove was in her civilian clothes picking something up before she headed out. Yanni was standing by my desk – the one that I'd barely sat at – and it looked like she'd been pacing. 'Bea, what happened?' she demanded. 'We've had calls about you performing some crazy magic at Sonny's.'

'Crazy magic? Me?' I scoffed. 'Come on, Yanni, you know better than that.' I gave a self-deprecating laugh that was only thirty percent bitter. Okay, fifty percent.

Her brows furrowed. 'So what *did* happen?'

'It was Old Jacobson. He saw me and absolutely flipped out. Honestly, that's the truth. Fraser Banks saw and heard it all – he got caught in the crossfire.'

'Is he okay?' she asked with real concern.

Huh. She really did like him. That gave me pause, because I trusted her judgement. If Yanni liked him, maybe Maddie and I were off base. And I was totally ignoring how much that thought made me happy.

It was noticeable that she didn't ask after *my* wellbeing, just about the ridiculously handsome shifter with the mysterious past and questionable wealth. Priorities, Yanni.

'Yeah, Fraser's fine.' A slight pause filled the air before I spoke again. 'Do you know anything about Old Jacobson? He seemed really freaked out. And he has power, a lot of it.'

She shook her head. 'To be honest, that's a total surprise. Most of us have never said more than a word or two to him, if that. He's never caused any trouble, not until now.'

'Not until I came back, you mean?' I sighed. This was starting to feel too familiar and too coincidental: murder in Witchlight Cove right after I returned; Old Jacobson causing chaos for the first time. There was definitely a pattern and I was at the centre of it.

'Are you okay?' I knew instantly that it wasn't the police chief who was asking, it was Maddie's grandmother. The woman who had looked after me when my parents had died. Who made the best sausage rolls in the whole village and was impossible to beat in a game of Shithead. A woman of many talents, none of which included minding her own business. That was why we'd always got on: we were cut from the same nosey cloth.

'I don't know,' I said truthfully. I struggled to find something else to think about. Luckily, I had just the thing: murder. 'Honestly, I'd feel a lot better if we could get some evidence to help Mrs D. That's what I have to focus on. Do we have any leads on Angelica yet? Or Toby. Has anyone seen either of them?'

Yanni squeezed my arm and let the personal stuff slide. She nodded briskly and dived straight into business. 'There have been no sightings of Angelica, and we're still following up leads on Toby.'

'Isn't it odd that both of our other suspects are missing?' I asked.

'It's definitely unusual,' Yanni agreed. Her acceptance caused a spark of hope in me.

'Does that mean we can let Mrs D go?' I tried.

'Mrs D wants to stay in custody.'

'*What*? Why?'

'She's shaken up and I don't think she wants to be alone. She's still very jumpy.'

'Then let her stay with you!' I suggested. I wasn't the first waif and stray Yanni had helped out and she had plenty of room in that big house of hers.

'I can't do that, Bea, and you know it.'

'Then she can live with me!' I folded my arms across my chest like the petulant teenager she knew so well, but even as the words slipped out I knew that was impossible. If Mrs D came to my house, she'd see that the Eternal Flame was gone.

'No, she can't,' Yanni said matter-of-factly. 'Amara wants to stay and I think it's good for her. She's here if we need to ask her more questions and it gives her a sense of security. Don't try to take that away from her. We're happy to keep her and she's happy to stay. I promise she's perfectly comfortable.'

Great. The murder suspect didn't want to leave custody and the other two suspects I wanted to question had vanished. Textbook police work, really. I sighed. 'I'd like to talk to Mrs D, if I could.'

'Let her be for now. She's upset so give her space. I'm sure you'll be here when she wants someone to talk to.' She touched my shoulder. 'Look, you had a late night yesterday. I shouldn't have asked you to come back so early this morning, not after the rough day you'd had. Why don't you go home?'

'I don't mind covering the phones,' Dove chimed in from her desk. She'd obviously been listening but she had an amazing skill of making herself near-invisible. 'Sam's working at the moment, and I'd like the excuse to get off earlier and be with him.'

'Are you sure?' I asked, surprised by her kind offer.

'Absolutely. You'll be doing me a favour. Though maybe I shouldn't have said that. That way, I could ask you to cover some of *my* shifts in the future.' She winked.

'Just say when and where,' I replied. 'And thank you. I appreciate that.' Yanni was right – though not about the lack of sleep. I *was* tired but, more worryingly, I was off my A-game. The shit in Sonny's had rattled me more than I cared to admit and a few hours to get my head together would be appreciated.

'No problem,' Dove beamed.

I looked at Eva, who was once again lying on her back, sprawled out and already snoring, despite us having been back in the office for less than ten minutes. Oh, to be able to sleep in public.

'Can you be back by seven?' Yanni asked as I picked up my bag. 'It'll mean doing the night shift so someone's here with Amara.'

Seven that evening: that meant six hours to eat, sleep and make myself feel a bit more human. That was something I could do.

'Absolutely. I'll be back at seven,' I promised. 'Ready to work.' A quiet night-time shift would hopefully give me the chance to look into this mysterious Fatima Crawley.

Sleep, then time on the clock digging up dirt. It was a win-win.

Chapter Thirty-Four

The minute I opened the front door, the smell hit me. 'Maddie? Is that...?'

'In the kitchen,' she called happily. She was standing over the stove, stirring something with a wooden spoon.

'You didn't!' I said, feeling the grin stretch my lips.

'Yanni rang and said you'd had a bit of a rough morning so I thought I'd make us hot chocolate. And if you look in that bowl there...'

I glanced into the dish she pointed at, and my heart surged with affection for my best friend. 'You've picked out all the pink marshmallows for me?'

'I did, because I'm wonderful,' she said smugly.

'You are,' I agreed over the sudden lump in my throat.

Maddie eyed me curiously. 'So, what the hell happened? My phone's red hot with calls about you and Old Jacobson getting into some kind of magical fight.'

I sighed. 'A magical fight implies you can both do magic, which we both know isn't the case. But ... it was weird. He got so freaked out when he saw me,' I paused then told her the only conclusion I could draw in the circumstances. 'I think he knew my grandmother and I guess we look alike. He saw me and totally lost it.'

Maddie frowned. 'But he moved here *after* your grandmother's ... incident.'

She was right. I hadn't thought about that; I'd been too distracted by the muttering, the heavy stares and hearing my name being whispered. 'I guess he must've heard about her,' I said. 'Maybe seen some photos. But honestly, it was like he thought he was *looking* at her and seen a ghost.' I paused. 'A terrible, evil ghost.'

'Don't take this the wrong way, but do you actually look like your grandma? I mean, I saw her too, with her scary hair and crazy eyes. She looked nothing like you.'

'Right.' I'd thought that too. The image of my grandmother isn't something that will ever fade from my memory – I don't even think the strongest amnesia spell could shift it. Given all the time she'd had me, I'd had a pretty good look at her and I hadn't seen any similarities between us. I hadn't even twigged that we were related until Dad showed up.

'Do you think Old Jacobson knew her before she came here?' Maddie said. 'When she was young? Your age?' Her eyes widened. 'God, is he a sorcerer?'

'Honestly, I have no idea. I'm guessing he didn't mean to hurt me though, because he definitely had the power to do that if he wanted to. I feel bad that Fraser got hurt trying to protect me.'

'Sorry, what?' Maddie turned to me, her mouth hanging open. 'Bea! Please don't tell me you're talking about Fraser Banks?'

I rolled my eyes. 'Do you know any other Frasers?'

'What the hell were you doing with him? Bea, he is the *enemy*.'

I sighed. Maddie could be a little black and white at times. 'He was at Sonny's and he offered to pay for my drink so that I could go and talk to Jacobson. Actually, he offered to pay for our drinks from this morning and buy me another.'

'I have a horrible feeling you're starting to like him,' Maddie scoffed. She narrowed her eyes. 'You realise he's manipulating you, right? He wants to get into this house – and we *cannot* let that happen.'

I held my hands up to placate her. 'I know, I know. We won't let him in, I promise.'

I'd considered Fraser's motivation for trying to get close to me, but everything about him felt genuine. The chemistry between us was unreal and you couldn't fake the rush that I'd felt at his touch. Then there was the small matter of me feeling his emotions even when my shields were up: his compassion had swarmed all over me. Still, there was no way I could tell Maddie about any of that because it would open a whole new can of worms.

'Are you enjoying your new job?' Maddie changed the subject as she stirred another spoonful of sugar into the hot chocolate.

'It's a little more active than Yanni promised. So much for sitting around answering phone calls all day – I've barely been at my desk. But I absolutely prefer it that way.'

She lifted two large mugs from the cupboard above her. 'Any closer to working out who's behind Warren's death?'

'No – but it wasn't Mrs D. It *couldn't* be.'

'I know, and for what it's worth I think Yanni knows it too. It's...'

'It's her job,' I finished for her.

'Exactly,' Maddie said. 'How long have you got before you go back to the station?'

'I need to be back by seven.'

As she handed me a mug, she grinned. 'Great. Plenty of time for a midday film while we drink our hot chocolates. What do you think?'

'Sounds good. I fancy some sort of crime thriller. Something actiony?'

'Too late,' she said with a smirk. 'I've already picked one.'

I should have known. Maddie loved romantic clichés like a moth loves an open flame – and with about as much self-preservation.

Two grown women curled up under blankets in the middle of the day sipping hot chocolate with marshmallows while we watched a cliché-ridden romcom was ridiculous. Maddie hadn't managed to get whipped cream for the drinks but I couldn't hold that against her after she'd picked out all the pink marshmallows for me. Her choice of film, however, I *could* hold against her. And I totally would.

'I can't believe you still love these ridiculous movies,' I said as we watched a couple embrace in the pouring rain after ninety minutes of will-they-won't-they tension. 'No kiss in the rain could ever be nice.' I huffed. 'That girl's got cold water running down her spine, soggy socks and a ruined blow-dry. If I were her, I'd be more focused on getting to a radiator than snogging some bloke with suspiciously perfect hair. It's unrealistic and completely unsexy. Who actually kisses anyone in the rain in real life?'

'We get it. You're not a romantic.' Maddie grimaced. 'Though I was hoping Ezra might change your mind.'

I threw a cushion at her head. 'Will you quit it with the Ezra thing? He's a great guy but there's no attraction there, no spark. Not on my side, at least.'

'You haven't given him a chance,' Maddie objected. 'Maybe you'll see things differently on Friday.'

I knew that she only wanted me to be happy but I really needed her to see that Ezra and I wasn't going to happen. 'Maddie, I've got to survive the week first. Let's see how I feel on Friday.'

'Fine.' She sounded crochety. 'Just as long as you're not giving him the brush off because you've got a crush on our sworn enemy Fraser Banks. Because if you are, I swear on my best tattoo gun that I'll stage an intervention.'

I didn't answer. But my stomach did a little flip. I was doomed.

On the floor by our feet Eva was gnawing on a meaty treat that Maddie had given her. It looked rubbery, tough and altogether grim. I didn't bother asking what kind of animal it came from; my limits for 'gross' had shifted dramatically since I'd become a dog owner. Letting Eva chew on a pig's trotter in my living room? Sure, why not. A knucklebone at the end of the bed? Absolutely.

Maddie's eyes were already drooping. Considering how early she'd gone to bed the previous night, I found it difficult to believe she wasn't getting enough rest. I frowned. 'Hey, Mads, are you okay? You look shattered.'

'Yeah, I did a big tattoo session this morning – Shady the vampire. He doesn't usually bother with them given that he owns a nightclub, but he's doing a bit of travelling. He wanted to make sure he wasn't confined to night-time sightseeing. It always takes a bit more out of me than normal when it's not a regular customer.'

'You still haven't explained how you're doing these tattoos without the Eternal Flame,' I noted.

Given that I'd been right beside Maddie when she'd learned to harness her powers, I had a pretty good grasp of her methods. I certainly understood more about her magic than the elementals' magic, or Old Jacobson's. But everything I'd seen Maddie do had involved the Flame and I couldn't figure out how she was enchanting her ink without it.

'I've been doing it the same way any alchemist who doesn't have access to an Eternal Flame,' she said sassily. 'Good old hard work. I'll get the hang of it eventually. It takes practice.'

I wanted to believe she was alright, but I knew how stressed and worried she was about the Flame being missing and keeping it from Yanni. I'd only been doing it for two days and already I couldn't imagine doing it for a whole week.

I twisted around on the sofa so that I was looking directly at her. 'Promise me you'll tell me if you're overdoing it, right?' I said.

'Says the woman trying to solve a murder, protect her home and deal with a vicious ancient sorcerer.'

I shook my head. 'Old Jacobson wasn't vicious. He was ... startled. And I'm not even sure that he's a sorcerer. I still think he might be a really powerful witch.'

Seeing his power had only confirmed that I needed to speak to him again and make him talk. He had power and a lifetime's worth of experience. He wasn't associated with a coven so he was the perfect person to talk to about the Eternal Flame – if he'd let me get near enough to actually speak to him.

'I think I need to close my eyes,' I said as the film credits started rolling. 'Can you wake me up in a couple of hours so I'm not late for work?'

Though I'd asked Maddie the question, it was Eva who looked up from the floor. She replied with a bark.

Maddie laughed. 'That sounds like a yes. Go to bed – we'll make sure you wake up. Well, one of us will, anyway.'

I didn't need telling twice. I left Eva chewing at her snack, whatever it was, and headed upstairs to my bedroom

I was asleep before my head hit the pillow.

Chapter
Thirty-Five

As I probably should have expected, Eva woke me up by licking my face thirty seconds before my alarm went off. 'Alright, alright. I'm up,' I grumbled.

Slobbery dog kisses were better than an alarm in one way at least: you couldn't press snooze on them. Particularly not when the dog was standing on your chest as she did the licking.

'You know you're not a little puppy any more, right?' I groused as I gently pushed her aside and clambered out of bed. 'One of these days you'll crush my ribs and then who will feed you? Think about that.'

After getting dressed, I gave my teeth an extra clean to banish the sugary hot-chocolate residue and headed downstairs. Despite saying she would make sure I got up for work, Maddie had fallen asleep on the sofa. I briefly contemplated waking her, but it didn't seem fair to disturb her if she needed rest. Instead I took the blanket from where it lay crumpled by her feet and pulled it up to her shoulders.

For a moment I considered leaving Eva with her. After all, Maddie had been insistent that we guard the house properly to make sure that no-one found out about the Flame, and she didn't look like she was in much of a state to do any guarding. But my retriever was already waiting by the door; something told me she was enjoying this new job as much as I was – or maybe it was the sofa in Yanni's office she liked. Either way, I knew she was coming with me.

Strangely, I didn't mind the split shift. It felt familiar, like balancing PI work and martial arts classes. I was missing my lessons; that physical exertion and the satisfaction of throwing someone to the ground had become a regular fix.

I immediately wondered what it would be like to wrestle Fraser over my shoulder, although a bed might be a better landing spot than a mat. Yes, I could definitely wrestle him on a bed. For purely strategic reasons, absolutely nothing else. Soft landings reduce injury.

Uh-huh. Bad Bea, I thought. It was a crush because I knew he was off limits. He was tasty because he was forbidden fruit, that was all. It would pass. And for now, I needed to focus on my job.

I strolled into the station ready to make myself comfy at my desk, but I hadn't even reached it when Yanni came out of her office, slipping on her coat. 'Don't get comfortable,' she said. 'We're going out.'

Excitement straightened my spine. 'You've got a lead? Angelica's back?'

She shook her head. 'Not that the barrier guards have let me know. But one of the barmaids at The Smuggler's Rest said she saw Toby drinking there last night. I thought we'd check it out.'

She didn't have to ask me twice; anything to find the real killer and I was in.

Eva, with her weird extra sense, hadn't even come inside the building but was waiting outside the door as if she knew we were about to leave. When she saw us, she ran straight to the police car.

Yanni shook her head in wonder. 'She's no ordinary dog,' she muttered.

I knew it. When I'd first met Eva, there'd been a small incident with a demon; in my haste to get rid of it, I'd used a magical vial of who-knows-what that Maddie had given me. I'd flung the unstoppered vial across the room and a single drop had landed on Eva's butt.

Now, no matter how much I scrubbed, her golden fur bore a stubborn purple-black mark that refused to fade. It was pure speculation, but I couldn't shake the feeling that whatever magic was in that potion hadn't just stained her fur, it had changed *her*. Maybe Eva wasn't an ordinary mutt any more. Maybe she was something far more extraordinary.

'I can't believe The Smuggler's Rest is still standing,' I said, as we drove down the high street. 'It was always a total dive. I thought it would have been condemned years ago.' I certainly didn't think it was the type of place someone young like Toby would drink, though I didn't say so.

'It's changed a bit since you were last there,' Yanni said. 'It's the number-one destination now – apart from Shady's. Speaking of which, I hear you're going there on Friday night. Time for a proper catch-up with Ezra?'

'Jesus,' I muttered. 'You can't keep *anything* secret in this village. And for the record, I haven't agreed to go yet.'

'You should. It's fun. And Shady is definitely a more friendly business owner than Sonny.' She glanced at me sideways. 'I hear you've made *his* acquaintance.'

'He's the most unpleasant vampire I've ever met, and that's saying something.'

Yanni chuckled. 'People close to him only have great things to say about the guy. He has to warm to you.'

'There are people close to him?' I asked with faux incredulity. 'Are they all being held hostage? Did you get them to blink twice if they needed help?'

Yanni laughed again as she drew the car to a stop. 'Right. I'll let you go in first.'

The Smuggler's Rest looked exactly the same from the outside as it had always done: wooden doors with peeling paint, and chipped, dirty windows. I braced myself for the dim, damp interior and the smell of stale beer – and worse – that I remembered, expecting a place where gnarly old wizards and werewolves nursed drinks late into the night.

When I opened the door, I froze. The inside was … transformed. It was modern, well-lit and tastefully decorated. Families were sitting at tables, laughing and eating meals that smelled divine, while well-dressed waitstaff greeted us with warm smiles.

'I don't understand,' I said as I looking around. 'This isn't The Smuggler's Rest.'

'I can assure you that it is.'

My heart clenched at the sound of his voice. Trying to look as if my pulse had not tripled its pace, I turned to face him. 'Hey, how's the head?' I asked Fraser Banks.

He wrinkled his nose in a manner that was infuriatingly cute as he rubbed his hand over his dark hair. Once again he was wearing a sharp suit, and this time with the jacket; I couldn't decide if I preferred him with or without it. With it, he looked sharp, but without it, I could see those arms.

'I heal pretty quickly.' He flashed me a smile. 'It's good to see you again, Beatrix.'

There was nothing I could do. The butterflies in my stomach were in overdrive. I was a goner. 'You know, I'm starting to think I should be concerned. You seem to have developed a habit of showing up wherever I am,' I said.

Fraser looked amused. 'I don't mean to nit-pick, but technically you're in *my* establishment right now. If anyone is following anyone, you're following me.'

'Yours?' I asked. 'You own The Smuggler's Rest?'

'I do. I take it the establishment has changed somewhat since you were last here? For the better, I trust? I'd be happy to help you sample the drinks. We could share a bottle of wine one night, perhaps?'

I was strongly tempted to say yes. I loved a bottle of white wine and it had been entirely too long since I'd had a man look at me like he was doing.

He's manipulating you, Beatrix! I could hear Maddie's voice harrumphing inside my head. I didn't think she was right but there was too much at stake to risk it. I pushed my shoulders back, trying to act like his presence didn't have any effect on me. 'No, thank you.' I looked around pointedly. 'From what I remember, the locals liked The Smuggler's Rest exactly as it was.'

'You're right. The old pub definitely had a certain charm, which is why I left it exactly as it was.'

I frowned at him. 'But you've refurbished everything.'

'Have a look through there.' He pointed to a door at the far end of the room that looked exactly like The Smuggler's Rest's original front door that I had just walked through. 'Be my guest,' he said before pushing it open and stepping aside for me.

The moment I walked through the doorway I felt the rush of déjà vu. The space I had walked into was *exactly* like the old Smuggler's Rest: the same dark and dingy interior. The same smell of stale beer. I even recognised the old werewoman perched in the same spot she'd occupied a decade ago.

I turned back to Fraser. 'An expansion spell. You put an expansion spell on the building so that you could keep the old bar too. That must cost a fortune to maintain.'

'It does,' he replied matter-of-factly. 'But it's not about the money, it's about resources. The village needed The Smuggler's Rest but it also needed somewhere for families, a nice place that wasn't a coffee shop or bar. This setup brings in employment, supports local farmers and creates a space for the community. The upstairs room is used for council meetings and workshops.'

I narrowed my eyes suspiciously. 'So it's not about profit?'

He shrugged. 'Some of it's about profit, but it's also about balance and community.'

'And the Eternal Flame?' I asked, finally piecing it together. 'You want it to power these spells, don't you? To keep this place running without draining all your funds?'

He smiled faintly. 'It would take a lot more than this to drain all my funds, but yes, the Flame would certainly help keep this and the other projects I have planned running efficiently.'

Yanni appeared beside us. 'Sorry to interrupt. Beatrix, you have remembered that we're here on official business, right? Fraser, we need to speak to one of your employees, Pei.'

My cheeks warmed. Yanni thought I was flirting with Fraser. I wasn't – not consciously anyway.

Fraser looked nonplussed for a moment. 'Is everything alright?'

'We need some information about someone who popped in here last night. We've had a missing person report filed and Pei came forward and said she'd seen him. We need to ask her a couple of questions.'

'Of course. I'm sorry for keeping you waiting, Chief. I didn't realise. I'll get her for you now.'

As Fraser hurried off to find Pei, Yanni sidled up beside me. 'I guess I know why young Ezra isn't getting a look in now,' she said with a wink.

Chapter Thirty-Six

Pei was a tall young woman around twenty years old. Judging from the shape of her ears and her delicate features, I assumed she was at least part fae but I wasn't about to ask. Making a mistake about someone's lineage could be highly offensive, and considering some fae-folk specialised in curses that wasn't a risk I was in a hurry to take.

'You said you saw Toby Brown last night?' Yanni asked, gesturing for the girl to take a seat.

'He came in for a drink after he'd been out hunting. He catches hares and things – though not as a shifter. He uses a bow and arrow.' She sounded really impressed and her eyes went dreamy.

'Yes, his mother told us the same.'

'It's a real skill,' Pei cooed. 'Incredibly impressive.' There was something in her voice that made me think she was impressed by more than Toby's hunting abilities.

'Pei, do you know if Toby is seeing anybody?' I asked. I didn't know what line of questioning Yanni would take, and I wasn't trying to derail her conversation, but I had a hunch my question might lead us somewhere useful. If Pei liked Toby so much, there was a good chance she paid close attention to the little things – and little things could mean a lot in our line of work. 'Does he have a girlfriend?'

'Not that I'm aware of.' She blushed slightly. 'Not since he broke up with his last girlfriend.'

'And you and him?' I prompted. 'Are you friends or something more?'

'No, we're just friends,' she said quickly, her blush deepening.

'I've never met him myself but his mum seems lovely and I saw a photo of him. He's a good-looking guy, a bit of a catch. I'm guessing you wouldn't say no to it being more.' I smiled coyly, trying to give the impression that this was nothing more than a girly chat so hopefully she'd feel comfortable opening up.

'To be honest, he's knocked me back a couple of times.' Pei sighed. 'And not just me. He even turned down a date with Ciara in the kitchen when she asked him out, and she's part siren. The only people who can easily say no to a siren are either totally in love with someone else or have really strong magic.'

That was useful information. I tried not to look at Yanni and focused instead on finding out more. 'You're telling me Toby was in love with someone?' I asked.

'I don't know,' Pei replied. 'There was Jennifer, the water shifter. They were together for years.' Bitterness crept into her tone.

'You weren't a fan of hers?'

'If you ask me, they were the oddest couple. For a start, she was five years older than him and her family has all this money, but she acted like she was one of us. Just an average Jo – Joanne. Whatever.'

'She's a nurse, isn't she? I hear she's very good at her job.' I didn't know why I felt the need to speak up for Jennifer because I didn't know her, but I'd liked what I'd seen of her. And I knew what it was like when people assumed that you were rich or powerful because your parents were. From what I'd seen, Warren had made a concerted effort to raise children who stood on their own two feet and I admired that. Five years age difference was hardly a lot; no one would have batted an eyelid if Toby been the older one.

'I assume you're aware that Jennifer and Toby broke up several months ago,' Yanni said. 'Or at least their families *believe* they did.'

Pei shrugged. 'They never came in together after the incident with the mer-guy, so I guessed they'd split up.'

'Have you seen him with anyone else?' Yanni added.

'No, but he was talking on his phone last night. He seemed pretty ... I guess you'd say loved up. Lots of grinning and chuckling. He took his drink over to the corner while he chatted and he was still on the phone when he left.'

'Did he mention meeting anyone?' I asked.

'Not that I heard, but he seemed really happy, the happiest he's been in ages.'

'And you think it was because of a woman?'

'I don't know.' Pei's easy manner was fading and it was clear she was no longer enjoying our chat. 'I'm telling you what I saw. That's all.'

'Thank you, Pei.' Yanni said and gave me a small nod to indicate that we'd got as much as we were going to get.

'Yes, thank you. What you've told us has been very useful,' I added.

As Pei stood up to leave, Yanni asked, 'Just to check, what time would you say Toby left here?'

'It was before closing.' Pei replied. 'Probably around half-ten.'

Yanni glanced at me and I knew we were thinking the same thing. If Toby was last seen here at ten-thirty and his mother didn't notice he was missing until the morning, then he could have gone anywhere in that time.

Our search for Toby Brown had just got a whole lot wider.

Yanni's phone buzzed loudly. She frowned at screen before standing abruptly. 'Excuse me, I need to take this.' She moved across the room to answer the call.

As Pei disappeared, my attention remained on Yanni. I didn't need to lower my shields to feel the wave of emotion rolling off her; dismay and guilt struck me like a truck. Whatever she'd been told, it wasn't good news.

As she hung up the phone, I hurried towards her – only for Fraser to step out from the bar. He caught my eye but I shook my head, trying to convey it wasn't a good time. Thankfully he understood and stayed where he was, leaving me to speak to Yanni alone.

'That was a shifter,' Yanni said, her voice trembling as she looked at me. 'They were out for a run in the forest when they found them.'

'Found who?' I asked, already feeling dread in my stomach.

'There's been another murder,' she said grimly. 'And it looks like a double one.'

Chapter Thirty-Seven

Dove had cordoned off the area by the time we arrived. 'I'm so sorry,' I said. 'You were supposed to have the evening off after taking my shift.'

'It's okay,' she replied. 'Shit happens, and Sam understands. It's the nature of the job. I was closest and we needed someone here as soon as possible.'

'It's definitely two bodies?' Yanni said. Dove nodded grimly in reply.

'Is it a double murder?' I asked hesitantly.

'I'm not sure,' Dove replied. 'It's two bodies, but... ' She glanced at Yanni. 'I'll let you see for yourself. You can decide what you think.'

I turned to Eva. 'Come on, girl. You need to go on your lead for this.' She stood still whilst I snapped on her lead. The last thing I wanted was for her to go trampling over any evidence, but at the same time I knew she might pick up something with her nose that we couldn't see. I didn't want to leave her in the car when she could be the one to find us vital clues.

As we followed Dove deeper into the forest, my stomach twisted into knots. I wasn't sure what we were about to find, but I had a sinking feeling I already knew who one of the victims was. I desperately didn't want to be right, not when I'd already seen how upset Toby's mother was about him not coming home.

As I stepped into the clearing, the first thing I saw was a red plaid shirt. It was identical to the one Toby had been wearing in the photo. 'Oh my God,' I whispered. 'Poor Mrs Brown...'

The guilt that struck had me resting my weight on my knees. Twelve hours ago, I'd been talking to Yanni, saying how Toby was obviously Warren's killer. I *wanted* him to be Warren's killer. And while I knew my stupid thoughts had absolutely no bearing on what had happened here, I still felt guilty that I'd had them.

'Will you be okay?' Yanni asked gently. 'If you can't deal with this, you don't have to—'

'No, I'll be fine.' I straightened up. My voice was steadier than I felt. 'Where's the other body?'

'Just over there.' Dove pointed to a thicket a few feet away from Toby's body.

The grass was tall and thick. I held Eva close to me on a short lead, partly to stop her walking too far ahead but also because I wanted her near me to stop me being overwhelmed. The emotions filling the air were tense: fear and guilt prevailed. Yanni and Dove felt bad that they hadn't caught Warren's killer in time to stop this – and they were also worried that this wasn't the end. I needed Eva's steadying presence.

As we approached the thicket, the first thing I noticed was a shock of white hair with blue streaks running through it. 'Is that... ?'

'Angelica Loren.' Yanni said solemnly.

'What the hell?' I didn't know who I'd expected the other body to be, but if Warren's murderer wasn't Toby then it had to be Angelica, right? Seeing her there, lying on her back, threw that theory straight out the window. If they were both dead, who the hell had killed them *and* Warren?

Wordlessly, Yanni slipped on gloves and handed me another pair. She edged a little closer. 'It's difficult to tell from the blood loss, but those look like claw marks on Angelica's chest,' she said as she crouched down.

Dove agreed. 'It's the way they've cut through the fabric. There are five gashes, four long and one shorter. Do you know what type of animal claw leaves marks like that?'

I didn't know if Dove's question was rhetorical, because Yanni and I certainly knew. It was a bear. Just like she was. And like Toby.

'How do we think Toby died?' Yanni asked, avoiding having to respond.

'A bullet wound,' Dove replied grimly. 'Looks like a silver bullet, possibly the same type that killed Warren.'

I took in a moment to process her words. Maybe I hadn't been so wrong with my first assumption that one of the pair had killed Warren. Only maybe it hadn't been *one* of them, maybe it had been both of them. 'Hold up. Are we thinking that Toby swiped at Angelica, probably with the intention of killing her, but she fired off the shot before she bled out?'

'That's certainly what it looks like,' Yanni said. 'But why?'

I remembered what Gilbert had said in Jennifer's house about Angelica liking younger men. Pei had sensed that Toby was seeing someone again, someone whom he loved so much that he could resist a siren's advances – well, a half-siren, at least. And while Jennifer had only been five years older than him, maybe Gilbert was right in thinking that he liked older women.

'Could it be...? Do you think they were together and Warren found out about their relationship?' I mused.

'And that was why they killed him? Maybe there was an altercation.' Although Angelica and Warren were in the middle of their divorce, it wasn't final. I could imagine Warren would be upset to discover the relationship, particularly as Toby had dated Jennifer.

'It's possible.' Yanni nodded slowly. 'Very possible.'

As I stared at the bodies, another thought struck me. 'Wait! Mrs D is still at the station, right? She wanted to keep herself in custody?'

'She is,' Yanni confirmed.

'So she has to be innocent because there's no way these deaths aren't connected to Warren's. They *have* to be. Dove already said it looked like the same type of silver bullet.'

'I said it was *possibly* the same type,' Dove corrected. 'We can't know that until the forensics come through. But I agree, these deaths are connected to Warren Storcrest's and Mrs D couldn't have had anything to do with them.'

'It does look that way,' Yanni agreed.

'We can let her go?' I asked, desperate to have one positive from all this mess.

Yanni nodded. 'We can let her go.'

I waited for the bolt of relief to hit me, both my own and a mirroring one from Yanni, but after a moment I realised they weren't coming.

It turns out that good news isn't so good when there are already three dead bodies on the ground.

Chapter Thirty-Eight

Mrs D's eyes filled with tears as I opened her cell door. 'Have you caught whoever did it?' she asked.

'We think so.' I couldn't tell her that the evidence was pointing to Toby and Angelica working together, not until it was confirmed by forensics. Letting her know she could go and that she was no longer a suspect would have to be enough for now.

'Poor Jennifer.' Mrs D was still wiping her eyes. 'First her father and now Toby. And she's such a lovely woman. She works so hard. Honestly, I think the way her father raised them, without any handouts was the making of her. She's dedicated her life to being a nurse. No one should have to go through loss like this, but especially not someone as kind as she is. And young Rory, losing both his mother and his father days apart. It breaks my heart.'

'I'm sure Yanni will do everything she can to give them as much support as possible,' I said. 'But you should get yourself home. Go and relax.'

The old woman shot out a rheumaticky old hand to clutch mine. 'Thank you so much, Beatrix. Thank you for believing in me. It really helped knowing you were on my side.'

'Everyone believed in you, Mrs D, but we had to follow the evidence.' God, I sounded like Yanni; next I'd be telling people to 'trust the process' and keeping a colour-coded case file.

Given that Yanni was still at the crime scene, there was something else I knew I had to tell Mrs D. 'We'll need you to stay in Witchlight Cove until we've got everything wrapped up, just in case we need to ask you more questions.' With Warren dead, the likelihood of Mrs D being charged over the pasty incident was low but it was still possible. Still, I trusted Yanni's better judgement to let sleeping dogs lie.

'I understand.' She dipped her head slightly. 'And don't worry. You know I never go away, not unless I'm taking the kids on a trip somewhere. And talking about staying put, I hope you will too, Beatrix. It might not have been the best of circumstances but it's been wonderful having you back.'

I didn't need to feel a rush of emotions from her to know she was telling the truth. 'I figure I'll be here for a little while longer, at least,' I admitted, only for an image of Fraser Banks to flash into my mind. Fingers crossed it was because I was thinking about stopping him getting into the house. Yup, that was it.

Even though Mrs D was free to leave, it took her a while to gather herself and her things. As she finally left, Yanni was walking into the office. Their exchange was brief – smiles and a handshake – before Mrs D disappeared through the doors.

'So?' I asked as Yanni approached. 'Any more information?'

'The coroner still needs to do a proper investigation, but it looks like a lovers' quarrel turned into a murder-suicide.'

'They were together?'

'It fits.' Yanni gave a long sigh. I felt guilty that she'd sent me home during the day when she looked like she needed a holiday, a bottle of rum – and possibly an exorcism.

'Those poor families,' I murmured. 'That's the last thing they'll want to deal with. Are you going to tell them today?'

She nodded. 'I have to. But you don't have to come with me. I can do this on my own.'

My immediate instinct was to say that I *would* go with her but I hesitated when a wave of her emotions hit me. She was thinking about another loss. I'd felt those same feelings flow from her before: she was thinking about me, about what it had been like to tell me what I'd already known, that my parents were gone. Her feelings would be even more intense when she spoke to the Browns and Storcrests and I wasn't sure that I could cope with them.

'I'm sorry,' I said quietly. 'I'm not sure if I can. Unless you need me to—'

'No, you need space. It's okay.' She managed a small smile. 'Besides, that dog of yours looks like she needs a walk.'

I glanced at the office chairs, but rather than lying over them asleep Eva was sitting up, looking at me. I nodded. Yanni's understanding had brought me both a relief and a guilt I couldn't quite shake. 'Come on, Eva,' I said. 'Let's go for a walk.'

I wasn't really thinking about where I was walking or how far I wanted to go; I wasn't really thinking at all because my head too full of emotion. Poor Mrs Brown. I hadn't lost a son, but I had *lost*. I could empathise so strongly it made me want to crawl into my bed and not come out.

People expect to lose their parents eventually, though not as young as I had, but to lose a child? And in such a violent way? And there would be no escaping the Witchlight Cove gossip. I wished there was something I could do to shield her from the heartbreak I knew was coming but there wasn't.

'Where do you want to go?' I asked Eva as I unclipped her lead. Without so much as a pause for breath, she bounded toward the beach.

I shouldn't have been surprised: in London, she'd ended up dripping wet more than once after bolting toward any body of water she could find. The sea, though, was an entirely different treat, the fun of chasing the waves, the softness of the sand beneath her feet. I understood why she wanted to go there; I loved it too.

As we approached the shoreline, a figure emerged from the water. He was chest-deep at first, his broad shoulders cutting through the waves, then his torso came into view as water streamed down his sculpted muscles. My eyes stayed locked on him, unwilling – or unable – to look away.

When I realised what was about to happen – and the part of his body that was about to be revealed – I slapped a hand over my face. At the same moment, he noticed me. 'Beatrix!' he called. 'Sorry, I didn't realise—'

'No, no, it's fine!' I said quickly, my voice muffled by my hands. Nothing to see here, nothing at all. Just a naked man emerging from the waves like a mythological thirst trap.

'My towel's over there. Give me a second.'

'Yes, of course!' I squeaked, turning my back and squeezing my eyes shut. There was absolutely no way I was going to look, absolutely not. Even though every part of me was screaming to have a quick glance.

'It's alright,' he chuckled. 'I'm decent now.'

I turned cautiously to find him buttoning his trousers. His shirt and leather jacket were draped over a nearby rock and it was that jacket that held my attention. It was far more casual than the suits I'd seen him wearing before and there was something about the material... There was a glimmer to it, as if it were infused with some deep magic.

'You're a selkie,' I said.

'I am,' he replied.

'And swimming in ... you know ... with actual skin. Like human skin.' I was babbling. Someone help me.

'Human skin. Wow, very technical.' He smirked.

I felt a warm sensation spread from him and settle behind my sternum. Why the hell did he always make me feel like this?

'I like swimming skin-on-water sometimes,' he said. 'Feeling the struggle of it. As a selkie swimming is easy, but sometimes I like to work for my pleasure.'

'"Working for your pleasure" isn't something you hear often.' I raised an eyebrow.

'Well, I'm not like most people,' he replied. 'But from what I hear, neither are you.'

The warmth I'd been feeling cooled instantly under his gaze. 'You've been asking about me?' The thought made my gut clench.

'No, I haven't but people talk. I promise that if I want to know something about you, I'll ask you,' he said firmly. 'But I will confess that I'm curious as to why everyone seems so fearful of your family name.'

He held my gaze steadily. He wasn't lying, he hadn't been gossiping about me – but why not? It would be easy for him to satisfy his curiosity. Then again, maybe it was a chance for me to satisfy my own. 'How about this?' I gambled. 'I'll tell you about me if you tell me about Fatima.'

His eyebrows rose. 'Well now, you *have* been digging, haven't you?' He bit his lip and for the first time I sensed he was nervous. Whatever this was, it was my ticket to ensure he didn't get the Eternal Flame, I was sure of it.

'You want to know about Fatima?'

'I want to know why you've sent her millions of pounds.'

'And if I tell you, you'll tell me your history?'

'That's the deal.'

Wordlessly, Fraser sank onto the rocks. He ran his tongue over his lips and for a second I assumed he'd refuse, but then he cleared his throat and lifted his gaze to mine. 'All right.' His gaze was serious. 'Beatrix Stonehaven, you've got yourself a deal.'

My skin chilled as I wondered if I'd made a deal with the devil.

Chapter Thirty-Nine

Fraser was still shirtless and I couldn't help but feel like he was using his abs to his advantage. Ab-warfare. 'I didn't grow up in Witchlight Cove,' he said finally. 'But you already know that.'

'I do, but it sounds like there's more of a story there.'

'There is,' he admitted. 'It's quite a long one.' He glanced at Eva who was pacing impatiently in the sand. 'Why don't we take her for a walk? We can talk as we go.'

'Sure.'

It was a crying shame when he pulled on his shirt and buttoned it. When he pulled on his leather jacket, I found myself focusing on how well it fit him. It really worked on him; then again, I doubted there was much he could wear that I wouldn't like the look of.

He snagged his shoes but didn't put them on, preferring to stroll barefoot in the sand.

'Fatima?' I asked impatiently as we started walking.

'I didn't grow up here,' he repeated, picking up where he'd left off. 'I grew up in a small village off the northern coast of Scotland.'

'You're Scottish? Your accent isn't very strong.'

'Well, you tend to mix a lot in magical communities – and I've worked hard to lose it. There are too many memories associated with that time of my life that I'd rather forget.'

'What happened?'

'The plan was to leave with my mum,' he said quietly. 'She was the reason I stayed as long as I did – I'd wanted out for years. My dad... He wasn't a nice man. He was a walrus shifter, a big, ugly brute in both his human and animal forms. He caused us a lot of pain, especially my mum.'

'I'm sorry,' I said, and I meant it with every fibre of my being. I was lucky to have grown up in a warm, loving home and my heart ached that he hadn't experienced the same.

He pressed his lips together as he tried to maintain his composure, but I could feel his agony. Grief and anger were intertwining until you could hardly separate the two. 'So you got out?' I prompted softly after several long minutes.

He shook himself. 'I did, but not soon enough. My mum ... she was a planner. She wouldn't leave until everything was in place. If we'd gone a day earlier, Dad wouldn't have found out and she'd have been okay.'

There were so many things I wanted to say, but none of them felt like enough.

'She was in the hospital for months, but in the end there was nothing they could do. God, I looked for any type of magic to heal her – and that was how I learned about the Eternal Flames. The day I found out there was one here, I went to the hospital – I was going to kidnap her and bring her here. But that was the day she finally lost the battle.'

'I'm so sorry,' I said helplessly.

He nodded. After another minute, he cleared his throat. 'In answer to your question, Fatima runs a retreat for women like her – like *us*. She found us at the hospital and promised there'd be a place for Mum when she got out. But Mum never did get out.'

He drew in a long breath. 'I came here for a fresh start. I'd already saved enough money for both of us to start over, but I was on my own. Working helped me to avoid thinking about Mum, so I focused on earning all the money I could and giving it to the community.'

As I watched him, a faint smile touched his lips. I couldn't reciprocate it. I'd suspected him of being something dark and nefarious and here he was – a philanthropist giving money to a shelter to save countless women from the fate his mother had suffered. In my own way, I did a similar thing by empowering women with self-defence training. I'd met women like the ones that used Fatima's shelter; I'd seen them coming into my class shaking with nerves and with fear rattling their teeth.

I always felt proud when I knew I'd replaced an anxious, fear-filled mindset with confidence and self-belief because no one should feel scared all the time. I saw it as a privilege to empower my women, especially the ones like Fraser's mum.

Maddie and I had been so mistaken about him and Yanni had been right – as always. I'd let my emotions cloud my judgement. 'Fraser,' I said softly, 'I'm so sorry you had to go through that.'

He stopped walking and turned to face me. 'Everything I did was so focused on forgetting my past and making the world a better place for other people – people like my mum – that I never stopped to think about what kind of future I wanted.' He paused. 'Not until I saw you.'

Oh fuck. I hadn't expected that.

My heart was so far up my throat, I could barely breathe. Was I meant to say something? I had to – but what?

Had I imagined what Fraser looked like beneath that highly tailored suit of his? Hell yes. But as far as the future went, I never thought further ahead than the next weekend, not with jobs and certainly not with men. He wanted something I couldn't give him.

The silence was threatening to swallow me whole when Fraser spoke again. 'So, Beatrix Stonehaven, I held up my part of the deal.' His voice was falsely jovial. 'I told you my story. Now it's time for you to share yours.'

As my eyes met his, I knew that I could refuse and tell him I didn't feel comfortable sharing with him. He would drop the subject because he was a *good* man. But the truth was, I *did* feel comfortable sharing it with him; more than that, I *wanted* him to know the truth. My truth, not the rumours whipping through Witchlight Cove.

Besides, I needed to balance the scales.

I looked down at Eva, who had found a long stick and was struggling to decide which end to pick it up from. Only when she'd found the point in the centre, her balance point, did I take a deep breath in and look back at Fraser. 'You've heard about the sorceress that attacked the village ten years ago?' I began. 'That started when she tried to kidnap a girl?'

'Of course.'

'The sorceress was my grandmother, my father's mum.'

His eyes widened then narrowed instantly. 'But your name's Stonehaven. The sorceress's name was something else, wasn't it?'

I nodded. 'Dahlia Bleakman.' Saying it aloud felt weird after I'd cursed it so many times in my head. 'Dad took my mum's name when they married. It was important that their children carried the Stonehaven name because she was an only child like me.'

'You're a sorceress, too?' He obviously assumed he'd figured out what I was about to tell him. He hadn't.

'No,' I said quickly. 'But if you heard about the attack, you'll know that a lot of magical people died or were badly injured that night. It really shook the community.'

'I heard a couple of things, and obviously there's the memorial in the square, but I didn't do any digging. I tend to keep my nose out of any place where loss has happened. People don't need strangers searching for titbits of gossip, not when all they want to do is trade details about someone's hurt. That's not a currency that I use.'

Any doubts I'd had about Fraser well and truly faded. Maddie had been so wrong about him.

'Sorry to sound stupid here,' he said, interrupting my thoughts. 'Isn't a sorceress and a witch the same thing? I always thought they were.'

My eyes widened and I shook my head quickly. 'No, they're *absolutely* not the same thing. And be careful saying things like that – no member of a coven will be happy with the comparison!'

'Sorry, I didn't mean any offence.' He sounded genuinely apologetic.

'None taken,' I gave him a small smile. 'I'm made of tougher stuff than that.'

'What's the difference between them?' he asked. 'They both use magic.'

'It's *how* they use it. Witches like me or Maddie use the power that's gifted to us. Maddie, for example, is an alchemist and a protection witch. She can cast wards for things like safeguarding kids or shielding vampires from the sun. There are fire witches, air witches, water witches – you get the idea.'

'What about you?'

'Me?' I laughed bitterly. 'I'm a hot mess. I've no real magic at all, just a bit of empathy that makes me feel what others feel.' I glanced up and found him staring at me so intently that my pulse quickened. I could tell that his gaze wasn't pitying, but it wasn't an easy expression to read. 'Dahlia didn't use her own magic; she took it from others. She was so powerful, she could pretty much steal whatever magic she wanted.'

Fraser's brow furrowed. 'And you were the girl she kidnapped?'

He'd joined the dots correctly. 'Yeah. I think she believed I had the powers she was looking for.' I shook my head.

'But she'd have been sorely disappointed. I'm a magical dud. Anyway, she grabbed me and got as far as the barrier – she didn't realise there was a ward on it.'

'A ward?'

'The border around Witchlight Cove prevents children under eighteen from leaving, unless they're with an adult whose intentions for them are pure.'

His eyes widened slightly. 'I didn't know that.'

There was a reason why I'd stayed in Witchlight until my eighteenth birthday and not a second more. 'You don't have kids and you're an adult, so why would you? Dahlia didn't know about it, either. The ward set off an alarm and every powerful witch, wizard, elemental – everyone with even a hint of magic – came running. It took everything they had to stop her.'

I swallowed hard. 'I wasn't the only one who lost my parents that night. Too many people died.'

Fraser's eyes were unblinking. 'And when people see you around, they're reminded of it.'

'The guilt. The pain. I can feel it all.' My voice was almost a whisper.

'I'm sorry,' he said. 'It took a lot of courage to come back here.'

I met his gaze and held it. There was something between us, I was sure of it. 'It did. But I can't let you have my family home.'

He nodded slowly. 'I understand what you're saying, and I understand your reasons for saying it, but the Eternal Flame could do so much good. There are ways to harness its power.'

I felt my stomach twist. 'That's the whole point. *You* can't harness it because you're not a guardian. Look, I believe that you have the best intentions and you think you could use the Flame for good, but it's too dangerous. It's in my blood. I was trained from birth to deal with it, to handle its strength and make sure I never abused it.'

'But Maddie has held it for the last ten years. It's not in *her* blood,' he pointed out.

'No, but she's been my best friend since before we could walk. She's not a bloodline guardian but she did a lot of the training with me – she thought it was fun. You don't have that and it would take you decades to learn.'

'Then I'll learn. You can teach me, that way you'd know exactly what I wanted to use its powers for. That would work, wouldn't it?'

I opened my mouth, not sure whether to agree or list of a dozen reasons why that wasn't feasible, not least because that would mean me staying in Witchlight Cove for the next decade and a half. I couldn't commit to that.

But before I could say anything, Eva started barking. 'Eva, what—?' I started, but she was already running away from the waves and bolting up the hill towards the village.

Something was wrong.

Chapter Forty

'Eva! You come back here now!' I didn't care that I was yelling – I *needed* to yell. Eva was running away from me and straight towards the village. As she reached the first road, she didn't even pause before dashing across it between two cars.

'Eva!' I screamed in panic. Relief flashed through me as the cars missed her. 'What are you doing, you stupid dog! Come back!'

She had never run off, not once – and I wasn't going to lose her.

My legs pounded the ground and my lungs heaved in air as I forced myself to run faster. I saw her take a left turn on the high street past Shady's and then go right, but I couldn't catch up with her. She was pulling away from me.

'Eva, what are you doing?' I yelled. This time she responded with a loud bark. Blasted dog! She could hear me, but she wasn't responding. What the hell? This was so unlike her.

As I watched her take another turn to the right, my stomach plummeted. I hadn't been sure, but now I knew exactly where she was going. She was bolting home. Why?

'Don't worry, I'll get her!'

I hadn't realised Fraser was running with me; in fact, he was level pegging until he spoke, at which point he pushed his pace faster and overtook me. Damn selkies with their proper fae magic making them stronger and faster.

Still, I could keep going for hours – my stamina was something special. My mum had made sure of that. Once, she'd made me fight for twelve hours straight, not even stopping for food or the toilet. It was supposed to be a simulation of how I might have to act if someone came for the Flame. If only she'd realised the Flame could disappear all on its own. There had been no drill for that particular scenario.

Stamina didn't equal speed, though, and I had to exert every last shred of energy to catch up with Eva. Finally, I turned the last corner and saw my house.

My girl wasn't running anymore; instead, she was barking non-stop, not even pausing for breath, and it was easy to see why. Smoke was billowing out of the window – and it wasn't normal smoke. The pearlescent mist shimmered with a pinkish hue and there wasn't a hint of grey in it.

'Maddie!' I yelled.

'Stand back! I'll go in.' Fraser held out his arm to stop me.

'Like hell!' I snapped and shoved him aside. He tumbled back in surprise but I didn't have the time to apologise, not when he was slowing me down.

Not wanting to waste time looking for my house keys in my bag, I leaned back, raised my leg and slammed my heel straight into the door next to the lock. The wood buckled and the door flew wide open.

'Wow,' Fraser breathed behind me, and I felt a wave of awe radiate from him. Any other occasion that might have been nice, but I didn't have time to dwell on it.

The house was thick with smoke but there were no flames – or heat. Whatever was causing this, it was some sort of magic. 'I'll look for the source,' Fraser said, as if he were reading my mind. 'You go find Maddie.'

Eva leapt ahead of us both, bounded into the house and through to the back of the building. Fear gripped me; the last thing I needed was for something to happen to her too. 'Maddie! Maddie, are you in here?' I screamed, trying not to panic.

I couldn't imagine being in any kind of magical smoke for long would be good for her – or us – and I covered my mouth with my sleeve. I prayed that Eva and I were wrong about our suspicions and that Maddie was far, far away, but when I followed my dog through the house I saw my best friend lying face down on the floor.

'Maddie!' Her name ripped from my lips as I dropped to the floor beside her and pulled her up to a sitting position. A moment later, a hissing sound filled the air. I twisted my head to find Fraser behind me holding a bucket of water and extinguishing the magical flames. The last few drops fell onto the large pink cauldron that Maddie had been using. Immediately, the smoke stopped billowing.

'Is she okay?' he asked as he crouched down beside me.

'She's not responding,' I said. 'She's breathing, but there's nothing...' I was shaking, panicking so hard I could barely see. I couldn't lose Maddie, not now that I'd found her again.

Eva licked Maddie's face and for a moment I held my breath. Maybe she could bring Maddie round like she'd done when my friend had fainted in my flat. But as I sat there, cradling her in my arms and Eva kept on frantically licking her, I realised it wasn't going to happen.

'She needs help. We need to get her to one of the covens,' I said. Still holding her like a baby, I moved to stand up but before I was upright, Fraser grabbed my arm.

'I don't think you can go to a coven with this.' His voice was a harsh whisper.

'What? We have to – she needs help!'

'I know. But *look*, Beatrix.'

I followed his eyes down to her hands. The cuticles of Maddie's nails had started to turn black. There was no denying what it was a sign of: black magic. My stomach lurched. The honey fungus outside hadn't grown because the Eternal Flame was missing; it had grown because Maddie was dabbling in evil magic.

'Correct me if I'm wrong, but don't witches get cast out by their coven if they're found to be involved in black magic?' Fraser asked.

'She wouldn't... She couldn't...' I stammered, but each time my voice trailed off. Maddie would work herself to the bone and do whatever it took to meet her obligations to her customers. With the Eternal Flame gone, she had needed to find another way to 'give the magic a little bit more'. That's what she'd told me.

'Maddie,' I whispered. A tear ran down my cheek and fell onto her face. 'What have you done?'

I sat there wishing I could feel something from her – anything, even pain. Pain would have let me know she was still there. But there was nothing but a terrifying emptiness.

'We need to take her somewhere else. Is there anyone you can trust with this?' Fraser asked. 'Would Yanni know someone? Could she protect her?'

There was no way I could take Maddie to Yanni. She didn't deserve to see her granddaughter like this, and besides it would put her in an awful position between her role as chief of police and her role as Maddie's grandmother. No, Yanni wasn't an option.

As for people I trusted, the only other one was Ezra but he couldn't help. He was a shifter, and I needed a witch. Suddenly a thought struck me. 'Find Maddie's car keys.' I stood up with Maddie in my arms. 'We need to get her to Old Jacobson,' I said grimly.

This time, I'd be prepared for the old man and his flip outs, and this time I wasn't taking no for an answer. He was a powerful witch and he *would* help Maddie.

Fraser had turned away from me so that all I could see was the back of his leather jacket. I assumed he'd wanted to give me a moment of privacy as my tears were falling, but when I called him again he still didn't move. 'Fraser, did you hear me? We need to get her to Old Jacobson.'

'It's gone,' he whispered.

'Fraser, you need—'

When I realised what he was looking, the air rushed from my lungs and panic gripped me. Oh this was bad. This was very bad.

'Fraser—' I began.

He turned to look at me before I could continue, not that I had the faintest idea what to say. 'The Eternal Flame has gone,' he said. 'And you've been hiding it from everyone.'

Chapter Forty-One

Silence filled the room. I was still holding Maddie; she was so light that at any other time that would have been easy, but at that moment my own body felt heavy and sluggish.

'How long?' Fraser demanded. 'How long has the Eternal Flame been gone?'

I bit the inside of my cheek. 'Fraser, please. Can we deal with one crisis at a time? We can talk about this later, but we need to get help for Maddie now.'

His eyes remained locked on mine for a second longer before he nodded. 'You're right. We'll table it. I'll find her keys.'

My relief was absolute. 'They'll be in a bowl by the door or on the kitchen worktop.'

I don't know where he found them, but by the time I was out by the car he was unlocking the doors. 'Here, let me do that,' he said. He took Maddie from me and lowered her gently onto the back seat, then I slipped in next to her to hold her body in place.

Fraser slid into the driver's seat. Eva promptly jumped over his lap and into the passenger seat before he had the chance to open the other door.

'We need to go to Shingle's End. You know where it is?' I asked.

He didn't reply but he started the engine, which I took to mean yes. As he reversed away from the house, I held Maddie's head in my lap, stroking her limp hair and pushing it behind her ears. I had lost her because of my own stubbornness and heartache and I had only just got her back. There was no way I could lose her again. I just couldn't.

As I fought my tears, I promised myself that if she was restored to me, there would be no more running. I would stay in Witchlight Cove forever if that was what she wanted.

'How long?' Fraser asked again from the front of the car.

'Sorry?' For an instant, I thought he was talking about how long Maddie and I had known each other – but I'd told him that less than an hour before. Then I realised he was talking about the Flame.

'How long has it been out?' he clarified.

'About two weeks,' I said quietly.

'That's why you came back.'

I nodded then realised he couldn't see me. 'Maddie didn't know what had happened. She'd got wards in place and no one had broken in. There was no evidence that the Flame had been extinguished. It had just ... disappeared.'

He let out a 'hmm'. I tried to sense his emotions but my own were too much of a mess to focus. 'Who else knows?' he said after a pause.

'No one.'

'Yanni. She's Maddie's grandmother, isn't she? She must know.'

'No. Maddie didn't want to put her in that situation. She wanted to see if me being here would help it come back, or if we could figure something out together before we worried anyone else.'

'I don't know if that was sensible or stupid. But let's keep it that way for now until we work out what's going on here.'

Tears pooled in my eyes. How had everything become such a mess?

'Could what's happened with her now have something to do with the Flame going missing?' Fraser continued with his questions.

'Maybe, ' I said, swallowing hard. 'Possibly. Maddie's used the Flame to make her wards. I didn't know how she'd managed to continue without it, but she said she'd found a way. I guess... I guess...' I couldn't say it out loud.

'Do you think Old Jacobson will know how to help her?'

'I've no idea,' I admitted truthfully. 'But like you said, we can't go to the covens. He's all we've got.'

I'd had two meetings with the old man so far: the first had ended with him throwing me out of his garden, and the second had ended with him hurling Fraser across Sonny's coffee shop. I really hoped this was a case of third time lucky because if it wasn't I was about to have another impromptu flying lesson and, frankly, I was sick of them.

'It's up here,' I pointed down towards Shingle's End over Fraser's shoulder. A minute later, Jacobson's house came into view. The knot in my stomach twisted even tighter. If he turned us away, I didn't know what we'd do. We'd have to go to the covens and that wouldn't end well for any of us.

'You go and make sure he's in,' Fraser said, as we juddered to a stop. 'I'll carry Maddie in.'

I flew out of the car, raced across the garden and pounded on the door. I didn't care what wards Old Jacobson had in place. He could throw me off his property a dozen times, but I would get right back up every single time and knock again. I was *not* giving up. He *had* to see me.

'Who's there?' came a voice from inside.

'It's Beatrix! I need your help – my friend needs your help!'

'Beatrix who?'

'Beatrix Stonehaven! I'm not my grandmother,' I added desperately. 'And I need your goddamned help!'

When the door opened I wasn't faced by the scowling face I'd seen on previous occasions; instead his expression was one of pinched concern. 'What's happened?'

'It's my friend, Maddie. She's been doing some magic, magic that normally uses the Eternal Flame, but she hasn't been able to use it recently. She'd been getting really tired and then we came home today and there was pink smoke everywhere and she was unconscious and I can't wake her up. And... And...' I didn't want to say this last bit, but I knew I had to. 'And her fingernails have started turning black.'

He recoiled. 'She's been doing black magic?'

'I don't think it was on purpose. I know her and she doesn't have an evil bone in her body. Please, can you help her?'

As I waited for a reply, Fraser appeared beside me clutching Maddie. Jacobson immediately picked up her hand and examined her nails. 'This isn't good. It'll take some time to fix. Come in, I need to look at her properly.'

Relief washed over me. He'd said it would take time, not that it was impossible. Maddie would be okay; I wouldn't let myself think any other way.

I wasn't sure what I'd imagined Jacobson's place would look like – maybe something damp and mouldy with overgrown plants spilling out of pots. But it was nothing like that. His living area was whitewashed, with books meticulously ordered along the walls. Beside them was a shelf with small glass vials and jars of herbs, tinctures and powders.

'Please tell me there's something you can do,' I begged.

'We'll see,' he said crisply. 'I need time. Space.'

As Fraser placed Maddie gently down on the table, Jacobson placed his hands on either side of my shoulders. 'She'll be alright. Just let me do my thing.'

I knew that's what I had to do, but it was so hard to see her in this state. I felt that same sense of helplessness I'd experienced when I'd seen my mother and father running towards me, when I'd seen my grandmother wielding her power as she'd tried to steal me from my family. But this couldn't end badly. It just couldn't.

'He'll do what he can,' Fraser said softly. He stood beside me as the old man's hands started hovering above

Maddie's torso. 'And if he can't, we'll find another solution. This isn't the only magical place, remember? We'll go somewhere else, somewhere with another Eternal Flame. I'll help you.'

'Fraser, about the Eternal Flame...'

'It's okay,' he said. 'That's not a discussion we need to have right now.' His eyes flickered towards Jacobson.

I nodded again. At some point, and without being conscious of doing it, I'd folded myself into him and my head was resting against his chest. When I realised what I was doing, I couldn't bring myself to move away from him. Not until my phone buzzed in my pocket.

I saw the name on the screen and fresh panic flooded me. 'It's Yanni,' I said, my voice trembling. 'What do I say?'

'Do you need to answer it?'

Yanni was my employer, my friend and my family. She deserved a response no matter why she was calling. I nodded. 'Yes. Just ... keep an eye on Maddie, won't you?'

'Of course,' he promised solemnly. 'You can trust me.'

And despite everything, I did.

Chapter Forty-Two

I didn't want to leave Maddie but Old Jacobson had started chanting. If Yanni heard him, she'd ask what was going on and there was no way I'd be able to think of a believable explanation in my current state of mind.

'I'll keep an eye on her. We both will.' Fraser gestured to Eva, who was sitting behind Jacobson and watching his every move.

'Okay. I won't be long.' I moved into the kitchen. Only when I had closed the door did I answer the call. 'Yanni?' I tried to keep my voice as neutral as possible. 'Is everything okay?'

'Not exactly,' she said. 'We've had the forensics back on Angelica and Toby's murders.'

'Okay.' It was hard to shift gears from black magic to murder most foul. 'Was it like we thought? A silver bullet and blood loss from a bear-shifter attack?'

'Dove was right about the silver bullet...'

'But...?' I suddenly had the feeling this wouldn't be as straightforward as we'd first thought.

'Angelica wasn't killed by a bear shifter. Her wounds were inflicted with a knife,' she said grimly. 'A knife designed to mimic the patterns made by a bear's claw.'

'Someone was trying to frame Toby and make it look like he was responsible,' I said darkly,

'It would appear that way.'

My head spun. It was almost too much to take in, but I forced myself to focus. If that was the case, there was a good chance that the killer was still out there with three kills under their belt and feeling cocky as fuck.

'That's not good,' I said in the understatement of a century. 'It has to be someone who wanted both Toby and Angelica out of the picture – and someone that Warren trusted enough to turn his back on.'

'It looks that way, yes.'

The answer hit me like a physical weight. 'It's one of his children. It has to be.' The divorce wasn't finalised; after Warren's death everything would pass to Angelica, so she had to die too. Toby was collateral damage, there to neatly wrap up the case so that the killer could slink back to their house and count their new inheritance.

'That was my thinking. I've already seen Jennifer – she was at Mrs Brown's when I told them the news about

Toby. She was in pieces. It turns out that the person Toby was in love with was her – they'd been seeing each other secretly again. They'd planned to elope once the merman drama calmed down. There's no way she would have killed him, and she had no idea why he would have been with Angelica. She said Toby hardly knew her.'

'So someone lured them both there?' Who would have the power to do that?

'Rory?' I tried it on for size: Angelica would surely meet her own son. 'Do you think he'd kill his own mother? But no, I don't see it,' I murmured, thinking aloud.

That was when I remembered what Mrs D had told me.

'Gilbert hated that Warren made them stand on their own two feet, and he was furious that his dad was paying Angelica money that he thought was his inheritance. He was angry that Jennifer was "selling out" their family line by going with a land shifter. He worked with his dad in the yachting business, meaning he would have had access to his emails. I bet he's the one who sent that email to Mrs D saying there would be no more donations, then he siphoned the money off himself! He's trying to frame Angelica. I'm betting he logged into his father's email account on her computer to make *her* look guilty.'

'I came to the exact same conclusion,' Yanni said grimly.

I chewed my lip. 'Yanni, if we've both figured it out that means Jennifer and Rory might do the same. They could be in danger.'

'We need to find Gilbert before he can hurt anyone else. Can you come? It would be useful to have another pair of fighting hands if things get messy – we're woefully understaffed for things like this.'

I look at the closed kitchen door behind which Maddie was lying unconscious on the table. There was nothing I could do here. Jacobson was working around her and he'd said that he needed space.

I had to stop Gilbert Storcrest from hurting anyone else; besides, maybe using him as a punchbag would help work off some of my anger. I was willing to put that theory to the test.

'Just tell me where to go,' I said grimly.

Chapter Forty-Three

'I need the car keys,' I told Fraser as I marched back into the living room.

'What? Why?' Concern shadowed his face.

'I have to go – Yanni needs help. She's worked out who killed Warren Storcrest, and the same person has killed his stepmother and his sister's fiancé. We have to stop him.'

'Who does she think did it?' he asked.

I sighed. I didn't need an interrogation, what I needed were the bloody keys. 'Warren's son, Gilbert.'

'He's a water shifter?'

'Yes.'

Finally, Fraser pulled the keys out of his pocket, though he didn't hand them over. 'I'm coming with you,' he said.

'What? No, I don't need you.'

'You absolutely do. First of all, you're not in any state to drive. You've been through an absolute trauma with your best friend and there's no way you should be behind the wheel of a car—'

I opened my mouth to object but he continued before I could get a word in. 'Secondly, he's a water shifter and I'm second-in-command of the water shifters. If he bolts, there's a good chance he'll head for the sea. You need someone who can swim. You need me.'

I bit down on the inside of my cheeks. He was right. Yanni might be a massively powerful bear shifter but her swimming skills were average at best. And while I could splash about fine in a pool, my guardianship training had been very much focused on dry land.

'Fine, but you stay back! This is police business,' I said, as if I were an actual member of the police rather than someone hired to answer phones.

As I prepared to leave, fear struck me again. Did I really want to leave the most important person in my life in the hands of someone who had attacked me twice? Like he sensed my apprehension, Jacobson raised his eyes to mine.

'Nothing will happen to her while she is with me,' he promised, as if he knew exactly what I was thinking. 'She's as safe with me as if she were with her family.'

'That doesn't mean much in my bloodline,' I muttered.

He gave a dry chuckle that faded into a sad nod. 'I'm sorry. You're right. But you have my word – the witch's bind – that I won't let anything happen to her. And you can leave that one to keep an eye on me, if you want.' He nodded at Eva. 'I'm pretty sure she'd take my leg off if I hurt your friend.'

That was one thing we agreed on. 'If anything happens to Maddie I will hunt you down,' I swore darkly.

Jacobson smiled. 'I would expect nothing less.'

I knew I didn't have a choice. Gilbert had killed a member of his own family and he wouldn't think twice about putting a bullet through Yanni. There was no way I could let her face him on his own. 'We'll come straight back as soon as we can.'

Jacobson didn't bother replying; he was already working on Maddie again.

As Fraser and I raced to the car, my phone buzzed again. 'Yanni?' I answered.

'We've got a sighting of him,' she said without needing to clarify who. 'He was around the back of his father's house. He kicked a charter customer off one of the yachts.'

'He's taking a yacht?' I said, looking at Fraser as I spoke. He nodded and turned the car to the waterfront. It seemed that having a water shifter might come in handy after all. 'Okay, I'm on my way. Wait until I get there,' I said before I ended the call.

'If anything looks dangerous, let me handle it,' Fraser said as we drove toward the waterfront behind Warren's house. 'I know you don't want to hear it, but I have my skin to protect me.' He pinched at his leather jacket. 'You don't.'

'You don't know what powers I have,' I replied indignantly.

'You're right, I don't. But you said not much power, and I know you're a witch who chose to break down a door by kicking it rather than bursting it or burning it down. This is my territory. I'd never forgive myself if anything happened to you, not after all that's happened with Maddie.'

Guilt radiated from him, thick and sharp. My emotions had been too high all evening to sense anyone else's, but now I could feel his as strongly as if they were my own. 'What happened to Maddie has nothing to do with you,' I said, confused.

'If I hadn't been trying to get to the Eternal Flame, it wouldn't have put her under such stress. None of this would have happened.'

Instinctively, I placed my hand on his. 'Fraser, the Flame would have gone out anyway. And Maddie would have carried on doing her spells regardless.'

My mind flicked back to my first day back in Witchlight Cove. Was it really less than a week ago? It felt like a lifetime had passed. But I remembered the giant ward Maddie had placed on the house to keep Fraser out while she tracked me down.

In some ways he was right: his actions had put pressure on Maddie to increase her magic at a time when she was at her weakest. But it was no more than the pressure I'd put on her by leaving her to manage the house alone while I sought my own space.

There was no point in us both harbouring guilt. I'd shoulder it; at this point in my life, it was virtually my other half.

'Look, I know how to fight,' I said. 'If we're on dry land, I promise you don't have to worry about me. But if Gilbert heads to the water, he's all yours. How about that for a deal?'

A smile crossed Fraser's face. 'Another deal? Done.'

We pulled up outside Warren's house and raced around the back to where the jetty protruded into the sea. Several boats were still boarded up, but one – a giant yacht – was rocking from side to side in the water. 'Why's he sailing away when he can swim?' Fraser asked.

'The same reason Gilbert has done everything so far,' I replied without hesitation. 'Money. I'd bet that yacht has a load stashed on it.' Not to mention that the vessel itself was worth a small fortune.

As we climbed out of the car, I saw Jennifer at the water's edge, tears streaking her face. 'He did it!' she cried. 'He was already on the boat saying he needed to think stuff through. He said he didn't kill Dad, but then the police car turned up and he started firing a gun. He told Yanni it had silver bullets in it. He killed Toby, didn't he? He killed Toby and Dad?'

I suspected she already knew the answer. She was all but hysterical but we had no time to stay and comfort her. 'Where's Yanni?' I asked urgently.

Wordlessly, Jennifer pointed to the back of the boat where Yanni was hoisting her giant body up a ladder. So much for waiting for me before doing anything.

'You get to the water!' I yelled to Fraser. 'You need to be there in case he jumps.'

'A boat is *not* dry land!' he yelled after me, but I didn't stop.

I needed to get to Yanni.

Chapter Forty-Four

I would have to practise sprinting if I stayed in Witchlight Cove; that was the thought running through my head as my legs pounded the ground for the second time in less than two hours. Stamina alone wasn't good enough; I needed to improve my speed.

Thankfully my body seemed to know what was required of it this time. The boat was pulling away from the dock but only slowly, the gap between the land and the vessel growing inch by inch.

By the time I reached the end of the pier, it was three feet away. That was a jump I could make – at least, I hoped I could. Before I had a chance to second-guess myself I bent my knees, pushed off the ground and flew toward the boat.

'Gotcha!' Yanni's hand grabbed mine as she pulled me up in one swift jerk. 'Talk about cutting it fine!'

'Where is he?' I asked, breathlessly.

'On the bridge,' Yanni said. 'And he's got silver bullets in that gun,' she added grimly.

'I know. Jennifer said.'

'We need to get the gun if we can,' she continued. 'I'd bet my pension that's the murder weapon he used on Toby. We don't want to lose it in the water.'

'We've got support in the water if we need it,' I confirmed.

Yanni raised an eyebrow. 'Really? Of the selkie variety, I assume?'

'This isn't the time, Yanni,' I muttered. 'We need to stop Gilbert and make sure no one else gets hurt. How are we going to do this?'

'Well, I'm pretty sure he knows I'm here but I doubt he's seen you. I'll keep him distracted while you cuff him.'

'I don't like the idea of you being the target,' I said. 'Not when he has silver bullets.'

'Have you got a better idea?' she asked pointedly and crossed her arms.

As a matter of fact, I hadn't. I was all out of ideas and I was running on adrenaline and panic. Maybe if my head had been clearer I could have come up with something smart, but part of my mind was still with Maddie, hoping I hadn't made an horrific mistake leaving her with Jacobson.

The next few minutes, when Gilbert was having to focus on steering the boat away from the jetty, were probably our best chance of getting him.

'Fine. But you need to keep a good distance from him, okay?' I said. 'Just make some noise and keep out of his line of fire.'

'Surprisingly enough, that was part of my plan,' she sassed.

Given how infrequently murderers popped up in Witchlight Cove, I should have been surprised at how calm Yanni seemed. Her composure was impressive, but that was the reason people trusted her to oversee disputes between the magical sects: she didn't flinch under pressure.

'The bridge is on this level,' she whispered to me. 'I'll go down a deck – it'll make it harder for him to get a clear shot.'

'Okay. I'll go around this side.'

Without another word, Yanni transformed into the majestic black bear I remembered from childhood. When I was a kid, I'd thought her colossal size made her invincible but now, impressive as she looked, she seemed heartbreakingly vulnerable. One silver bullet and she'd be gone.

I watched as she clambered down to the lower deck, making as much noise as possible to draw Gilbert's attention. Then something silver-grey in the water caught my eye: a sleek, glinting figure was diving beneath the waves, its shimmering skin matching the jacket Fraser had worn earlier. There could have been a thousand seals in the sea, but I knew from that moment on I'd always be able to pick him out.

'GRRAAWWRR!' Yanni's roar reverberated from below as she went into full animal mode, distracting Gilbert with her considerable might. It was working, too. A shot rang out as the boat swayed beneath me. I needed to act before one of those bullets hit her.

As I moved forward, I tried to stay steady on my feet. Fraser hadn't been joking – this was nothing like dry land. Yanni's movements were rocking the vessel as she tried to unsettle Gilbert; unfortunately they were unsettling me, too. Add to that his lack of control as he tried to shoot Yanni and steer at the same time, and it was like being high up on a fairground ride.

Knowing that every second's delay could be fatal, I grabbed the rail with my left hand and edged forward.

'I'll kill you! Don't think I won't!' Gilbert screamed. 'I've lost too much to give up now!'

When I was close enough to peer through the glass into the bridge, I stopped to see what I had to deal with. My breath caught in my lungs. We'd been right about the money: open crates filled with cash were piled high. And while I didn't know how many silver bullets Gilbert had in that gun of his, he wasn't slowing his shots at Yanni.

With my heart pounding, I waited for his back to turn then broke through the glass. My only weapon was my fists, but they were what I'd been trained to use. The edge of my palm slammed into the back of Gilbert's neck, sending him stumbling – but he held on to the gun.

'Yanni, stay back!' I shouted, in case she got any ideas.

'Get off me, you bitch!' Gilbert snarled, spinning to face me. His body writhed unnaturally, slippery and ungraspable like an eel's. So that was what he was – an eel shifter.

I tried to reason with him. 'This is over, Gilbert. There's no way out. Drop the gun and at least give yourself a chance in court.'

'This is mine!' he bellowed. 'I'm owed this! It's my inheritance! He wanted to give it all away!'

I tried to tighten my grip on his neck but I couldn't hold him, so I drove my knee into his groin instead. He howled and the gun finally slipped from his hands and rolled toward the edge of the deck.

'Yanni! He's disarmed!' I shouted. The gun teetered, millimetres from plunging into the sea. 'Fraser!' I yelled. 'Grab the gun! We can't lose it in the water!'

'Got it!' his voice called from below.

Beside me Gilbert was whimpering, doubled over in pain. 'It's over, Gilbert,' I said.

'Damn right it is.' Yanni shifted back to human form beside me. 'We're turning this boat around and heading home.'

As she took charge of Gilbert, I moved to the edge to check that Fraser had retrieved the gun. When I reached the railing, Gilbert spoke again, his voice laced with malice. 'You may have got rid of my silver bullets,' he sneered, 'but I hear bog-standard ones work perfectly well on witches. Let's see, shall we?'

I froze as I tried to make sense of his words. A moment later his hand flicked to his waistband and I saw the flash of metal in his hand. Oh fuck! He had another gun!

Yanni lunged towards him, but I knew she would be too late.

I stared down the barrel of the gun, the muzzle flashed and then pain consumed me.

Chapter Forty-Five

The sensation of falling was what I remembered the most. I don't know how high the deck was, but I seemed to plummet downwards forever. Heat was rolling off my body and the pain was so intense it almost forced my mind to go blank. A second later, cold hit me as if I'd slammed into a wall of ice.

'Beatrix!'

I could hear voices, full of fear and panic, but I didn't know who was calling my name. Was it my parents? They'd called my name in the same way the night I'd been taken. That was the last time I'd ever spoken to them.

I had felt so far away from them for so long, but now I could feel them moving closer...

The darkness surrounded me – was it going to consume me? Fear stilled my heart.

But then it was as if I were being wrapped in the softest, warmest blanket, every inch of me held in a gentle, comforting embrace. I didn't know who or what was doing it, but I knew that I was safe. And it was wonderful.

Water filled my ears. At first all I could make out was the crash of waves but then something changed and there were voices too, faint words as if they were coming from miles away.

'Fraser, is that...? What have you *done*?' That was Yanni's voice.

'I didn't have any choice.' His voice was slow, sombre.

'You must have had!'

'No, I didn't. It was this or we lost her. We'll talk about it later.'

'She has to—'

'We'll talk about it later.' His tone silenced her. How peculiar: it wasn't like Yanni to be silenced so easily. Was she hurt, too? Please don't let her be hurt!

My concern for Yanni forced my eyes open. Blinking against the light, I tried to focus. 'Did you get him?' My words were barely audible.

'We got him. Don't worry about that.' Fraser's voice was soft and his touch was like the cosy blanket that had caught me when I fell. But surely that had been my imagination?

'He's in the car with magic cuffs on him so he can't change or move,' Yanni confirmed. She sounded fine. *That's good*, I thought to myself. *That's good.*

I closed my eyes again and let the warmth surround me. I couldn't remember the last time I'd felt this way – safe, whole, like something that had been missing from my life for years was finally back where it belonged.

The thought of Gilbert and the fight flickered through my mind. We had got him. That was done. But Maddie... I needed to see Maddie. I needed to tell her we'd done it.

I jolted awake. How could I have forgotten? I needed to get back to her. I sat upright, only for the blood to rush from my head. The entire world swayed as I glanced down at my bloodstained side. Blood? What the hell? God – I'd been shot.

Now I remembered. Gilbert had a second gun – and he'd shot me! The little prick.

Expecting pain, I pressed my hand against my side but I felt nothing more than dampness. When I drew my hand away, I saw the hole in my T-shirt the size of a bullet wound. 'What? I— I...'

Shrugging off the leather jacket from my shoulders, the one I recognised as Fraser's, I lifted my top. There was no sign of any injury. Confusion overwhelmed me. Had I caught my top on the railing on the way down and torn it? But the blood...?

I shook the thought away. It didn't matter. Maddie was what mattered. 'We need to get back to Old Jacobson's.' I twisted my neck so that my eyes locked with Fraser's. 'We need to make sure Maddie's okay.'

'Maddie?' Yanni said tightly. 'Why wouldn't Maddie be okay? Beatrix? What's wrong with Maddie?'

Oops. The chill I'd expected from the water finally hit me, though it had more to do with Yanni's sharp voice than the actual temperature.

'Beatrix, tell me! What's going on?' she pressed. 'Why do you need to get to Maddie?'

I kept my eyes on Fraser; for some reason I trusted his judgement now more than ever. His chin moved the smallest fraction, but I knew what he meant: I had to tell Yanni what had happened.

I was trembling as I turned to her. 'I swear I didn't know how bad it was.'

Her face blanched and her lips curled in a way that reminded me more of her bear form than the human police inspector I was used to seeing.

'Take me to my granddaughter. Now,' she snarled.

Chapter Forty-Six

Dove arrived to take Gilbert to the police station. A triple murder was beyond Yanni's usual scope and the main magic council would need to be brought in to handle it.

As we walked towards Maddie's car with Yanni leading the way, I tried to hand Fraser's jacket back to him. 'It's fine. You keep it,' he said softly.

I'm not one to keep things that don't belong to me, but I wasn't going to say no. The moment I'd taken it off earlier, I'd felt an unusual chill. Now I was wearing it again, the jacket seemed to fit me perfectly – which was bizarre given that Fraser was twice as broad as I was. It had to be something to do with the water: the leather must have tightened or reshaped itself.

'So, let me get this straight,' Yanni said as we drove toward Old Jacobson's house. I could tell she was trying to piece it all together so I stayed quiet and let her work through it. 'As far as you know, the Eternal Flame disappeared about two weeks ago. It wasn't stolen, no alarms went off, it just disappeared? Was it extinguished?'

'I don't know,' I replied. 'Maddie just said it was gone. But it's not possible to extinguish it. We should know, we tried often enough as kids.'

Yanni ignored that piece of idiocy. 'Okay.' Her voice was still sharp. 'But rather than coming to me, or consulting a coven, Maddie waited a week. In that time, she somehow mastered black magic so she could keep on making her tattoos. Then, when the Flame still hadn't come back, she brought you back to Witchlight Cove – and on top of that, she convinced me to hire you at the police station. Was that so you could keep an eye on me? Make sure I didn't find out what was going on?'

'No,' I said quickly, stung by the accusation. The idea that Yanni thought I'd manipulate her like that hit hard. 'I've hated you not knowing. Honestly, I wanted to tell you but it was so difficult. We didn't want to put you in an awkward position. And, for what it's worth, I've loved spending time with you. Apart from the early starts and answering the phones.'

Yanni snorted. 'It's not like you've actually done much of that, is it?'

'Well, no,' I conceded.

'I think it's best if you go back to doing what you're best at. Being a PI.'

I blinked. 'Are you firing me?'

Her expression softened. 'I'm setting you free with one month's severance pay. I'll try and get someone else to man the phones. Someone who'll actually do it.'

I winced. 'I'm sorry,' I said piteously. 'I didn't mean to hurt you.'

I could feel the pain radiating from her, sharp and raw. She was scared, and no wonder. She'd already lost her daughter and she barely ever saw her son. Maddie was all she had left.

'I know.' She reached out and took my hand. 'But I wish you'd both trusted me with this earlier.' Silence descended, painful and prickly like my conscience.

'Well, that has to be a good sign.' Fraser's voice drew me from my thoughts.

As I looked up and followed his gaze out of the windscreen, my heart leapt.

Maddie was standing at the window of Jacobson's house. Even from this distance, I could see how pale she was. Her skin looked almost translucent but she was standing upright, her eyes open, and the ghost of a smile played on her lips when she saw us.

The car had barely stopped when Yanni flung open the door and raced toward the house. As she struggled with the front door, Jacobson appeared and opened it. Eva barrelled out and raced towards me.

'I'm alright, I'm alright,' I said as she placed her paws on my chest and nuzzled her head against me. She always sensed when there was danger, like during the fire at the house, so perhaps she could sense what had happened to me, too. Not that I was entirely sure what that was.

'I should leave you here,' Fraser said.

I immediately stopped fussing over Eva and looked at him. 'Are you sure? You could stay ... to see if Maddie's okay. If you wanted to?' I wasn't sure why I didn't want him to leave yet, but I didn't.

He smiled gently before leaning forward and planting a kiss on my forehead. 'It's okay. You need time with your family. But you and I ... I'd like us to talk soon, if that's okay. Maybe over dinner?'

'That would be nice,' I said.

I remembered thinking the same thing when we were at the beach talking about our families. I had wished then that we could sit and talk for hours. I wanted that now, but it felt different. It wasn't a want but something more – a *need*.

'Message me when you get back to the house,' he said. 'Just so I know you're alright.'

I nodded. I couldn't remember the last time I'd needed to text a guy to tell him I was home safe, and it wasn't as if I was going home alone. But it didn't feel like an unreasonable request given all that we'd been through.

Fraser bent down to ruffle Eva's ears before turning and heading back down the lane.

Inside the house, I hugged Maddie so tightly I was pretty sure I heard some of her joints pop. 'You're gonna have to let go of me or I'll suffocate,' she said with a shaky laugh.

I drew back to look at her. 'You scared the life out of me! Don't you ever do that again! Old Jacobson said you were dealing with black magic. What the hell, Maddie?' I prodded her chest with my index finger.

'I didn't realise... I mean, I knew it was different from what I'd done before but I thought you had to be – I don't know – evil or something to use black magic. Everything I was doing was to help people, so I assumed I was tapping into something different. I swear I didn't know I was doing black magic.'

I couldn't be mad at her. I wanted to be absolutely furious, but I believed her completely. Maddie didn't have a bad bone in her body; there was no chance she'd ever tamper knowingly with that side of magic.

'But you're okay now?' I glanced at her fingernails. The black had gone, though they were definitely redder than normal.

Rather than replying immediately, she bit down on her lower lip. For the first time I noticed how much older she looked, and not because of the years we'd spent apart. She was the same age as me and yet there were crow's feet at the corners of her eyes and thin lines around her lips.

'Jacobson's going to help me, but he says there'll have been effects. Using my life source instead of the Eternal Flame has taken something from me.'

'It's taken something? What does that mean?'

She looked away from me. 'It could be a couple of months ... could be a couple of years.'

Her words hit me with as deep a physical pain as the impact of the gunshot. 'Are you serious, Maddie?' I whispered.

She lifted a hand to silence me before I could continue. 'I know, alright? I know. But like I said, Jacobson will help me. There's a way to work around this with white magic to put back whatever ... whatever it was I've taken away. I don't know how it will work exactly, but he's going to help.'

I felt the weariness radiating from her. She was absolutely exhausted; this wasn't the moment to push her further, but I needed more answers. 'Where's Old Jacobson now?' I said. I might not be able to question her but I could definitely question him – and hopefully I'd get some answers.

'I think he's in the kitchen with Yanni.'

'Actually, I'm here,' a voice said.

We turned to find Jacobson standing in the doorway. 'And if you don't mind,' he added, 'a little less of the "old". The name's Ernie, Ernie Jacobson. And Beatrix, it's time you and I had a conversation.' A smile flickered on his lips but it faded almost immediately, probably because of the way I was glaring at him.

'Maddie told me about the life source thing. She said that the magic has drained her, drained her actual life.'

'We will talk about Maddie later. For now, she is stable. It's not her I want to talk to you about, it's you. About your parents.'

I blinked. 'My parents?'

'I think you might want to sit down.'

I didn't want to sit down. I couldn't think of a single reason why Ernie Jacobson would want to talk to me about my parents. He hadn't even lived in Witchlight Cove when they were alive. Yet there was something radiating from him, something that told me I had to listen.

'Maddie,' he said, glancing at my best friend. 'Do you mind? I would like to speak to Beatrix alone for a moment.'

My response was instant. 'Whatever you want to say to me, you can say in front of Maddie,' I said. 'And Yanni too,' I added, when I saw her standing in the doorway.

Jacobson's cheeks sucked inward and for a moment his scowl nearly returned, but he shook it away. 'Please?' he asked.

I relented. 'Just give us a moment,' I asked the others.

'We'll be through here if you need us,' Yanni murmured as she shut the door to the lounge behind them.

Ernie Jacobson sighed. 'There's no easy way to say this.' His gaze flickered. 'I don't want you to be upset.'

I gave a dry, humourless laugh. 'Whatever you're about to tell me, I've had worse. Trust me.'

He nodded and exhaled sharply. 'Beatrix. I'm your father's father.'

'Sorry?' The word fell from my lips. My father's father? Who even spoke like that? The repetition made it worse, made it harder to process.

Then it hit me and a cold dread crept through me, as if every window in the world had been thrown open. I knew what he meant, but my mind refused to accept it. Rejected it outright. I opened my mouth to speak but no words came. I needed him to say it, *really* say it so there was no room for misinterpretation.

He stepped closer and took my hand. His grip was firm. His throat bobbed as he swallowed, his eyes searching mine in a plead for understanding.

'Beatrix,' he said slowly, deliberately. 'I'm your grandfather.'

If you desperately need more Witchlight Cove adventures, then you can grab this **free bonus scene,** all from Fraser's point of view, here: https://BookHip.com/FASGDCS

Pre-Order the next book in Witchlight Cove, *Secrets of the Deadly Nightshades,* here: https://readerlinks.com/l/4606344Coming 1st May 2025!

About Heather

Heather is an urban fantasy writer and mum. She was born and raised near Windsor, which gave her the misguided impression that she was close to royalty in some way. She is not, though she once got a letter from Queen Elizabeth II's lady-in-waiting.

Heather went to university in Liverpool, where she took up skydiving and met her future husband. When she's not running around after her children, she's plotting her next book and daydreaming about vampires, dragons and kick-ass heroines.

Heather is a book lover who grew up reading Brian Jacques and Anne McCaffrey. She loves to travel and once spent a month in Thailand. She vows to return.

Want to learn more about Heather? Subscribe to her newsletter for behind-the-scenes scoops, free bonus material and a cheeky peek into her world. Her subscribers will always get the heads up about the best deals on her books.

Subscribe to her Newsletter at her website www.heathergharris.com/subscribe.

Heather's Patreon

Heather has started her very own Patreon page. What is Patreon? It's a subscription service that allows you to support Heather AND read her books way before anyone else! For a small monthly fee you could be reading Heather's next book, on a weekly chapter-by-chapter basis (in its roughest draft form!) in the next week or two. If you hit "Join the community" you can follow Heather along for FREE, though you won't get access to all the good stuff, like early release books, polls, live Q&A's, character art and more! You can even have a video call with Heather or have a character named after you! Heather's current patrons are getting to read a novella called House Bound which isn't available anywhere else, not even to her newsletter subscribers!

If you're too impatient to wait until Heather's next release, then Patreon is made for you. Join Heather on Patreon here: https://www.patreon.com/c/heathergharrisauthor/

Contact Heather

Website: www.heathergharris.com
Email: HeatherGHarrisAuthor@gmail.com

Reviews

Reviews feed Heather's soul. She'd really appreciate it if you could take a few moments to review her books on Amazon, Bookbub, or Goodreads and say hello.

Other Works by Heather

The *Witchlight Magical Mysteries Series* with Ella Stone

Secrets of the Frostbound Cottage – Book 0.5 (a prequel story),

    Secrets of the Forgotten Heir – Book 1,

    Secrets of the Deadly Nightshades – Book 2; and

    Secrets of the Eternal Flame – Book 3.

The *Portlock Paranormal Detective* Series with Jilleen Dolbeare

    The Vampire and the Case of her Dastardly Death - Book 0.5 (a prequel story),

The Vampire and the Case of the Wayward Werewolf – Book 1,

The Vampire and the Case of the Secretive Siren – Book 2,

The Vampire and the Case of the Baleful Banshee – Book 3,

The Vampire and the Case of the Cursed Canine – Book 4,

The Vampire and the Case of the Perilous Poltergeist – Book 5,

The Vampire and the Case of the Cozy Christmas – Book 5.5,

The Vampire and the Case of the Hellacious Hag – Book 6; and

The Vampire and the Case of the Malevolent Mermaid – Book 7.

The Other Realm Universe:

The *Other Realm* series

Glimmer of Dragons- Book 0.5 (a prequel story),
Glimmer of The Other- Book 1,
Glimmer of Hope- Book 2,

Glimmer of Christmas – Book 2.5 (a Christmas tale),

Glimmer of Death – Book 3,

Glimmer of Deception – Book 4,

It is recommended that you read *The Other Wolf books 1 to 3* before continuing with:

Challenge of the Court– Book 5,

Betrayal of the Court– Book 6; and

Revival of the Court– Book 7.

The *Other Wolf* Series

Defender of The Pack– Book 0.5 (a prequel story),

Protection of the Pack– Book 1,

Guardians of the Pack– Book 2,

Saviour of The Pack– Book 3,

Awakening of the Pack – Book 4,

Resurgence of the Pack – Book 5; and

Ascension of the Pack – Book 6.

The *Other Witch* Series

Rune of the Witch – Book 0.5 (a prequel story),

Hex of the Witch– Book 1,

Coven of the Witch;– Book 2,

Familiar of the Witch– Book 3; and

Destiny of the Witch – Book 4.

The *Other Detective* Series

Frustrated Justice – Book 0.5 (a prequel story),

Veiled Justice – Book 1,

Mystic Justice – Book 2,

Arcane Justice – Book 3; and

Savage Justice – Book 4

About the Author - Ella Stone

About Ella

Ella Stone has always been enchanted by the magic of stories. From sneaking late-night reads of The Magic Faraway Tree and The Borrowers to getting completely lost on the staircase with Harry Potter, books have been her doorway to other worlds.

Now, as a writer of urban fantasy and magical mysteries, Ella weaves her own worlds filled with intrigue, humour, and a touch of romance. When she's not crafting stories, you can usually find her hiding in a quiet corner of her tiny house surrounded by her cats, trying to squeeze in "just one more chapter."

Stay in Touch

Ella has a great website, which also offers you some free books if you join up for her newsletter, so have a rummage around at: https://www.ellastoneauthor.com/

Social Media

If you're a social soul, then track Ella down at her Facebook page, Ella Stone Writes!

Other Works by Ella Stone

The *Witchlight Magical Mysteries* Series with Heather G. Harris

Secrets of the Frostbound Cottage – Book 0.5 (a prequel story),

Secrets of the Forgotten Heir – Book 1,

Secrets of the Deadly Nightshades – Book 2; and

Secrets of the Eternal Flame – Book 3.

The *Dark Creatures Saga*:

Dark Creatures - Book 1,

Dark Destiny – Book 2,

Dark Deception - Book 3,

Dark Redemption – Book 4, and

Dark Reckoning - Book 5.

The *Bloodsucker's Blog Trilogy*:

Life Sucks – Book 1,
Love Bites - Book 2, and
Lost Souls - Book 3.

Review
Request!

Thank you so much for reading our book. We hope that you loved it, and if you did, we would be super gratefuf if you could leave a review of the book! We call that "social proof" and it persuades other people to pick up the book and give it a try! We are indie authors, without a huge publishing and marketing team behind us, so every review or rating really does help.

If you can review on Goodreads, Bookbub, Amazon, Storygraph or on social media, you will have earned our eternal gratitude. THANK YOU!

Printed in Dunstable, United Kingdom